JODI
THOMAS

MISTLETOE
MIRACLES

HQN™

ISBN-13: 978-1-335-00592-2

Mistletoe Miracles

MISTLETOE MIRACLES

MISTLETOE MIRACLES

CHAPTER ONE

Maverick Ranch, Texas
Griffin's Problem

LOOKING AT HIS two brothers was like staring at one of those paintings with hidden figures masked in the folds of dots. There had to be depth in them, something that made sense, but damned if he could find it.

Griffin Holloway considered his own faults. Well, his one fault, really. That's all he'd allowed himself in this lifetime. Some people might consider being born Texan a flaw, but he loved his state and this land that generations of Holloways had been born to.

He cussed, though. Far more than allowed, he figured. His mother had washed out his mouth so many times when he was a kid that he'd grown to like the taste of Ivory soap.

But his two younger brothers were not nearly as disciplined. If they had to carry all their shortcomings in a sack, they'd both be permanently bent over.

Holloway men might all top six feet and they were reasonably good-looking, but Griffin wasn't sure any, including him, could claim to be long on brains.

Cooper, the youngest at twenty-three, was lanky and limber as a bungee cord. He thought the ranch was his private playground. Hell, he should've been born free like a coyote or a hawk. As a kid, he hadn't bothered to wear clothes unless their mother made him when she was expecting company.

He was so wild, she swore if he'd been able to grow fur, she could have sold him to the circus. Griffin wasn't sure, even today, that his little brother wasn't more critter than human. Growing up hadn't changed him much.

Right now, Cooper was standing, covered in mud, in the headquarters' great room, and it wasn't even eight o'clock in the morning. He didn't seem to be paying any attention to the weekly family business discussion, but that was nothing new. He obviously wanted to get the talking over with and head out to roam the land—fishing, hunting, exploring for Aztec gold— doing anything but work.

Elliot, the middle brother, tried to look like he was following Griffin's weekly lecture about how broke the ranch would be by Christmas. At least Elliot did his share of the work and had since the day he'd come home from college to help run the place. But Elliot's heart wasn't in ranching, never had been. He spent ten hours on his computer for every one he spent on a horse. He made Griffin think of a bit actor who'd accidentally stumbled onto the wrong set.

Facing them both, Griffin cleared his throat and got straight to the point. "We have a problem with a simple solution. I'm thinking we've tried everything else and now it's down to only one answer."

They both looked clueless. Elliot started texting and Cooper scratched his brown hair, dry and dirty as a tumbleweed.

I'm adopted, Griffin thought. *It's the only explanation. Or they are.* He'd been around when his mother went to the hospital to deliver them both, but he hadn't actually seen the births. He'd been eight when Elliot was born and eleven for Cooper. He could have handled watching. After all, he'd seen his dad pull dozens of calves by then. Even helped with some. How much different could it be?

Cooper frowned. "What's so important, Griff? I got thirty head lost out in Mistletoe Canyon. They need to be found and herded to the north pasture before it gets too late for me to get some fishing in."

Elliot nodded. "I got calls to make. The market's down and what little cash we had in reserve seems to be evaporating."

"All right." Griffin straightened, facing his problem head-on. "It's simple. The ranch is broke. We've got two months to come up with the loan payment and all I see is money going out."

"We're always broke." Elliot shrugged. "We'll find a way to pay the loan come January. We always do. Sell cattle or gravel, or lease a few sections out for winter wheat crops."

Closing his eyes, Griffin ran through the long list of things they'd tried before. A few, like leasing land for grazing or farming, had helped get them through last winter. But others, like the expensive barn his father had once built to board racehorses that never came around or Cooper's plan to raise miniature horses to sell to city folks, hadn't paid off.

Griffin frowned, knowing he was out of ideas. "There is no easy answer this time. Selling gravel or leasing wouldn't be enough. Selling off our best breeding stock will only hurt us next spring. I see only one way out of the mess we're in. One of us has got to get married."

Glaring at Cooper, Griffin clarified, "And I'm not talking about someone like the new waitress at Dorothy's Café. One of us has to find a woman with money or land we can borrow on. I'm not particular as to which. We need fresh blood flowing into the Maverick Ranch."

Cooper grinned. "Dang, Griff, you sound like we're vampires. I don't want to marry some girl for her money."

Griffin realized how callous he sounded. "Of course we'd love her, treat her right and all that. It's just time one of us got married, and her being rich wouldn't hurt."

Elliot looked up from his cell. "I was engaged during my freshman year of college to Bella Brantley, remember? Her family owned a few blocks in downtown Dallas. But then Dad died and within six months I had to quit school and come home." He glowered at Cooper. "She broke off the engagement after a weekend visit here. I blame him for that. One look at little brother and she didn't want anything to do with our gene pool."

"I wasn't the reason. I was only a kid. That woman was a plague of problems." Cooper puffed up like a horned toad. "I just took her for a ride across the place. It wasn't my fault she kept falling off the horse. Then she got all crazy when I offered to rub liniment on her backside. Like I wasn't being considerate or something. And that accidental bumping together in the hallway was her fault, not mine."

Old anger fired in Elliot's eyes.

Griffin stepped between them before a fight broke out, again. "I'm serious and I have a plan. Come hell or high water, one of us is walking a wealthy girl down the aisle before Christmas. We're land rich and cash poor, and I see only one way to end that. Two months should be enough time to find a woman, date her, propose and get married. Way I see it we won't take any of her land or money. That wouldn't be right. We'll just borrow against her land to make the payment. Next spring we'll make it back and pay her back."

"That's what you always say," Cooper groaned. "We're always living off next year's money."

"We could sell off a few sections," Elliot suggested.

Both brothers stared at him so hard he took a step backward.

Never selling land, any amount, had been drilled into them like it was the eleventh commandment Moses forgot to write down.

"I'll be long buried in Holloway dirt before I sell a square foot. It's part of me. I might as well cut off a leg or an arm." Griffin's hands molded into fists.

"We get it, Griff. We feel the same. It was just an option." Griffin nodded once.

Elliot tried again. "You're the oldest, Griff. You go first. At thirty-four, you're about to go from ripe to rotten anyway."

"But you're the best-looking one, Elliot. Remember those tourists who stopped us in town and wanted to take your picture? Perfect profile of a cowboy, they claimed. Put the word out that you're available and women will come from all over the state. I wouldn't be surprised if Bella Brantley didn't come back. Last I heard she's still single. Maybe she just planned a long engagement?"

Elliot shook his head. "We broke up seven years ago, and she's not exactly single. She might be between husband numbers three and four for all I know."

"What about me?" Cooper jumped in. "I'm the youngest. Women like men who are still young and wild."

They both looked in his direction, but Elliot spoke first. "Good idea. There's a kind of woman who's attracted to stray dogs. Cooper might have a chance. We could advertise him as a makeover project. Flipping houses is popular. Maybe someone could flip Cooper."

"We'll talk about it at supper. Right now, we're wasting daylight." Griffin ended the meeting. "Just think about it and come up with some ideas by tonight."

Neither of his brothers looked challenged. Griffin had a feeling he'd be doing all the thinking, all the work, all the sacrifice.

Shoving on his battered hat, Cooper headed outside.

Elliot turned toward the huge study where each brother had a desk, but Elliot was the only one who ever used his.

Griffin passed through the kitchen, smiling. He'd introduced his plan. At least that was a start. Step one.

Next step: make a list of possibilities, and he knew exactly who to ask for help. The Franklin sisters. The two old ladies might never have married, but they knew every eligible woman in the county. All he'd have to do was line up the ladies and parade them by. The Holloway men might be a little rough around the edges, but their ranch was one of the oldest in West Texas.

"It'll never work," whispered a voice, scratchy with age, from across the wide bar lined in stools with saddles for seats. "It will take all three of you boys to fill the qualifications to any girl's list."

Griffin glared at Mamie, the cook at the Maverick Ranch for thirty years. "Why won't it work? You turn into a fortune-teller in your old age?" He tolerated the round little woman and made a point of never taking her advice. "And, Mamie, we're not boys. I took over the ranch at twenty-four, remember? Dad was getting sick and Mom was dead."

"I know. I was here. Who do you think was cooking three meals a day for you boys? Don't need to be a fortune-teller. None of you will ever find a woman dumb enough to take any one of you on." She giggled and all the rolls from her neck to her stretch-pant-covered knees wobbled like Jell-O. "The three of you can't get along. What makes you think bringing a woman in this house will solve anything? Besides being rich, she'd have to be crazy and blind to even think of taking one of you Holloways on."

Griffin frowned. "Fair enough. I'll add those to the list of requirements."

Cramming on his hat, he decided talking to Mamie was like taking a once-per-day depression pill.

As he stepped out into the crisp November air, Griffin smiled. For a moment he just closed his eyes and breathed. This was his home, the place he'd always belong, and if he had to marry a rich, crazy, blind wife to keep it, he would.

By the time the town put up their eight reindeer on the light poles, he'd be engaged, and by Christmas he'd be married.

CHAPTER TWO

Midnight Crossing

DEEP WITHIN THE shadows of hills too rough to be broken by a road sat one lone cabin at the edge of Shallow River. Local history claimed that a hundred and fifty years ago, cattle drives crossed in the shade of these hills after midnight, hoping to move unnoticed by outlaws.

In the '20s, the story went, several ranchers had been sitting around playing poker. The hour was late and most of their pockets were lean, so they played one last hand. The loser had to claim ownership of Midnight Crossing. Since three of the eight men were from the O'Grady clan, the odds were against them avoiding ownership of the worthless land.

Nearly a century later, Jaxson O'Grady never cared about any legend, or poker, for that matter. He was the fifth O'Grady to move onto the worthless five-mile-square of land called Midnight Crossing. The rocky plot was bordered on one side by the Double K, Kirkland land, and on another by Maverick Ranch, owned by three Holloway brothers. Neither neighbor had ever offered to buy O'Grady's land.

Now and then, in a family as big as the O'Gradys, a loner would be born who didn't want to run with the pack. That man would lay claim to the cabin on Shallow River and live there until he either died or finally decided he'd rather join society than be driven insane by the winds that whipped through the rugged rock formations.

The old cabin had stood empty for more than twenty years when Jax claimed it, along with his right to loneliness. He'd been broken, and the family backed away, giving him time to heal.

He loved the spring and summers, but as fall turned into winter his second year alone, Jaxson reconsidered his choices. The wind howled down from the black hills, keeping him awake most nights. The river froze over for days, ending any hope of fishing.

Jax grew restless on cold nights, but he couldn't go back among people, not yet. He never longed for company. Only peace. Summer's calm cool nights gave him that. So he decided to stick out another winter, waiting for spring. Maybe then he could look people in the eyes. Maybe he'd forget, even for a while, what he'd done.

Over the months he'd been on Shallow River, his body had healed but he grew thin, as fear and regret ate away from inside. There were times when a man wasn't fit for company, and Jax had decided he was living in one of those times.

No modern-day outlaws haunted the dark hills behind his cabin. No one crossed his piece of land except a cousin now and then checking on him. All Jaxson's demons roamed in the dark corners of his mind. They whispered of what he should have done in the one moment when he hadn't reacted.

Tonight, he faced November winds as he walked the edge of the river and let the noise of the water drown out his thoughts. Later, he'd run the hills until his muscles burned so he'd be able to collapse in dreamless sleep. When it grew too cold to run, he'd work with the pine and mahogany stacked in his workshop and pretend all was normal in his life…and in his mind. He'd spend late hours studying for online classes he'd taken without any direction of a degree.

At thirty-six, Jax felt like he was an old man inside. He couldn't remember ever being young. He might look straight and tall, but he feared if he turned around too quickly, he'd catch sight of his shadow, all twisted and deformed.

He had nothing to live for, and worse, nothing to die for.

On rainy nights like tonight, he put on a black slicker and moved into the shadows. He walked the edge of sanity, tempting crazy, but not stepping off the cliff.

As he did almost every evening lately, he climbed an easy two miles to the north edge of his property and sat on a mound high enough to see the ribbon of a two-lane highway a mile away. Part of him wondered where all the people were going, racing along like fireflies low to the ground. Part of him didn't care. He just liked following the lights on a road shiny with rain.

After a while, the lonely stream of cars and trucks relaxed him, and he stood. The rain was so slow he almost felt he had to bump into it to feel the moisture. The air was heavy, weighing down his lungs and pressing against his chest.

Just as he turned to head back to his cabin, Jax heard the squeal of tires and saw a lone car suddenly fly off the pavement as it missed the one bend for ten miles along the county road.

In a quick blink, the driver's door flew open and the driver tumbled out, rolling across the uneven ground like a broken toy.

With his heart pounding, Jax climbed down the mound, barely noticing the sharp edges cutting into his palms. He carried no phone. No way to call for help, and no doubt the driver was in crisis.

By the time he reached the base of the hill, two other cars had stopped to help, and he was still almost a mile away.

Jaxson began to run, but crossing the rough terrain wasn't

easy. He slipped several times and had to turn back twice to find a shallow place across the river.

By the time he was a hundred yards out, an ambulance had pulled up. Paramedics rushed toward the body crumpled in the muddy field. The crew was loaded down with about fifty pounds of equipment and yelling.

"She's hurt bad," shouted one man, who'd stood guard over the unconscious motorist.

"We're here to help," the first EMT answered. "Stay back."

The driver hadn't been moved, but one of the men who'd stopped had knelt close to her, which Jax saw as a good sign that she might be still breathing.

Jax hesitated in the shadows, knowing he could do nothing to help. Even though he'd been trained, he had no equipment, no lights, no way to transport a wounded passenger. The cavalry was already on-site. They didn't need him stepping in.

All he could do was watch. Within minutes, the woman was lifted into the ambulance, and the silent flashing lights had pulled away from the scene.

The two cars that had stopped moved on down the road and the only evidence that a drama had played out was the dark outline of a red sports car flipped ten feet off the road. In watery moonlight, the vehicle appeared twisted and trapped by a barbed-wire fence as if it were no heavier than a plastic bag.

Jaxson stood stone still. Like his life, someone else's had changed in a fraction of a second. He didn't know if the driver was dying or simply knocked out by the blow. But if she lived, this moment would alter her and the world would never be the same.

Something moved in the tall grass beside him. A whimper whispered in the wind.

Jax remained still. The whimper came again. More movement in the grass.

He glanced back to the road. Not a car in sight. Curiosity got the better of him. Snakes wouldn't be out in this cold weather, and a rabbit or prairie dog probably wouldn't attack.

Moving slowly, soundlessly, Jax studied the tall grass. A long form, almost the size of a coyote, shown dark against the sand-colored grass.

A pickup rattled along the road a hundred feet away. For a blink, the lights shone on the animal lying so still.

A dog.

Jax advanced and knelt as a low cry of pain came again.

"Where'd you come from, boy?" Jax whispered as he slowly moved his hand toward the animal.

The dog showed no aggression.

Jax lightly brushed the animal's side. Halfway down the body he felt the thick wet warmth of blood.

The dog raised his head a few inches but didn't growl. He was comfortable around humans, even appeared to trust.

"I can't see how to help you." Jax guessed that if he left the animal here until dawn, he'd bleed out or, worse, be eaten by some predator. He tugged off his rain slicker and wrapped it around the dog, tying the jacket's arms to hold the animal in the wrap.

With little effort, he lifted what looked like a half-grown collie pup and headed toward his cabin. Within a few minutes, he was on familiar ground, moving slowly, making his way home.

The pup didn't make a sound. He was either too far gone to fight or somehow sensed he was being helped.

As Jax neared the light shining from his cabin porch, a dozen possibilities sparked through his mind. There were no neighbors close enough to have an animal wander onto his place, but folks from town did drop off dogs and cats from time to time on country roads. Maybe they thought they were giving the pet a chance at another life. In truth, all they were giving him was starvation.

This collie might have been dumped out here. Maybe he was

in the road when the red sports car passed. He might have even caused the accident.

Or, like the driver, he might have been thrown when the sports car rolled. If the driver hadn't bothered to belt herself in, she probably hadn't secured her dog.

Maybe she'd glanced over at him and missed the bend in the road. Any way Jax looked at it, there was probably a fifty-fifty chance the animal caused the wreck.

A head poked out from beneath the slicker. Big black eyes, golden hair, blood shining across his long nose. The collie pup stared up at Jax and tilted his head in question.

"Hello there, buddy." Jax climbed the three steps to his porch. "How about you let me take a look at you?" He laid the dog on a workbench and started unwrapping his coat.

The dog pressed his nose against Jax's palm and gave a low cry.

"I know, buddy, it hurts. I've been there."

Slowly Jaxson slid his hand along the animal's sides. Blood. Lots of blood.

Gathering his fishing gear and a pile of rags, Jax put together his emergency kit. Hot water. Duct tape. A few boards to act as splints. Not exactly the medical supplies he needed, but he'd work with what he had.

Not once did the animal growl or snap, but his low cries let Jax know that he was hurting.

Jax tried to make sense of what happened. The dog must have crawled away from the accident. If the driver was unconscious, she couldn't have told anyone. The men on-site were too interested in saving her. They probably never noticed the dog.

Slowly, trying to cause no more pain or damage, Jax began cleaning the wounds and stitching up open gaps with fishing wire. The light was good but the night was cold, almost freezing.

The emergency medical training he'd taken while he'd been a fireman was of little help on an animal. One broken leg. One deep gash just behind the dog's ear. When he moved his hand over the animal, the dog jerked slightly. His shiny coat of fur hid other wounds.

For the first time in two years, Jax forgot about his scars, his pain, his problems and went to work on a dog that had been overlooked.

"If you live, I think I'll call you Buddy." He talked to his patient in low tones. "If you could talk, you could call me Jax. I'll fix you up the best I can, but I'm no doc. You'll have scars."

Buddy raised his head and licked Jaxson's right hand in a silent thank-you.

Jax smiled for the first time in months. The dog had paid no attention to the knotted twisted skin crossing his hand. "Yeah, boy, looks like we all have our share of scars. If you don't mind mine, I won't mind yours."

CHAPTER THREE

Griffin's Quest

MIDMORNING, AFTER COLLECTING his mail and picking up a load of groceries for Mamie, Griffin Holloway pulled up in front of the Franklin sisters' bed-and-breakfast just off the main street of Crossroads, Texas. He couldn't put off what had to be done any longer. He was in town. Might as well stop by and talk to the chatty Franklin sisters.

Their big old house looked newly painted, and apparently the three-story Victorian had gobbled up the tiny bungalow next door, because now both homes were joined by a rose garden path lined with faded garden gnomes. Maybe because Crossroads was growing, the sisters thought their place should also. Rumor was the town would be big enough to have its own Walmart soon.

He cut the engine of his truck and frowned as he set his mind to what he had to do. Sometimes, you had to take action no matter how dumb the plan was, and marrying for money was the only idea he had.

Lately, the sisters had been putting up billboards outside of town calling their place The Franklin Destination Event and

Wedding Center. They'd even created a fairy-tale slogan: *where your heart's desire and midnight dreams become reality.*

No one dared to mention that for half the town, *heart's desire* fit more into a topless club than a bed-and-breakfast. And Griffin didn't want to think about the definition of *midnight dreams.* One evening at the Two-Step Bar, a dozen drunks had got together to list what they thought *heart's desire* meant, and not one of the choices had the word *wedding* in it.

"Hell," Griffin mumbled as he walked up to the newly painted purple door. He'd rather spend the day at the smelly, loud and smoky Two-Step than have to talk to the sisters. But he had a real problem, and they were probably the only ones who could help.

Rose Franklin answered the door and looked at him like he was planning to sell her expired Boy Scout popcorn. "How can I help you, Griffin Holloway? Don't tell me that rambling old ranch house of yours burned down and you need a place to sleep."

"No, the Holloway headquarters is still standing. Electricity even works now and then." He grinned. "I'm here to ask for your advice, Miss Franklin. If you've got a few minutes to spare me?"

That one sentence seemed to be the magic open sesame. She stepped back and welcomed him into a cluttered entrance, then marched him to a sunny breakfast room decorated in Peanuts Halloween characters.

"Little late for Halloween," he mumbled.

"We're getting there," she answered. "Decorating is an art that can't be hurried by a calendar. It saves time if we take down one holiday as we put up the next."

Several of the two-foot fluffy not-so-scary statues started talking as he passed, and Griffin fought the urge to take a swing at them. He hated any kind of decorating, and this old house was ground zero.

When he raised an eyebrow, Rose Franklin huffed. "We're

getting out Thanksgiving tomorrow. You are welcome to join us." She turned toward the kitchen.

Griffin guessed, if he hit Snoopy just right, all the decorations would tumble off the table at once. She might even see it as helping with the takedown. Only he had no hope Thanksgiving would look any better.

He hated cute decorations. Hell, he hated all decorations. He hated holidays, period. Halloween to Christmas was not a happy time for him. But if he wanted Miss Franklin's help, he'd better leave her creepy menagerie alone.

She offered him the seat at the end of the table.

"Daisy!" she yelled without noticing her sister standing three feet away at the door Griffin guessed led down a hallway. "The oldest Holloway boy has come to ask for our advice."

Daisy made a squeaky noise, then answered, "I'll get the muffins and coffee. Don't start talking until I'm in the room. If a Holloway thinks he's got a problem, it must be huge 'cause them boys were all three spoiled by their mother to think they were perfect and knew everything."

"I heard that." Griffin plopped his Stetson down on the table just to irritate the ladies. "Mom has been buried for over a dozen years. Perfection seems to have slipped a bit among her offspring."

Rose picked up his hat and set it brim up on the windowsill. "Except for being nearsighted about her sons, your mama was a good woman."

Griffin nodded and took the seat offered. He had no idea if he was being ordered to the head of the table or the tail. "That she was and I'm hoping the next Mrs. Holloway will be the same."

Rose's bushy eyebrow raised slightly. He'd caught her interest.

A few minutes later when Daisy rushed in with apple muffins, honey butter and a pot of coffee, he realized he was beyond dumb. Who goes to two women who've never married for advice? The gang at the bar would probably have better ideas. He shrugged. On the bright side, the gang at the bar wouldn't offer apple muffins and coffee along with their advice.

Besides, it was too late to bolt now. He'd set his course. While the ladies downed their coffee and two muffins each, he laid out his problem as quickly as possible.

One of the Holloway men needed a wife, one with money or land. One willing to marry by Christmas. Leaning close, he lowered his voice and added, "I wouldn't want this out, but come January, we're liable to lose the place if we don't come up with cash." He winked at them. "You'll keep that quiet, ladies?"

They both nodded, swearing to a secret everyone in the county already knew. If the Holloways weren't low on cash, now that might be something new. Word was, several ranchers were already planning to make the bank an offer as soon as the land was foreclosed on. Of course, no one would want the whole ranch, but the bank could split it up into a dozen smaller parcels.

Griffin would rather have someone carve up his heart than sell off the ranch in pieces. Five generations were buried there. His father's trees. His mother's honeysuckle. Over a hundred years of Holloways had worked the land, and Griffin wanted another hundred years more to do the same.

To his surprise, the sisters didn't ask one question about the *why* to his plan. They were far more interested in the *who*.

When he admitted he didn't have a bride in mind, the Franklin sisters just stared at him as if they'd accidentally let in a serial killer.

Griffin ate his muffin in silence and waited. The plan had sounded better in his head. Maybe he should have been more detailed, but the whole thing seemed simple. Find a rich woman, marry her, add her money or credit potential into the bank account. He'd heard a dozen women over the past year say they'd love to marry into his family. Only they didn't seem to be around now.

The only other choice was to sell part of the ranch, and every

Holloway buried on the land would come back to haunt him if Griffin did that. He was out of options.

"What about love?" Rose whispered. She said the words slowly, as if fearing he might ask for an explanation.

"Of course we'd love her." Griffin wanted to scream that love had nothing to do with this. The Franklin sisters didn't seem to realize the sacrifice he, or one of his brothers, was willing to make. He quickly added, "Franklin men tend to fall in love fast. We're kind of the at-first-sight types. So the falling-in-love part won't take long, but meeting eligible women is hard when you're busy from dawn till dark ranching."

Rose leaned so close he started counting the hairs on her upper lip. "Is only one of you boys looking to marry or all three?"

"It don't matter. We're all unattached. We're willing, ready and ripe for the picking." When he'd been in his twenties, single women seemed to be everywhere, but now, those same women were all in their thirties and wanting to show him pictures of their kids.

Both Franklin women frowned and crossed their arms over their ample chests as if deciding to be the guards at the gate. Griffin figured he'd said the wrong thing. He didn't have a romantic bone in his body, and he didn't plan on pretending now.

"I mean, ladies. My brothers and I have talked it over, and we all three think it's time we settled down, but the chance of us all three finding love before Christmas is slim. Though that would be all our hearts' desire." It couldn't hurt to toss in the slogan the sisters used in their advertising. Now all he had to do was close the deal with his proposition. "If you ladies could help just one of us find our forever mate before the end of the year, we'd like you to also plan the biggest wedding this town has ever seen right here in your beautiful home."

Griffin knew he was laying it on a little thick, but the idea of making money might entice them to help. After all, the offer wouldn't cost him anything; the bride's family paid for the wedding.

Rose stood and reached for the coffeepot. For a moment, he thought she might slam it against his head. She probably saw right through him. Hell, he didn't like himself much at the moment either. Maybe they'd be better off to try the miniature horse idea again.

He didn't plan on losing the ranch. They were down to the Hail Mary play. There was no plan B.

Daisy reached into one of the drawers of a sideboard that had to be a hundred years old and pulled out a pen and paper. "Write down exactly what you're looking for in a wife. We'll do what we can."

Griffin reconsidered his idea. The longer they stared at him, the dumber it seemed. He'd never put much thought into what kind of woman he wanted, but he had enough sense to know long-legged and big-breasted probably shouldn't be at the top of the list.

Pretty. That was a start. He didn't care much about *smart*, but Elliot might, so he wrote that, too. *From a good family, but she should be financially independent.* He guessed they'd figure out that meant rich.

He'd never thought about marriage before. It was just something in the far future. Usually by the fourth date, he was making a list of why he'd never want to spend the rest of his life with a woman. He'd had a few serious girlfriends from time to time. The kind where he'd had to remember birthdays and get Christmas presents, but the ladies always drifted away.

Maybe it would be easier to come up with what he didn't want. It usually took him about three months to add a *never-want-to-marry-this-kind-of-woman* to his list.

Griff wrote *likes children*. The Franklin sisters might like that. And *tall*. Short women made him nervous.

Glancing up, he saw them both waiting, so he handed over his list. He had the essentials. That should get them started.

Rose finally stood and glared down at him. "We'll think it over, Mr. Holloway, but don't get your hopes up. Women have careers today. They don't always want to live on a ranch half an hour from town. You three men are good-looking enough, but I'm guessing none of you knows the first thing about how to treat a woman."

Griffin stood and grabbed his hat. Hell, she was right. Even if they hooked one bride, she probably wouldn't stay. The only woman on the ranch was Mamie, and she only stayed because they paid her.

But if a bride did stay, until spring anyway, the ranch would have survived another winter. He'd settle for that. Even help her pack if the marriage didn't work out. After all, marriage was a percentage game. The odds were low on finding a keeper, but he was willing to roll the dice.

He raised his head and stared at the two women twice his age. "You're right. I don't know much about women. But I'm willing to learn."

Rose stared at him a full minute, then nodded once. "All right, we will do our best. First, all three of you make a list of the last five women you've dated and text it to us. We'll get the whiteboards out and start our list. We'll expect you all three back at eight."

Daisy nodded her agreement to Rose's plan. "It won't be easy, but we'll give you a crash course." She giggled. "And tell Cooper to be sure and wear clothes. That afternoon he streaked past the ladies book club still haunts me."

"He was five," Griffin commented.

Neither sister acted as if they'd heard him, so he nodded and stood to leave, more confused than when he'd walked in. The sisters seemed to have forgotten about him. They were busy pulling a six-foot-wide whiteboard out of the closet.

As he walked out, Charlie Brown squeaked, "Trick or treat."

Griffin knocked the stuffed toy backward, but Charlie didn't tumble. He just rocked and settled back into place. Swearing, Griffin fought down the urge to take another swing. If he couldn't put up with a stuffed Charlie Brown, what hope did he have at tolerating a real wife?

As he turned into the foyer, he heard Rose order, "Eight o'clock sharp. And tell your brothers to bring a detailed list of exactly what they're looking for."

Daisy giggled and added, "There will be homework after our first session."

He stepped into the autumn air and took a deep breath. How was it possible to fall into hell without dying? If there was going to be homework, the chances were good that there would also be more sessions. Great.

There had to be an easier way. Maybe he should drive over to Lubbock and sell all nine pints of his blood. That and both kidneys might be enough.

No, that wouldn't work. The Franklins would follow him into the afterlife and kill him for standing them up. He'd heard rumors that they barely tolerated men. If he crossed them, there was no telling what trouble the two might cause.

All the Holloway men would show up tonight even if he had to drag Elliot and Cooper. Griffin grinned. The sisters would probably be surprised when they discovered he was the easiest one to get along with.

CHAPTER FOUR

Midnight Crossing

JAXSON O'GRADY LEANED FORWARD, his head resting on his arm atop the workbench. He wasn't asleep. He couldn't sleep until he knew the dog was going to make it.

His fingers lightly stroked Buddy's neck. The collie hadn't moved for hours, but they were both covered by a wool blanket. Buddy's breathing seemed fast and shallow. Jaxson figured the pup was about half-grown. Paws too big for his legs right now. But, if he lived, Buddy would be a beautiful dog, scars and all.

Funny, he couldn't think of a single person he'd worried about as much as he'd worried over this tossed-away pup. He'd thought of starting up the Jeep and taking him into town to the vet, but he had no claim to the dog. What if whoever threw him away tried to take him back so they could finish the job?

Jax sat up for the tenth time and checked Buddy's wounds. The bleeding had stopped. He'd made a splint for the leg and it didn't seemed to be bothering the dog. If he lived, it would be a while before he'd heal and there was no guarantee he wouldn't have a limp.

As the sun came up, Jax stood, thinking he'd fry up bacon for breakfast. If the dog would eat a little, that would be a good sign.

When he turned to leave, Buddy whimpered and opened his sad eyes.

"All right, boy, you're coming with me."

Jax wrapped the blanket he'd covered Buddy with and carefully carried the dog into the two-room cabin. "You're my first guest that isn't related to me. Sometimes I think the O'Grady clan has a raffle every month to see which one will come out here to check on me. They bring the mail, like I care, and more food than I could ever eat, even though I tell them every month that I can drive into town to buy groceries."

He lowered the dog to the floor beside a fireplace still warmed by dying coals. "If I see them coming, I act like I'm not home. I'd appreciate if you'd do the same."

As Jax cooked breakfast for two, he told Buddy about every one of his relatives. The dog just watched him moving around, showing far more interest in the bacon than the cousins.

When Jax sat down on the hearth with two plates, Buddy managed to raise his head.

"Join me for breakfast, boy. I seem to have cooked far more than I can eat."

Buddy leaned his head just a little to the right.

"You've figured me out, haven't you?" Jax smiled. "I guess it's about time I had a little company. As long as you don't snore, you're welcome to stay." Looking around the open room, he added, "I can kind of see why no one visits. I tossed out the old furniture. All I needed was a desk for my computer and a bed in the other room to sleep."

One desk. One chair. No place for company to sit. Simple living made for one. He liked his basic decorating. He'd built shelves on every bit of wall space. Paperbacks, magazines and thick manuals mixed in with the books he'd used in every on-line course he'd taken.

An hour after breakfast, Jax had read last week's Crossroads paper to the dog. He slept through most of it but did seem to show some interest in the weather report.

Jax patted Buddy and silently decided after two years of being alone, he was finally cracking up. Without much thought, he spread out on the floor next to the dog and was sound asleep in minutes.

The dog laid his nose atop Jaxson's hand and did the same.

CHAPTER FIVE

The Johnsons

Captain James Wyatt Johnson walked away from the cargo plane at Sheppard Air Force Base near Wichita Falls, Texas. For once he didn't look up to study the sky. He was too tired. He knew it would be dark soon, and he needed to find a hotel before the storm rumbling above hit.

He wondered why the only part of his body still working seemed to be his legs. His brain was mush. He'd been on patrol three days without more than a few fifteen-minute naps when he should have been eating. Then he boarded a plane, thinking he'd sleep for twenty hours or so and let a few of the bruises he'd collected heal on the way back to the States.

No chance. Bad weather, terrible food and the fear of nightmares haunting him kept him awake. Now he was in the center of the US. He was safe. No one was after him. He'd done his job. Now all he had to do was find a bed and spend the next two weeks alternating between sleeping and eating.

He picked up his rental car and heard the attendant say he

should stay on the farm-to-market roads. There was a bad wreck on the interstate heading into Wichita Falls.

If he'd been smart, he would have asked for directions to the nearest hotel. But within a few miles, the local roads would cross Interstate 287. Hotels along a major highway were probably within sight of one another.

Wyatt didn't bother to change into civilian clothes. He'd strip as soon as he got to the hotel, put the Do Not Disturb sign out and sleep around the clock. Ten minutes. That was about all he had to stay awake. Surely he'd find a hotel by then.

The rain warped his view as he drove off base. The few streetlights fused like huge balls and then faded. He saw a gas station but didn't recognize the tiny hotels until he'd passed them.

No problem. The places near the bases were never quiet. He'd be in Wichita Falls in a few minutes. Dozens of hotels there.

Following the attendant's suggestion, Wyatt took a county road. Drive. Just drive. It didn't matter if he turned right or left. He'd stop soon. How far apart could towns be? He was in Texas, not in the middle of nowhere.

"Texas," he said aloud. "Why the hell am I in Texas?"

Talking to himself seemed as good an idea as any. No one was around and he couldn't sing.

Laughing at his poor attempt at humor, he answered his own question. "You're in Texas because neither coast wants you home."

His words stung a bit, but he never hid from the truth. His folks in California hadn't spoken to him since he dropped out of college ten years ago to join the army. They'd been divorcing; both had met a second, younger, soul mate. Neither wanted him around to remind them they were getting older and that they had been married once before.

When he'd called from London twelve hours ago, his latest girlfriend told him she was engaged to a guy who dropped by more than once every six months. She added that her fiancé planned to beat him up, if he ever came to Maryland, for making her cry.

Funny, when he was overseas, all he'd thought of was getting home. Now it looked safer to go back. He couldn't think of one old friend that would put up with him for two weeks, and the thought of staying at a hotel the whole time was the definition of *purgatory*, but it was starting to look like his only choice.

The last time he suggested staying over with his high school buddy Ryan in Tennessee, Ryan had said his wife was gunning for Wyatt because he'd broken her sister's heart.

Hell, Wyatt couldn't even remember the sister's name. She'd been a bridesmaid at Ryan's wedding, Wyatt was pretty sure, and she'd stripped for him between the wedding dinner and the champagne toast. Then she left with one of the groomsmen before Wyatt had time to introduce himself.

Wyatt rubbed his eyes, trying to make anything out in the rain besides a ribbon of black highway. If he didn't find a hotel soon, he'd start remembering other states he didn't need to stop in. Like Georgia and Washington. He made a great boyfriend, even fiancé, but once he was gone, women were not his priority and emails or letters or even a call seemed a waste of time. All he had to say was the same thing over and over again. Basically nothing.

By the time he landed back stateside, the woman he'd left crying usually had a list of what was wrong with him, if she answered the door at all.

Now and then, when he let himself, he pictured having a wife to come home to. Someone waiting. Someone who cared. Someone who'd smile when she saw him walk through the door. He'd step into a simple ordinary life. She'd cook the big meals his mother had never had time to. He'd mow the lawn and fix things around the house. They'd watch movies together and try restaurants with funny-sounding names. They would laugh and talk and watch sunsets, like that was something important to do. She'd be his calm in the storm.

Fat chance of that ever happening. He kept driving, pushing through the rain.

If possible, the storm got worse, and Wyatt swore he was the only one on the road. An hour passed, maybe more. He hit the steering wheel with his forehead, fighting sleep.

He had to get home soon, and tonight home was any hotel with a vacancy sign still on. From the looks of it, there were no shoulders or rest stops. Nowhere to pull over. No sign of stations to swing into for directions.

He pulled out his cell. No signal.

The possibility of having to pretzel his body onto the back seat wasn't appealing, but it was starting to look like his only choice.

He shook his cell as if a few jolts might wake it up. Still nothing. Where was he? Maybe he'd finally found the one place he'd feared going. Nowhere. Deep down, he knew that was why he'd studied the stars as a kid, learned to map his way by the constellations. No matter what continent, what state, he always liked to know exactly where he was.

Only tonight he had no map, no cell service, no stars.

He had to push on. "Home," he said as if that was a place to him. "Home."

Wyatt nodded off for only a few seconds and slid his car off the road into a line of poles holding up a barbed-wire fence. His forehead slammed hard into the steering wheel this time, but he barely felt the blow when his car bumped to a stop against a short tree with branches ten feet wide.

He'd reached the breaking point. Without any thought, he grabbed his pack and climbed out. As long as he could hear the tap of his boots on the blacktop, he was heading somewhere, and that had to be better than the nowhere he was right now.

The nights in boot camp when he'd been in training had prepared him for this. March, soldier. March. Numbness blanketed him. He didn't feel the rain or the cold.

March, soldier. March.

AN HOUR LATER, the bright lights of Sheriff Jerry Cline's patrol car passed beside the figure of a man walking down the center of a deserted county road.

Sheriff Cline pulled alongside the soldier who looked more like a ghost from an old World War II movie than real. The vision didn't stop moving or even look over; he just kept going, in slow motion, straight into the storm. The guy was big, over six feet and looked solid as a rock. The pack he carried had to weigh fifty or more pounds dry.

The sheriff moved closer beside the soldier, taking in every detail, but the man ignored him.

"You all right, Captain?" Cline yelled as he made out the bars on his collar.

The stranger kept stomping, one boot in front of the other, seemingly unaware that he splashed mud with each step.

The sheriff radioed in. "Thatcher, you close to the Holloway spread?"

"Maverick Ranch?"

"Yes."

"I'm a few miles out. You need help? Got a wreck?"

"No," Cline answered. "I got a man in an army uniform marching down the center of the road."

"He armed?"

"Not that I can see, but from the size and look of him, if he fights, I wouldn't come out the winner, and there's no way I'm pulling a weapon on a soldier."

"I'll be there in five."

The radio went dead, and Cline climbed out of the patrol car. He fell into step with the soldier. There was no law against walking down a road twenty miles from town, in the middle of a storm, carrying a full load of wet gear.

"Where you heading, Captain?"

"Home," the soldier answered, without even looking toward the sheriff. "I got a wife waiting for me. I got to get home to-night. I missed watching the sunset with her."

Cline had a feeling the captain was talking to himself.

A white pickup with the county sheriff's seal on the driver's door pulled up. Before the deputy could reach him, Sheriff Cline watched the soldier deflate like a huge blowup toy. He had no idea where the man had come from, but he knew the captain had given all he had trying to make it home.

"Who is he?" the younger patrolman yelled as he ran toward Cline.

"Captain Johnson, according to his name tag. He must have pushed as hard as he could, then passed out cold. That's all I know. From the looks of it, he ran off the road about an hour ago, and he's been walking through this rain ever since. Even with the pack and the storm, he's crossed more ground than most joggers could have."

"Captain Johnson." Thatcher smiled. "That could be the new drama teacher's husband, I'm guessing. Her name's Jamie John-son, and she told the whole church last Sunday that her husband was off on assignments for the government. I reckon the army is part of the government. She said she never knows when he'll be coming in. He's got a top-secret job, and the few days she gets to be with him are usually times when she flies to meet him." Thatcher looked down at the soldier. "He must be com-ing home to surprise her."

"You know a lot about the new teacher." Sheriff Cline liked to stay out of people's business if they weren't breaking a law. Thatcher, on the other hand, seemed determined to know ev-eryone in the county. Still in his twenties, he was on his way to serving first as a highway patrolman and then a Texas Ranger. At the rate he was going, he'd know everyone in the county before he got transferred to Austin.

"I didn't plan to know about him, Sheriff, but info just seems to fall into my lap."

"Could be because you talk to everyone."

Thatcher straightened and continued, "I was sitting next to Rose Franklin at the church supper. The old lady does like to talk."

The sheriff leaned down over the soldier's crumpled body. One of his hands looked to be professionally bandaged, and a long dark bruise ran the length of his jaw. "Help me lift him in the back of your truck, and we'll take him the last few miles to his home. It's the least we can do."

"But he'll get wet back there in the bed of my truck. Maybe you should take him in the back seat of the cruiser?"

Cline shook his head. "I don't think he'd fit sideways. He's already soaked to the bone. Fifteen minutes more in your truck bed won't matter."

Thatcher slipped the pack off the soldier's back and tossed it in first, then both men struggled to get Johnson in the truck.

"I think he's made of lead," Thatcher commented.

The soldier mumbled something about going home when they accidentally thumped his head against the toolbox.

"We'll get you home, Captain. Mrs. Johnson is going to be real surprised to see you."

As Cline followed Thatcher's pickup down into the tiny lake community outside Crossroads, Texas, he wasn't surprised Thatcher knew where the new drama teacher lived. The little lake house was built in a crescent shape so all the back windows faced the lake, but even in the headlights, the sheriff could see that it was freshly painted and decorated with enough yard art to start a store.

Like all locals did, Thatcher pulled his truck around back near the lake. Cline stopped at the front, walked up the winding path and knocked.

To his surprise, Thatcher unlocked the front door from the inside.

"She must have been expecting her husband. The back door was unlocked." Thatcher turned lights on as he moved to the kitchen door. "I remember someone saying the drama team was at a meet in Lubbock. She must have gone with them."

Cline frowned. "What do we do with the captain?"

"Wake him up and tell him he's home alone."

"Good luck with that. If he didn't wake up rattling around in the back of your truck, he's out for the night. And I'm guessing if his wife isn't home, he'd just as soon sleep."

"Maybe he's hurt?" Thatcher lowered the tailgate and began tugging on the captain's boots.

"No. I can hear him snoring from the front porch. He's just tired."

Cline jumped into the pickup and lifted Johnson's shoulders. "How about we put him to bed? Mrs. Johnson may be gone all weekend, and from the looks of him, he'll sleep it through."

Thatcher nodded. "I'll drop by tomorrow morning and leave a bag of donuts and coffee. I'll make sure he's alive but won't wake him if he's still sleeping."

With great effort, they managed to half walk, half carry the captain to the bedroom.

"You all right, Captain?" Cline asked when the soldier kept standing as they both let go.

"Where am I?" he mumbled.

"You are home, sir."

"Finally," the captain said, and he took a deep breath. He stripped off his uniform, then Captain Johnson fell across the bed like a tree.

The sheriff floated a quilt over the man's bare body, noticing the soldier had more than his share of scars along with fresh bruises and cuts.

The two lawmen backed out of the house, turning off lights as they moved.

"Mrs. Johnson is going to be real surprised to see him." Thatcher laughed. "I wish I could be a fly on the wall when she walks into the bedroom and there he is, naked and asleep."

Cline laughed. "I'm guessing the Johnsons wouldn't agree to any plan that involves you watching their homecoming. We need to tell folks to stay away for a few days and give them some time."

CHAPTER SIX

Griffin's Plan

"I DON'T CARE how important you think it is, Griff, I'm not going over to the Franklin house again. First, that big place is old enough to be haunted, and second, the sisters pick on me," Cooper yelled as he backed away.

"Yes, you are going this week and every week until we figure it out. We all are. We agreed that one of us would find a wife and be married by Christmas. That's less than six weeks away, little brother. Not even two months left." Griffin knew Cooper was their long shot for finding a bride, but they all had to try.

Cooper shook his head. "I don't see how the sisters can help. I know how to compliment a girl. I don't have to learn. We're all too old for dating school."

"Telling a girl that she has nice headlights is not a compliment, Cooper. Miss Franklin was right about that. The last girl you dated wrote her goodbye on the ranch gate."

"I remember," Cooper yelled again, as if he thought his brothers might be hard of hearing. "I'm the one who had to sand it off."

Elliot clicked off his computer and reached for his jacket. "Give up on him, Griff. Maybe we should tell the Franklin sisters to find a deaf girl. It would be easier than trying to domesticate Cooper."

All three walked out the side door of headquarters, still arguing. The first lesson at the Franklin sisters' home last week had been an hour lecture on how to talk to a woman. Griff figured out about halfway through that pretty much anything he'd ever said to girls from the playground all the way to the woman he met last month at the feed store was wrong. He was amazed how he'd made it past thirty without being killed by an angry mob.

Each brother climbed into his own vehicle. Elliot drove his Aruba metallic gray Land Rover. Cooper rattled down the dirt road in the old red Ford pickup that had been their father's. Tack and riding gear always loaded the bed of the truck.

Griffin drove his Toyota Tundra. It might be five years old, but there wasn't a challenge it wouldn't match. It never occurred to any of the Holloway boys that they should ride together during the thirty minutes to town. They all liked to drive.

On the way into town, Griffin listened to country music. Elliot liked jazz, and Griffin wasn't sure what Cooper turned his radio to.

For thirty minutes, they'd all have time to think about the assignment the sisters had given them last week. *Where do you see yourself in twenty years?*

Griffin had no idea why they needed to know that, but the question had bothered him. He might have been able to answer in his teens or even early twenties, but somewhere over the past ten years—while he'd been burying his parents, running the ranch and trying to finish raising Cooper—Griffin had settled. Not just on the land, but he'd given up on dreams for himself. He'd stopped wishing for anything in his life. Lately, he'd just tried to get through each day, getting as much done as he could, trying not to worry himself into an early grave.

He was a man who lived by the seasons, and ranch work never got finished. Not one day had he ever woken up and said, "I'm caught up." He'd never had one week when he'd decided to take off because everything could wait. Not one daydream that wasn't marked with the Maverick brand.

Adventure, excitement, even joy and heartache had been washed away in a river of responsibilities. It never got easy. It never stopped. There were no vacations. Hell, there weren't even days off. At some point, he'd given up on personal goals and decided to think of himself as more of a machine. He ate so he could keep going. He slept so his mind would be clear. He breathed to keep blood flowing, but somewhere amid all that had to be done, he'd stopped living.

He was a walking breathing corpse. The last thing he'd plant in Maverick soil would be himself—worn out, used up, broken-down.

The Franklin sisters wouldn't be able to bring him back to life with table manners or by showing him where he went wrong with other women. One reason he'd quit even trying to date was simply that the excitement at the beginning wasn't worth the arguments when it came time to break up. No matter what he did, dating wasn't worth the disappointment at the end.

Before he could think of saying, "I love you," women he'd dated were compiling his list of shortcomings. He never lived up to their hopes. Just once, he would have liked to be enough for a woman. Maybe not the greatest or the best, but enough.

Hell, maybe that's why he forgot about goals. He never reached any of them anyway.

Griffin had a pretty good guess as to why Cooper couldn't answer the Franklins' question about his future. Because twenty years from now, nothing would change for his little brother. He'd simply be twenty years older. Cooper had the life he wanted. Change could only be downhill for him.

When Griffin walked into the Franklins' sunroom that had

been converted into a classroom, he was surprised to see a tea set for five. Tea? Were the old ladies crazy? Beer might be more like it.

Cooper, who'd sworn he wasn't sitting through another lecture, took one look at the tiny cakes and grabbed a chair. While the sisters took turns lecturing about how to act and what constituted proper dinner conversation, Cooper ate a dozen of the tiny cakes.

Within an hour, to Griffin's surprise, the sisters dismissed both his brothers and ordered him to remain. He felt like he'd been kept after school, and the reason was bound to be something he didn't want to hear.

Griffin shifted uncomfortably as they turned a huge whiteboard over, and he saw the names of the last five women he'd dated, with what looked like a list of complaints about him under each name.

This was going to be bad, he decided, *real bad*.

"First—" Rose tapped a wooden spoon over each name "—as near as we can tell, you have no type. There is no common denominator among the women."

Silently, he wanted to argue. They were all women and they probably all hated him. Sure, one was ten years older, another eight years younger. Two were tall, two average and one too short. One blonde, one redhead, two brown-haired and one skunk-striped. He couldn't remember how much education any one of them had. It hadn't been a subject that had come up before he decided to run, or they made up some excuse not to go out with him again.

Rose lifted a sheet of paper Griffin had scribbled on before he'd climbed out of his truck. "Next, your vision of yourself twenty years from now." She unfolded the note. "In twenty years, you want to have a successful ranch."

"Right." He smiled, proud that he'd thought of one goal.

Hell, he'd always needed a successful ranch. One free of debt. One he wasn't always worried about losing.

Rose didn't look happy. "No wife? No children?"

Griffin was afraid to answer. Either way, he could sound like an idiot. He'd already asked them to help him find a wife, but the chances of her staying around for twenty years, with his record, didn't seem high.

Rose pointed her spoon. "You don't want a wife, do you, Griffin?"

He almost yelled that of course he wanted a wife, every man wants a wife, and kids, but deep down, he had no idea how he'd handle either. Women always made everything so complicated. In truth, he just wanted to keep his land. He wanted to see it prosper. He'd be happy watching his brothers have families. Hell, if he said he wanted offspring, the sisters would probably expect him to come up with names.

Maybe if the time ever came when he didn't have to worry about losing the ranch, he'd think about the rest later. Kind of fill out the puzzle one piece at a time.

Rose looked like she might stare him down until the Second Coming, so Griffin decided to tell the truth. "I was hoping to find a woman with land or money. Either for me or one of my brothers, it don't matter. I know you two ladies think it's selfish, probably borderline criminal, but that's about as far as I can reason right now. I'm hoping she'd bring an infusion of money or income to keep our ranch going. It's been in the family for over a hundred and fifty years and I don't want to be the one to lose it. I'll do whatever it takes."

When Rose didn't say a word, he added, "You find me a rich girl who likes living in the country, and I swear I'll be good to her. I'll even let her name the children." Griffin grinned. One future problem solved.

"But?" Rose coached as if she knew there was more to his request.

"But don't expect me to entertain her or keep her company or take on the job of making her happy." He might as well toss in another. "Or listen to her problems. I won't have time. If she wants that kind of partner, then she'd be happier with a cocker spaniel."

Rose nodded once at her sister, then straightened as if making a formal announcement.

Griffin stood to face the sentencing. They wouldn't have to kick him out. He'd thank them politely and leave with his head up. He might not have answered the way they wanted him to, but at least he'd been honest.

Rose cleared her throat. "Griffin Holloway, I think my sister and I have found just the woman for you. Meet me at Dorothy's Café at two tomorrow. There will be details to go over."

Two minutes later, Griffin walked out of the sisters' bed-and-breakfast, trying to figure out if he was happy or terrified. Mostly, he was just shocked that the old girls hadn't been put off with the truth. He realized he knew nothing about women or how to make them happy, but if they thought one woman might be interested, he'd try.

Nightmares haunted him until almost sunup about what would be waiting for him at two o'clock. A woman so ugly telemarketers wouldn't hire her. A rich girl with a dozen kids she planned to bring along. A lynch mob because he was the most insensitive man who ever lived.

The Franklin sisters hadn't told him anything, but Griffin knew one fact. This woman who was interested in marrying him didn't have very high standards.

CHAPTER SEVEN

Dorothy's Café

THE NEXT AFTERNOON, Griffin walked into Dorothy's Café to face his fate. He felt like he'd won the toss to be the first brother to stand before a firing squad.

As he looked around the almost empty café, he found himself hoping Rose didn't show up. Maybe she was simply testing him. After all, almost every woman he'd dated in the past mentioned how he was unreliable or never on time.

Two o'clock on the dot, and not surprising, both of the Franklins were at the back table. Griffin smiled. No prospective bride waiting. They were just testing him. He was so relieved, he couldn't have wiped his grin off with dynamite.

"Afternoon, ladies. May I join you?"

Rose rolled her eyes. "Of course you can, Griffin. You're the reason we're here."

He pulled out the chair across from them and folded his arms. He was reliable. He could be on time. He'd just proved it. Now they could take that fault off his list.

The waitress rushed over and offered him coffee, then refilled the ladies' iced teas. When she finally stopped chatting and wandered off, Griffin started, "I guess my future wife wasn't as easy to find as you thought."

Rose raised one finger. "Oh, we found her, but she has a few concerns about you, Griffin Holloway. We're just staying around to make introductions and warn you to be on your best behavior. You're not an easy sale, boy."

"Does she even know me?"

Rose straightened. "No, but she Googled you."

"Does she fit my criteria?" He hated that he sounded so cold, but Griffin didn't want to waste his time or hurt some woman's feelings because he didn't pick the first offer presented.

"She does." Daisy finally joined the conversation. "The question, Mr. Holloway, is do you fit her list of requirements?"

Griffin didn't like the lady already. Maybe the Franklins thought she was pretty, smart and rich, but he was picking her, not the other way around.

Before he could complain, a silver Denali truck pulled up out front. No one could miss the huge black crown on the truck's door.

"You ever hear of the Krown Ranch?" Rose asked.

"Yeah, I've heard of it. South of here a few hundred miles. Huge and powerful. The man who owns it spends more time in Austin than on his ranch. Never met any of the family, but I hear they raise some of the best registered Angus cattle in the state."

Rose stood. "Well, you're about to meet Sunlan Winston Krown. Be polite to her, Griffin, because she fills out your list."

Daisy joined her sister as she tried to gather up her purse and finish her tea at the same time.

Deciding now might be a good time to run, Griffin considered heading out the door. He saw a tall woman in a cream-colored wool suit step out of the truck. Her hair was sunshine-blond and pulled back in a neat knot. She was about his age, but way out of his league. Everything about her, from her handmade leather boots to her perfectly fitted jacket said money, deep-pocket money.

Griffin hadn't even worn his good hat.

Rose passed him, knocking her huge purse against his leg. "Don't look so worried, Griffin. When I told her you wanted to get married before Christmas, she said, 'Fine with me, but we'll have a few things to settle first.' At least she didn't turn you down right away. We'll leave you two alone to hammer out the details."

Griffin walked to the front door and held it open so the Franklin sisters could leave and Miss Krown could step in. As she passed him, he just stood there, staring like Dorothy's Café had a doorman.

"Mr. Holloway?" She nodded once without smiling.

"Miss Krown."

They stood assessing each other. He decided she wasn't pretty—stunning was more the mark, but on closer look, he didn't miss the dark circles beneath her beautiful blue eyes or the pale skin her makeup didn't quite conceal.

The lady had her problems, and at this point, he wasn't sure if he was adding to them or being offered up as a solution.

Maybe she's dying, he thought. For some reason, she wants to be married before she passes. Why else would a woman like her even be talking to a man like him?

"Shall we sit?" Her words were low, like she thought she might be trying to communicate with a lower life form.

"Sure." He waved her to the table where he'd been sitting with the sisters. "Would you like some coffee?"

"If I do, I'll order it." She took the chair Rose had vacated and shoved their tea glasses aside. "I'm not here to socialize, Mr. Holloway. I understand you are interested in getting married as soon as possible."

"Yes. We could spend a few weeks dating, getting to know each other, but a date before Christmas would be nice." He thought of adding *give you time to change your mind*, but that didn't seem a positive comment.

"That won't be necessary," she answered as she finished removing her gloves and waved the waitress over. "Anytime, as long as it's soon, will be fine."

Griffin studied her as she ordered a water with lime, not lemon. She was really beautiful in an untouchable way and confident like people with loads of money sometimes were, but maybe she wasn't too bright if she was considering his offer.

"I believe in being completely direct. Why do you want a wife, Mr. Holloway?"

He felt like he was on the witness stand. He wouldn't be surprised if she pulled out a Bible for him to swear on. "I'm thirty-four. It's time I settle down, but I work fifteen to twenty hours a day seven days a week. I asked the Franklins to help me find a wife."

Sunlan didn't react. She just stared at him. Griffin decided he was sounding like a nitwit.

"You're in debt." She didn't blink when she spoke.

It wasn't a question, so he nodded. "We hit a dry spell, but you probably understand that. You were raised on a ranch."

"Only until I was twelve. Then I went to boarding school. From there, college in Colorado. I have two degrees, one in art restoration and the other in European art history."

"You must enjoy the work." He hoped she didn't ask him what degree he had. Ranch management didn't sound nearly as interesting.

To his surprise, she smiled. "I don't work, Mr. Holloway. As an only child of an only child, trust funds run deep in my family."

He decided to turn the tables. "Why would you want to marry me, Miss Krown? Sounds like you're set for life."

For a moment, he saw surprise in her eyes, then a kind of deep sadness settled in again. "I've checked you out. Your father invested heavily in upgrades that didn't prove profitable. Your parents' long illnesses drained reserves. Eighty percent of your pasture was wiped out by prairie fires six years ago." She raised a perfect eyebrow. "Should I go on?"

"No. I obviously know the whole story. Once a ranch gets behind, it's hard to climb out. Interest on the loans drains profits."

She nodded, then lowered her voice. "Despite the money troubles, you appear to be a good man, Griffin Holloway. You deal fairly with your men and, as near as I can tell, you are a man of your word. You have never committed a crime. You've finished raising your brothers while taking care of sick parents. You come from sturdy stock. An old Texas family. My father would approve of you."

For once, she sounded like a rancher. Only this time she was buying a husband by the breed, he decided. "I have a feeling that has nothing to do with why you want to get married. Am I right?" Funny, he could read her emotions in her eyes. Light blue, the color of the plains sky. Hauntingly beautiful.

"Correct. If we marry, I'll move enough money to clear your debt completely, not just pay on the loan. That should put the ranch in good standing for a year. Each year we remain married, I will deposit the same amount on our anniversary into the ranch accounts to insure further growth."

"Fair enough." She was offering exactly what he was wanting, only not for one year but for as long as they were married. For the first time since he'd been old enough to study the ranch accounts, he wouldn't have to worry about money. "What's the catch?"

"I will allow no restraints on my time after we are married, but I will keep you informed when I travel. We will not share a bed or a checking account. Your accounts, as well as the ranch accounts, will be yours. My accounts will be mine. When I am on the Maverick Ranch, we will also not share a bed. I'd like my own suite of rooms, if possible. I'll need a bedroom, an office and a living area. From the size of that barn of a headquarters, that should be no problem."

"I can handle that. My grandpa thought he'd have a dozen kids. Turned out after four wives, he fathered only my dad. Half the house is closed off or used for storage." Too much information, he decided. Keep it simple. "We'll make room for you."

He didn't want to keep up where she was anyway, and the three bedrooms in the attic hadn't been used for years. She'd have her own bath and he could clean out every room up there if she wanted a study or maybe, from the looks of her, she'd be one of those women who needed a whole room for extra closets. When she did come home, she'd have the best views of his ranch from those high windows.

His room was completely across the house from her. He probably wouldn't even know she was on the ranch. Griffin was so pleased with the plan he didn't realize she was talking again.

"…agree to a few public appearances with me each year. My choice. No more than six a year, at the most I'd think, but you may have to fly to Austin or Washington. My father usually doesn't want to talk to me, but he needs to parade me around."

She hesitated.

"All right, I'll go with you," he added but it was obvious she had more to say.

Those blue eyes filled with tears, but her voice was so low he had to lean across the table.

"Tell me what you want, lady. If this is going to work, we got to lay it all out before either of us agrees."

She nodded. "As far as the world is concerned, we'll be happily married," she said, speaking up. "True to one another for the duration. The marriage must never have any hint of scandal. I'll have your word on that before any other details."

Raising an eyebrow, he whispered, "So I get to keep my ranch, but I become a monk?" He was willing to compromise, but setting forever rules seemed harsh. He'd never thought of having an affair after marriage, no matter what the ground rules were. He might have hoped that with marriage came a few benefits. Maybe even a closeness after a while. But that option didn't seem to be on the table.

Hell, why was he complaining? It had been so long since his last one-night stand he couldn't remember the woman's name. He was already living a monk's life.

"Those are my terms. You'll have your ranch. I'll have a husband I can trust."

Griffin pushed his hat back. He had so many questions he didn't even know where to start. "I'll think about it. In the meantime, do you want a tour of my ranch?"

"No. I saw the land before I considered the man." She smiled slightly and he thought Sunlan Krown was not the kind of woman who'd ever need to buy a husband.

"How'd we measure up?" He didn't know whether to be impressed that she cared about the ranch or insulted that it came first.

"You've got good grazing land and the plowed fields don't look overworked. Plenty of water year-round, I'm guessing. You could easily run double, maybe triple the cattle on your open pastures."

"That would take money."

"Of course, and good management." She looked him straight on. "Which you can provide. Everyone my investigator talked to said you run the place better than anyone could."

"My brothers help." Before he could add more, she changed the subject.

"Are you making use of that huge barn north of the headquarters?"

"You drove across my place?" He found it hard to believe she'd explored the whole ranch without anyone noticing.

"No, I flew. The barn and corrals surrounding the white barn didn't seem to be in use."

Of all the things she wanted to talk about, he never thought the fancy barn his father built would interest her. "No. No one uses the barn. My father thought to board racehorses, but it didn't happen. He kept pouring money into the place, but his dream never panned out."

"I understand." The waitress delivered her water and refilled his coffee. Griffin thanked her, but Sunlan took the time to stare at him.

"I'm glad the land measured up," he said, "but that still doesn't tell me why you want to marry."

Sunlan didn't reach for her glass. She simply sat still as stone until she was sure the waitress was out of hearing distance.

"I have to marry because I'm pregnant. My father will disown me if I bring even a cloud of scandal to our name this year."

Griffin remembered hearing the great Winston Krown might be running for office, but news like that didn't matter much in Griffin's world.

"If we do this, you claim the baby and no one, not even your brothers, will ever know it is not yours. I'll raise my child, but he or she will have your name."

"How far along are you?" He took her news calmly. He should have expected a few catches in the plan. A woman like her would never give a man like him a second glance.

"A little over two months. I might be showing by Christmas, I'm guessing."

"Women raise babies alone all the time. You don't have to marry anyone." He almost felt sorry for her, doing something so drastic when it wasn't necessary. "Or I've heard there are reasons to end the pregnancy."

"Will you marry me without asking questions? You need to understand from the first that you have no right to ask questions or make any demands. This is a bargain between us and only us. No one will ever know the details. We will seal the deal with a handshake. We'll marry and then go on living our separate lives, only my child will have your last name. You'll have your ranch, and you'll never bring any shame on my child's last name. Understood? You don't have to love my child but he should be able to respect you."

"Understood." Holloways never caused trouble. Forgetting to vote now and then was their only crime.

She'd said twice that the child would carry his name, he realized. For some reason that was important to her. Maybe the most important part of the bargain. Only, why would she need his name? She already had the powerful Krown name.

"One question," he added. "You planning to divorce me as soon as the kid is born? Right? Am I just your temporary stand in? I'm all right if that's the way it is, but I'd like to know the truth from the start."

"No. If I marry you, it will be for life. I'll not be the one to end it. Should you wish to end, we'll do so quietly but my child will always be a Holloway."

He thought of asking if she meant the end of the marriage or his life, but he didn't want to give the lady any ideas.

Lowering his head, Griffin pulled out a notepad he always kept in his pocket and stared at the back-flap calendar. She was watching him, waiting, but he needed to think. There were about a million ways this setup could go wrong, but she seemed to be taking most of the risk.

When he looked up, he thought he saw fear in her eyes again. He wasn't sure if it was because he might say yes or no. "If either of us does want to end this, I agree we do so quietly, no yelling or blaming each other. We just tell people we grew apart."

"No interviews. No news account. If you walk away, you'll do so silently."

"I won't walk away," he whispered more to himself than her. If she could stay in this, so could he. No matter what. Clearing his throat, Griffin began his new life's story. "A few months ago, I was in Fort Worth at a horse show. We had a one-night stand. I got you drunk, so you can blame it all on me. I didn't use protection, but I want to do the right thing now. How does that sound?"

She shook her head. "I wasn't drunk. We'd been having a secret fling for several months. I fly my own plane, so I'd meet you places. You'd drive up to my horse ranch in Denver when I was there. We fell in love almost at first sight."

"Right." He studied her as he made up their past. "We were into each other but keeping it quiet." *Fat chance of that*, he thought. "I insisted we marry when I found out you were pregnant."

"I agreed. We were getting serious anyway. We both figured that a hurried marriage was just moving up the wedding date that we both knew was about to be set."

Griffin nodded. "I like that. It makes it sound like neither of us got trapped."

"Then it's a deal?" She offered her hand. "You got me pregnant a few months ago in Fort Worth. I was actually in Dallas at the time, so the story will stand."

Griffin felt like he was stepping off a cliff, so he might as well jump. He was saving his ranch, and in a small way, he felt like he was saving her. He liked that feeling. "It's a deal. You set the date, and we marry at the Franklins' place before Christmas."

She opened her mouth to object, then hesitated. "I agree to the location, but I decide all the other details about the wedding. I see no point in bothering you."

"Your way or the highway, right, lady?"

"You guessed it, cowboy."

"You're going to be a bossy wife, aren't you?"

"Yes, but the good news is you won't have to see me often. I run my life, you run your ranch. When I'm with your family, I'll play the loving wife. When we're around my father, you play the loving husband."

Watching her closely, he added, "When I'm with your family, I'll stand with you. I'll always have your back. I promise."

She smiled for the first time. "Thanks. It may not be as easy as you think."

"I can handle it, Sunlan." The words seemed simple, but he felt like he was swearing an oath. "Any other details?"

She relaxed and picked up her straw without bothering to put it in her drink. "I'll deposit the full amount of the loan payoff the day we marry and you will give me that big barn as a wedding present." She smiled again for only a fraction of a second. "Since I'll be coming back and forth the next two months, I'd like to clear a strip near your place where I can land. I'll stay at the bed-and-breakfast until we're married and I'll remodel my space at your headquarters."

"Fair enough, but that barn won't fit on your finger and you'll have to leave it if you leave me."

"I won't leave you, Mr. Holloway. You're exactly the man I've been looking for."

He found that hard to believe. Any single man breathing would take this deal. She was offering a full payoff of a loan he'd been dealing with since he inherited and all she asked for was a barn no one was using.

They stood. He dropped a twenty on the table and they walked out together as the few people in the café stared.

Griffin noticed two men standing in the back of a pickup. They were trying to lift a plastic reindeer onto the light pole at the corner of the café's parking lot.

"What's that?" Sunlan asked.

It is time running out, he almost said before answering, "First sign of Christmas decorations. Seems those old reindeer go up earlier every year. Town starts decorating in November and last year it was almost Valentine's before they came down. Crossroads goes all out for Christmas. Lights in the gazebo. A town Christmas tree. We even have wagon rides full of carolers."

"Sounds like a great time of year for a wedding." She almost smiled.

While he was trying to decide if they should shake hands, she hugged him.

"Everyone in the café is watching." She fit against him. "It's time we began playing the happy couple."

"Right." He kissed her on the mouth, which felt as awkward as if he'd kissed Rose Franklin.

He pulled away, noticing she looked surprised but not angry.

"I'll try to get used to that. It's something married people do, I guess," she said so low no one could have heard her. "But warn me next time."

"I'll remember that."

She patted him on the shoulder as if understanding that he'd probably need house-training. "I'll be staying at the Franklins' place another day or two. Could you arrange to have breakfast with me, Mr. Holloway?"

"I can and if you have time, I'd like to invite you over to-morrow night to meet my brothers. They are part of the ranch. Part of my life."

"I understand."

"Should I meet your parents?" He had no idea how to move forward.

"No. My father will be at the wedding. You'll meet him then."

Several pickups pulled up, parking all around them. Cattle-men, obviously stopping in for afternoon coffee and pie. Griffin knew them all, but two seemed to know Sunlan, as well. Both tipped their hats to her and one winked at Griffin.

Once they went inside, Griffin leaned close. "They're still watching, aren't they?"

"I'm afraid so." She lifted her chin slightly and shrugged.

"Then we'd better make it look good." He grinned, thinking his part of the agreement wouldn't hurt a bit. "I'm planning on kissing you again, if you've no objection."

She moved her arms over his shoulders and pressed against him.

The kiss was quick, light, but not awkward. When he pulled a few inches away, he saw that bone-deep sadness again in her eyes. "We can do this," he said. "We'll work it out."

She didn't look like she believed him. "I can't give this baby up. I won't."

"I'm with you on this, Sunlan." Odd, he thought. This beautiful, rich lady was broken. Deep down broken. And he wanted to help. For a moment, he wished he could tell her that the marriage, the money, didn't matter. He just wanted to help.

He watched her drive away, trying to decide if he'd just signed on for a ride through heaven or hell. Then he realized he didn't really care. He had no plans of getting off.

CHAPTER EIGHT

The Johnsons

JAMIE JOHNSON CLIMBED from her old white Dodge Caravan feeling as if she'd been run over by the school bus while it was loaded with screaming teens. From noon Friday until sundown Sunday, she'd been in charge of thirty-seven high school drama students. They all practiced on the two-hour bus trip to Lubbock for regionals and either celebrated or cried all the way home.

This was their first meet, and her first time as sponsor. Jamie felt like she'd run a marathon in heels between all the events that went on at once. Add fights, constant noise, unauthorized room changes, underage drinking and the worse plague—sophomore lovers. To make it more difficult, the male sponsor, an English teacher named Mr. Thames, kept flirting with her while he ignored the students. He was more than ten years older than her and considered himself an expert on pretty much everything.

Finally, she made it back to Crossroads with all thirty-seven students and one pouting male sponsor. When she'd used her cover, *I'm married*, he'd simply said, "So am I." The next shield she used was, *I'm not attracted to you, sorry.* That made him mad.

After all, he'd read the classics, so what woman wouldn't be attracted to him?

Just before the sun disappeared, Jamie pulled up to her little place on the lake. "Peace," she said with a smile. The cabin had been over her budget, but the moment she saw it, Jamie knew this would be her home. She'd drifted through three different school districts in the eight years since college, but this place, this school, this town was the first time she felt like she could finally settle down and unpack. No apartment this time. She'd saved enough for a down payment and she wanted her own house.

A dozen wind chimes scattered along the front porch clanked a welcome in the chilly breeze, almost making her forget her problems from the weekend.

She unloaded her suitcase from the van and bumped it up the back steps while mumbling what she wished she'd said to that jerk of an English teacher. Something told her his behavior would hang around like food poisoning brought home from vacation.

There seemed to be a kind of man who thought he could push his advances on women who weren't too pretty or too slim. He thought they should be grateful. He'd flirt with the shy girl, the homely girl, the alone girl, probably because he thought she'd be desperate and accept sex without the wrappings. No promises. No future. He even walked in with the attitude that she should feel lucky to get his attention.

Jamie had never played that game, and she wouldn't do it now. She might not be slim and beautiful, but she had her pride. Only all weekend, Mr. Thames continued to advance as if he thought he might wear her down.

There was nothing she could do about Mr. Cheater's behavior. He hadn't touched her, except on the arm once and a dozen more times by accident, he'd claimed. He'd stood in the bus aisle twice when she was moving back to her seat. Both times, he'd made sure their bodies bumped.

He'd hinted at things they might do, but she'd look like a fool turning him in for sexual harassment. She'd watched her roommate in college try to file a complaint once. They'd done the paperwork, but nothing ever happened.

Jamie thought she'd solved the problem of unwanted advances this time. When she applied for the job at Ransom Canyon High, she'd said she was married. She'd seen what happened after she turned down a few advances at a new school. Once, a pushy vice principal turned the tables and told everyone she'd hit on him. Half the faculty avoided her after that. Another man, husband to the parents' booster club president, tried to get her fired because she wouldn't play along with his *harmless flirting*.

But this time, she'd been sure the *I'm married* lie would work. She'd even bought a ring and put Mr. and Mrs. Johnson on the mailbox.

As she pulled her bag across the tiny kitchen of her new home, she noticed three cereal bowls stacked by the sink.

Strange. She never left dirty dishes out. Maybe Goldilocks had visited three times while she was gone. If a robber broke in, he'd be hard-pressed to find anything worth carrying off. Books? A hundred old VHS movie classics? A mice teacup collection? A burglar would have trouble making a fast turnaround for cash with any of her stuff.

One glance at the dozen Precious Moments statues running along the top of her three feet of kitchen cabinets eased her mind. She'd bought one tiny figurine every year as her Christmas gift to herself since she'd left home. One box to open under her tree made the holiday.

She moved through the living room. The TV was turned to face the couch. Odd. The afghan she always curled up in was on the floor. An almost empty bag of donut holes sat between two paper cups.

Her tired mind began to put the obvious together. Someone

had been in her place. They'd eaten her cereal, brought donuts to the break-in and watched TV.

Slowly, she lifted the umbrella she kept by the front door and moved toward her bedroom. A runaway kid maybe? A drunk fisherman who got the wrong house? Mr. Thames making one more try?

She crossed the darkened hallway and slipped into the only bedroom. Watery moonlight shone through thin cotton curtains, giving the shadows a blue glow. As always, the house was as quiet as a crypt, except for the lake gently lapping against her tiny slice of shoreline twenty feet from her back door.

Jamie lifted her weapon, planning to strike if anything moved.

Clothes were scattered on the floor like it had rained khaki. A dirty pair of boots rested on one side of the bed. A white towel was looped over the corner of the headboard as though the entire room was surrendering.

Ignoring the clutter, the dripping shower drew all her attention. Not only had someone broken into her house and made a mess, he'd obviously just taken a shower in her bathroom.

Jamie's grip tightened on the umbrella as she moved toward the bathroom. The door wasn't completely closed. She pushed it slowly open as if she might be compromising a crime scene.

The shower door slid open, releasing a cloud of steam that fogged Jamie's glasses for a moment. She wiped them off in time to see one muscular arm reach out for a towel that no longer hung on the hook.

A male voice swore as he moved halfway out and grabbed one of her fancy towels only used as decoration.

Jamie froze, trying to decide whether to scream or attack. She'd had no training in using an umbrella as a weapon, and no one lived near enough to hear her yelling.

A moment later, a man stepped from the fog as he tied the towel to his waist.

He was tall, well built and scarred.

Jamie drew in a breath to try screaming as she looked up into his face. Rainy-day gray eyes met her stare as water dripped from his short dark hair. He showed no surprise, only awareness as he looked down at the point of her umbrella an inch from his middle. He raised one dark eyebrow, and she stepped back a few inches without lowering her weapon.

The intruder slowly smiled and said as calmly as if they were just passing one another on the street, "Evening, Mrs. Johnson. I was wondering when you'd be home."

The stranger knew her name! He must have been stalking her. That's what killers did, right? Find single women. Learn their routine. Break into their house. Murder them.

Do something! After all, she had the weapon. He obviously had none. That should give her the advantage.

Of course he knew her name. It was on the mailbox. *Stop thinking. Act.*

Pointing the umbrella directly at his chest, she decided to at least act brave. If he was going to kill her, she wouldn't go down without a fight.

"Who are you?" She paused to scream, but it sounded more like a hiccup. "And what are you doing in my house?"

He stood his ground, still smiling, still almost nude, still calm. "I'm Captain Wyatt Johnson with the United States Army. I'm not sure what I'm doing in your house or even how I got here. Best scenario I can figure out is the sheriff of whatever town this is found me exhausted and assumed I was your husband. He thought he was bringing me home, and I was so tired I must have seen the bed and crashed. When I woke up, my car wasn't here so I stayed."

She poked him about heart level with the metal tip. "You are not my husband."

"No, but neither is anyone else. After I ate the donuts left on the porch, I looked around. Not one picture, no clothes, no birth control or second toothbrush. Lady, near as I can tell, you're living a lie. Somehow, you managed to convince even the sheriff that you were married, but unless I've lost all sense of observation, you are not."

When she just stared, he added, "I don't mean you any harm, Mrs. Johnson. I'll keep your secret and be out of your house as quickly as possible. I won't tell a soul. I would have left yesterday, but no one was here and I just needed to rest awhile and get my head straight. I figured, since they'd already dumped me here and you weren't home, I'd—" he hesitated "—I'd house-sit till you got back."

She finally lowered the umbrella. "Would you mind putting some clothes on while I call the sheriff?"

"Of course. Sorry, ma'am." He slipped past her. "I'll need him to take me to my car. I think I ran it off the road a few miles back. It was dark and raining. I must have been sleep-driving because I have no idea where I was."

She didn't turn around, but she could hear him rummaging for clothes.

"I don't want to be any trouble, but I probably should mention that if you tell the sheriff I'm not your husband, he's going to start asking questions. Like, where is the real Mr. Johnson and why did I stay two nights waiting for you? I could plead exhaustion, but you might want to start thinking about what you're going to say. I've been thinking that once he knows I'm not your Captain Johnson, he'll spot the lie you seem to be living here."

She slowly turned to face the stranger. "You'd blow my cover?"

She glanced at him. The man was listening, but he had that *not my problem, lady* look in those gray eyes.

Jamie sat down on her bed. "I just want to be a teacher. I thought if I invented a husband, everyone would leave me alone. But no such luck. Two months into the school year, you show up and rat me out. Now everyone will know I lied about being married. That's not going to look good on my résumé when I have to leave and look for another job."

"I didn't think employers could ask that kind of questions," he added, more as a correction than interest.

"Maybe they can't directly, but it's there, hidden somewhere in the interview."

"Maybe so. I haven't applied for a job in years. I found the army and stayed."

"You have no idea what it is like to be a single teacher of a certain age. Most men are nice, but a few think it's open season to flirt, to try to hook up on the weekend while we're both chaperones on a school trip. After all, I'm over thirty and alone. I must have played that game before." Jamie knew she was rambling but she was too tired to care. Talking to this total stranger made more sense than rambling on to herself, which she usually did.

Some of the fear melted away since he was dressing. Rapists don't dress. Also, she'd seen no weapons, so that seemed to lean to the bright side. If the home invader stayed much longer, he'd be on his way to becoming a friend.

As he packed, she kept talking. "At every school there's always one teacher who tries to match me up with her unmarriageable brother or son. Or another who thinks something must be wrong with me and wants to help make me over or save me from the sin of being single."

He pulled on an army sweatshirt, then jeans and sat down beside her. "Man, I thought I had it bad in the war zone."

"It wasn't easy being the girl who never gets asked out in college." When he didn't comment, she continued, "Oh, I had lots of *boy* friends. Mostly study partners. I thought sparks might fly between one of them and me. Like one of those Hallmark movies where best friends look across the table and suddenly discover their one true love has been beside them all along.

"But that part of my life story seemed to be left on the cutting room floor. When I started teaching, I was too busy for a while to worry about dating, and then there just wasn't anyone around. The high school teachers lounge isn't exactly a singles bar. I wouldn't know how to get picked up anyway. I'm a total loser at dating skills. I either push people away or hang on too tight."

She paused to study the guy beside her. If Naked Man was going to kill her, she might as well tell him her problems first. What difference did it make? Maybe he'd figure loneliness was contagious and just leave.

Tears rolled down her cheeks. "I've had a terrible weekend fighting off a jerk who tried everything from telling me I should be glad he's even considering sleeping with me while we're both chaperones to threatening to cause trouble if I didn't *relax and take advantage of the opportunity*. All the time the skinny creep kept accidentally touching me and whispering dirty things while I was trying to keep up with thirty-seven kids. Then, I come home to a messed-up house and a naked man in my shower. This is my worst weekend ever, and believe me, I've had some bad ones." She looked up at him, hoping he had some answer.

He stared at her for a full minute. "You always talk so much, lady?"

"Yes. Occupational hazard. I sometimes lecture myself when I can't sleep."

He slowly stood and offered his hand. "How about you go take a shower, and I'll clean up my mess around the place. Then, if you still want to call the sheriff, it's fine with me. Since he brought me here in the rain, maybe he'll remember where I left my rental car and take me back. No harm done. I swear, I didn't break anything. I'll reimburse you for what I ate."

Jamie tilted her head and stared. He didn't look crazy, and he wasn't in any hurry to kill her. She might as well take a shower. His suggestion made about as much sense as anything else in her life right now.

She gathered her jogging clothes, which were good as new since she never jogged, and locked herself in the bathroom. Maybe, if she took her time, he'd be gone by the time she came out.

She stood under the water until it turned cold, then dried off with the other decorative towel and tiptoed to the bedroom. The bed was made. His clothes were gone. It occurred to her that maybe she'd just imagined the handsome man who'd been sleeping in her bed.

People who live alone might invent an imaginary friend. Someone to talk to. It made sense in a crazy kind of way. Why fight it? No one would know but her. Maybe she'd simply invented an intruder?

No, he'd been real. Her imagination wasn't that good. Gray eyes. A muscular body bruised and scarred.

She walked out of the bedroom, feeling almost normal. The donut bag and cups were gone. The cereal bowls must have been washed and put away. Her afghan lay over the arm of her grandmother's rocker, almost in the spot where she always left it.

The man was still there. Dressed in jeans and a cream-colored sweatshirt. Still staring at her with those intelligent gray eyes.

Without a word, he handed her a cup of tea and followed her to the couch. He took one end; she took the other. For a few minutes, she just drank her very bad tea.

"I'm sorry I invaded your house. It wasn't planned. I'd just made it stateside without sleeping for three days, then my car ran off the road, and I must have walked ten miles in the rain before I collapsed. I was asleep when they carried me in here. I stayed because, for a moment, I wanted to be home, or at least feel like I was. I've been deployed for months, and your place just seemed like a tiny piece of normal."

"You can't stay here."

"I know. I'll call a cab to take me to another rental car place instead. That way we won't have to involve the sheriff, after all.

Maybe they'll rent me another car, so I can drive around and find the first one."

She shook her head, and her long damp hair brushed against her cheeks. "Crossroads doesn't have a cab company. There is nowhere to rent a car for fifty miles. There is an old hotel down the road, but it's one step below the Bates Motel. But you're right about one thing. If you call the sheriff, he'll just ask questions, and within minutes, he'll know I lied. How are you going to fix that, Captain Johnson?"

He didn't say a word. If anything, he looked more bothered than guilty of blowing her cover.

"Is your name really Johnson?" she asked.

"Yep. Yours?"

"Yes. It's a very common name. I guess I can see how the sheriff would think you lived here. You must have family waiting for you. A real wife wondering where you are."

"No family looking for me. No real place to call home. When I left the States six months ago, I did have a girlfriend up near DC, but when I called to tell her I was coming in, she told me she was engaged."

"I'm sorry."

He shrugged. "It's happened before."

She looked up and caught his smile. They both laughed as if what he'd said was somehow funny.

"I'll be glad to pay you for the two nights I stayed here. This place was far better than a hotel. I loved just sitting out on the back porch and watching the sun sparkle off the water. Peaceful isn't something you find often. I kind of spent the day drunk on it yesterday."

Jamie leaned back, sipping her tea. "I like that, too. I bought a hammock, but I don't know how to put it up. I was thinking that next spring I'd fix it so I could sleep in it. Then I could listen to the sound of the water all night long. Once in a while, I can hear a fish jump and splash back into the lake."

She wondered if he was thinking what she was thinking. What if he stayed? It was a wild idea. The wildest thing she'd ever done, but it might work. He seemed to love it here. They could coexist for a few days. He probably needed some peace, and she spent almost every waking hour at the school.

No, it wouldn't work. She couldn't let a stranger live with her for a few days, even if she had figured out he probably wasn't going to kill her or rob her.

Neither said a word. Silence. She closed her eyes, trying to think of some way that this would work out. He needed rest. She needed to hold on to her lie.

"I've got a few weeks left on my leave," he said so low she wasn't sure he knew he was saying the words out loud. "If I could stay here, I'd be happy to put up the hammock. I noticed several other things around here that need fixing. I'm good with my hands."

She shook her head at the suggestion. "It wouldn't work. There's only one bedroom."

"I could sleep on the couch."

"No. I'd fit better on the couch. You could have the bed."

"No, I take the couch." He let out a breath he must have been holding for a while. "It could work, Jamie. We could be seen in town. I could pick you up from school. No one would doubt I was real once they saw me. We could pretend to be a couple in front of people and remain polite strangers here. I'll do my best to stay out of your way."

"It shouldn't be too hard. I usually stay late with the drama club and I go to bed early."

"It could work."

She shook her head. "I don't know. You seem like a nice guy, but…"

"How about we give it a day? Any problem, you say the word, and I'm out of here. That will give me time to find my car and get my bearings."

Glancing out the window, she noticed the night seemed to have darkened to inky black. This late, the only way he could leave would be to call the sheriff, and then they'd both have some explaining to do. Captain Johnson seemed nice enough, and there was a lock on her bedroom door.

"All right. We'll try it for one night."

He stood. "Where do we start? I've been eating cereal for two days. Do you think it might be possible for you to drive me to a fast-food place? I'm dying for a real hamburger with the works on it or a real meal of any kind."

She laughed. "Crossroads has a drive-through, but it's not very fast. But we can give it a try. I'll show you the town, too. It'll take about ten minutes."

"Thanks," he said as they walked out the back door.

"For what?"

"For letting me stay. Even if it's only one day, I have a feeling it's going to be the best day of my year."

CHAPTER NINE

The Johnsons

IT TOOK THREE tries for Jamie Johnson to get her old van started. Wyatt knotted his hands in the dark, trying not to comment. The engine sounded like it needed a good tune-up and the woman beside him was pumping the gas pedal too fast. But this wasn't his vehicle, he wasn't the driver and to be honest, he didn't much care where he was going as long as there was something besides cereal and donuts at the end of the journey.

Patrolman Thatcher Jones had filled him in yesterday morning on the news in town when he dropped by to deliver another bag of donuts. He wasn't much more than a kid, but Wyatt had the feeling if trouble came calling, he'd stand strong in a fight.

Thatcher claimed he'd only seen Jamie from a distance, and he had only heard great things about her. Thatcher didn't give Wyatt any details about her age, and Wyatt couldn't ask what his wife looked like.

Watching her now, he couldn't figure out if he thought she was pretty or not. Maybe because he'd seen her scared and panicked. Maybe once she settled down, if she ever settled, he'd take a second look. They had time. A day. For once, he'd wait.

Women were strange creatures. Some were beautiful when you first saw them. Then after talking to them for a few hours, you could hardly see any of that beauty left. He had a feeling he'd seen Jamie at her worst, so in her case it might be the other way around. Not that it mattered. He wouldn't be around long enough to get to know the chatty teacher.

Silence wasn't his usual reaction to any situation. Orders, criticisms and occasionally praise came hard and fast in his world. He felt like he'd been whispering around a fragile flower for an hour and now he needed to bark out a few commands.

But it wouldn't be Jamie Johnson. She was kind, and people like her were rare. Kind enough to give him a chance to stay when most would have kicked him out into the night.

"We've got a hamburger place that's open until ten and a café that's open another hour." She smiled at him once the car started, as if she'd accomplished something.

She backed out of her drive, almost taking down the two thin trees on her right. Wyatt swore he saw them both shake in fear.

"Which place is better?" he asked in a low voice, hoping not to distract her.

"The café, I guess."

"The café sounds great." He hadn't had a regular meal in months. "But show me where the hamburger place is, and I'll walk to town for lunch tomorrow."

"Aren't you going to ask what's on the menu?"

Everything was in shadow as they drove away from the homes along the lake. Peaceful. Calm. "I don't much care where we go and I'll eat anything as long as it isn't floating in milk." Since he couldn't see her face, he let any hint of a smile drop. Smiling had never come natural to him.

She laughed. "You're a lucky man, Captain. Dorothy's Café won't disappoint you. They have a special on Sunday. Usually turkey and dressing with all the trimmings. It's their best dish all week."

"You eat out often?" From the store of food in her freezer, he would have guessed she cooked.

"Once a week. I usually make a run to Dorothy's on Sunday night before they close. I drive in and get a dinner to go. I don't like to eat alone in a restaurant. People give you sad smiles."

"I know what you mean," he lied. He rarely ate alone, and when he did, he didn't care what people thought. "Will you eat with me at the café tonight? I'd like to watch regular people."

"It's a date," she said as she reached the lights of town.

He swore she was blushing. "It's a date," he echoed.

When they pulled into the café, he whispered, "When we get out, hold my hand. That way if anyone that you know sees you, they'll figure I'm your husband."

"I'll probably know half the people in the place by sight. I've been in town almost three months, you know. I'm guessing the sheriff has already told folks you're in Crossroads."

Climbing out, he waited for her in front of the van. When she came near, she offered her hand, and he folded it into his bandaged one.

She tried to tug away. "You're hurt?"

"No. Just put the bandage on to remind me to keep the stitches dry. It's almost healed."

Jamie nodded as they stepped inside.

A few diners turned their direction as they sat down in the last booth against the windows.

Wyatt didn't turn loose of her hand. "This is nice. Peaceful, you know. From here, I can watch the people and passing cars."

Jamie had her back to both. "I don't mind skipping watching crowds or traffic tonight. I feel like I've been surrounded with both all weekend."

A waitress hurried over. "Two specials I'm guessing." She was already writing. "And what to drink?"

Wyatt smiled up at the teenager. "Three specials, and I'll have coffee." He turned to Jamie. "What will you have, honey?"

"Tea." She didn't look up.

The waitress finished writing and grinned at Wyatt. "You guys expecting someone else?"

"No. I'm just hungry." He thought of saying that it was none of her business what he ordered, but Wyatt reminded himself he needed to at least try to be nice. Sometimes he felt like an alien who traveled between two worlds, and neither felt like his home planet. One he didn't seem to belong in, and the other he didn't want to ever feel comfortable in.

The waitress darted off like a rabbit, and Jamie raised her eyebrow. "You almost scared that girl. I don't know her name, but I've seen her in the sophomore hall."

"I thought I was being nice."

She smiled. "I have a feeling you're used to people looking at you with caution."

He patted her hand, still resting in the center of the table. "You're not afraid of me, are you, Mrs. Johnson." It surprised him how much he wanted his statement to be true.

"No, but I've seen you naked. Besides, if you were going to kill me, you'd have done it before you took me out to eat."

"True." He studied her. Average height. Rounded nicely. Hair that looked brown when it had been wet, but now it was naturally curly and blond. "Jamie, sitting here, talking to you, holding your hand, is the most normal thing I've done in a long while. I promise you won't be sorry that you gave me this chance. One day. If it doesn't work out, I'll walk away at sunset tomorrow."

"Fair enough, but you have to give my hand back."

"I do?" He liked her smile.

"Yes, but I'll let you hold it again when we walk out."

"Fair enough." He let go.

He relaxed as he leaned back in the booth and watched families come and go from the café. Just an ordinary night. "So, now that you're an old-timer in Crossroads, tell me about the town."

She talked until the food came, telling him all she'd learned about this one-light little town. He managed to ask a few questions while he cleaned both his plates. Polite strangers, he thought. Nothing more. He could handle that. He liked listening to her voice, a hint of a slow Southern drawl mixed with a peppering of Texas twang.

After he'd finished his third cup of coffee, he walked to the front counter, bought a whole pie and paid the bill. The waitress took her time boxing the pie. "You're Mr. Johnson, aren't you?"

"Yep, just home on leave." It was time he played his part. "You know my Jamie?"

"Sure, my brother is in her class. He says she's a great teacher."

"I'm a lucky man." Wyatt was surprised how proud he felt of his make-believe wife. His opinion of her climbed as the waitress rattled on about how Mrs. Johnson was helping her brother. Jamie seemed a bit of a chatterbox, but if her students liked her, that meant something.

He had a feeling she'd be an interesting person to get to know. If he left her as friends, maybe they'd keep in touch.

When he turned back to their place by the window, he noticed a tall thin man in his forties leaning into the booth. His hands were waving back and forth as he talked. He must have been whispering, but one long finger kept pointing at Jamie as if warning her.

Wyatt couldn't miss the way Jamie had slid as far away as she could from the guy. The stranger had his back to Wyatt, but he had no doubt from the look on Jamie's face that the man was telling her off or warning her, or maybe even threatening her. She kept pushing her glasses up as if they were somehow protecting her.

Anger climbed over his skin like fire ants. He didn't need to see the guy's face to know he was bullying Jamie.

Before he took one step, the thin guy turned and smiled as if he'd said what he came to say and headed out the door. He hadn't been one of the diners or Wyatt would have noticed him. Wyatt guessed he'd just walked in when he'd seen Jamie sitting alone in the booth.

"You know that man?" Wyatt whispered to the waitress, guessing his name wasn't Mr. Cheater like Jamie had called him.

"Yes. He's probably taught English here for fifteen or twenty years. Mr. Thames. Not one of the favorites, but they say he can quote lines from every Shakespeare play."

Wyatt glanced back at Jamie. Her head was down. Her hands laced together.

"Hang on to this pie for me for a minute," he said to the waitress without waiting for an answer.

Ten seconds later, he was out the door and beside the tall stranger. Just as the man opened his car door, Wyatt reached past him and closed it with a hard pop.

"Pardon me, Professor." Wyatt almost smiled. "I'd like to introduce myself."

The teacher looked bothered but not afraid. After all, he was used to being in control. "I've had a long weekend sponsoring a school trip. Parents can make appointments during my prep period. I—"

Wyatt cut him off. "I'm Captain Wyatt Johnson."

He let his name sink in and didn't miss the sudden flash of fear in the man's eyes.

The thin man straightened. "I wasn't aware you were home."

"Probably because it was none of your business." Wyatt's words came fast and cold. "I'm not out here to meet you, Mr. Thames. I just wanted to tell you that if you bother my wife again or ever say a word to upset her, I'll find you. I will gladly fly from half a world away and rip your balls off, then serve them to you as an appetizer before I even get mad enough to start beating you all the way into next week. You won't have to worry about quoting Shakespeare—you'll be visiting with him in the hereafter."

Wyatt smiled a big smile. Showing all his teeth like a predator. "And if you ever touch her, even accidentally again, I suggest you count your fingers because there will be a few missing. I always carry a knife and I've seen a few missing fingers become life-threatening. You'll probably bleed out before you can scream."

Anger flared in the thin man's eyes. "You can't talk to me like this! I'm calling the sheriff and telling him what you just said. You can't threaten to kill me! I'm—"

"I'm not threatening you, pal. I'm *promising* you." Wyatt patted the guy on his shoulder so hard the man's knees almost buckled. "Are we clear?"

Wyatt turned back to the café. Mr. Thames wouldn't call any sheriff. If he did, everyone would know why Jamie's husband had threatened him.

Wyatt grinned. Straightening the guy out had felt so good he was tempted to backtrack and hit him a few times. Maybe Thames would think of the hits as air quotes.

A minute later, he slid in on the same side of the booth with Jamie. She twisted in her seat and was staring out the window at the English teacher leaning against his car as if he was about to vomit. "What did you say to him?"

"I just told him who I was." Wyatt touched her shoulder lightly and was relieved when she didn't jerk away. "He'll never bother you again." What he'd just done felt good. It felt right, even if it probably wasn't very civilized behavior.

To his surprise she turned into him, burrowing into the thick cotton over his shoulder.

He tugged off her glasses and wrapped an arm around her. As she cried softly, he kissed the top of her head. "It's all right, Jamie."

With tears on her cheeks, she smiled up at him. "Thanks."

"No problem. How about we go home? I bought a pie we can eat while we watch a movie. You've got about a hundred to pick from."

"All right, but I pick the movie." She shoved tears away with the palm of her hand.

"Fine." He handed her back her glasses and helped her out of the booth. "But I drive home."

CHAPTER TEN

Midnight Crossing

THREE DAYS AFTER the wreck out on the county road, Jaxson O'Grady carried Buddy out to the dried grass by Shallow River. The dog tried to stand and Jax felt a pride in his doctoring as well as Buddy's determination to live.

His hairy patient was drinking water, eating a little and healing. Jaxson had made the same journey almost two years ago; he knew the drive and determination it took to push back against the pain.

Jaxson was still wrapped and hurting when his cousin, Tim O'Grady, had brought him out to Midnight Crossing three days after he'd gotten out of the hospital.

As Tim had unloaded Jaxson's two suitcases and half a dozen boxes, he'd complained, "You're a hard man to live around, Jax. If this were *Survivor*, the whole family would have voted you off the island. But we don't have an island so this old shack will have to do. One of us will drop by now and then to check on you. If you need us, just leave a white flag on the pole out front. One of the family will see it from the road when we pass."

Jax remembered saying that he wouldn't be needing anything, including a cell phone. He had enough supplies to last a few months and an old Jeep if he needed to make a run.

Tim had just stood there looking like he felt sorry for him. Jax wasn't sure he'd even thanked his redheaded cousin that day. They weren't close in age enough to be friends, with Jax being well into his thirties and Tim still in his twenties. As second cousins, even the O'Grady blood didn't run deep between them, but kin was kin.

About a week later, one of his uncles dropped off a pickup load of woodworking equipment and some rough boards. He taped a note to the pile that read, *When you were a kid, you used to love helping your grandpa work with wood. Now that you've got some time on your hands, I thought you might try it again. Build something.*

All Jax thought about was that he hurt everywhere, was barely mobile and appeared to be hooked on painkillers. The whole family had encouraged him to go into assisted living for a few months, but after two days of being constantly told to *cheer up*, he chose a stay at the cabin, until his legs were stronger. Until the burns on his hands had completely healed. Until he was back to normal.

Whatever that was. Whenever that might be.

He let the tools sit out for a week before he dragged them into the shed beside his cabin. When Tim dropped by a few days later, Jax had a list ready of tools to round out what the old uncle forgot.

"I'm not really interested in messing with the wood, but there doesn't seem anything else to do."

Tim grinned. "You could always shave. Your hair might be light brown, but I swear that beard is coming in with a bit of the O'Grady red in it."

"I hadn't noticed. There are no mirrors in the place."

"No problem, Jax. When you get to looking bad I'll tell you, or better yet, bring out a razor. But from experience, I've learned that a man trying to hide from himself can't disappear behind a beard. You're still there."

Somehow, Tim O'Grady, the crazy writer in the family, had understood and been on his side. Tim might never stop talking when he visited, but he didn't ask too many questions. Jax appreciated that. Healing was something he had to do on his own. Everyone called the day he was broken *the accident*. But it hadn't been an accident.

Jax had been a fireman for almost twelve years. He would have made captain in a few more years. Only one night. One fire. He froze. Almost killing himself. Almost trapping his men.

The scars would fade. The burns would heal. The muscles in his legs would strengthen, but Jax had to rebuild from the inside.

Whether Jax thanked him or not, Tim kept coming. He'd usually stay long enough to sit on the porch and tell Jax all the news from town. When Tim noticed Jax no longer seemed to be working with wood, he brought out a laptop and set it up.

"What am I going to do with that?"

"I don't know. Pay your bills. Watch porn. Email all those friends who keep sending letters you probably never open. Learn more about fires. What's that old saying? *Know your enemy.*"

Jax glared at him as if Tim had taken one more step into insanity. But when his cousin left, he did look up the newest techniques in dealing with chemical fires. Maybe if he'd studied them more, the blast wouldn't have surprised him. He wouldn't have frozen.

On one of the sites, they mentioned fire science and Jax was hooked. He had to learn more even if he never put on the uniform again.

While still healing, he signed up for his first class online from the University of Florida. Only he didn't mention it to anyone, not even Tim. Thanks to the internet, he could order books and turn in assignments. By the time his first year passed at the cabin, he was well on his way to a master's degree without even stepping foot on the campus.

When Tim dropped by to read his latest young adult story about vampires invading high school locker rooms, Jax told him how good it was, which he guessed was really what Tim wanted to hear. He was a rich writer, after all. Rich enough to spend his spring and summers in New York and his winters in a little lake house near Crossroads, Texas.

Rich enough to have women chasing him, but somehow Tim O'Grady always seemed lonely. He must be. He had time to come out and visit his hermit of a cousin living on a tiny piece of land not even big enough to be on any map.

A week after moving in, alone in the silent cabin, Jax had tossed the painkillers in the fireplace. He'd take the pain and if he came out on the other side of it one day, he'd be stronger.

And slowly he did. Now going into his second winter at the cabin, he'd recovered, but still wasn't ready to join the world.

As he watched the collie trying to stand, he said the same words he'd told himself a million times, "It hurts, doesn't it, boy? But you can take it."

Buddy tried again and again to put weight on the leg now in a splint.

"I know how you feel. Only I deserved my pain. You don't." He knelt and patted the dog. "I wish I knew who you belong to." The report in Crossroads's online paper had only mentioned the one-car rollover that sent one person to the hospital. No word about how it happened or that a dog was involved.

Jax guessed whoever dropped the dog off had no idea he could have caused an accident. Or maybe the driver, who didn't strap him into the car, had far more to worry about than the pup traveling with her. The gash behind Buddy's ear was deep. If Jax hadn't found him in the grass, the dog might have died in the dark that night.

"We'd best be turning in. You're in no shape to run and if

you stay out any later, the coyotes will make a snack out of you."
Jax picked up the dog and carried him into the cabin as winter's
first snowflakes whirled in the wind.

"I would take you to town to find a few answers about who
did this to you, but a few of my relatives would probably have a
heart attack if they saw me. My cousin Tim says most of them
have decided I'm no more than a ghost living out here."

The pup put his head atop Jax's scarred hand.

"Wish you could tell me if you know the woman hurt in
the crash. If she's in the hospital, she must be in bad shape. The
paper said her name was Mallory Mayweather. Never heard of
anyone by that name around here."

Buddy's ears shot up at the mention of her name.

"You know her?"

The dog settled back down, no longer interested.

Jax leaned back, keeping his voice calm. "Smith. O'Grady.
Kirkland. Wilson. Franklin. Jones." Buddy's eyes remained
closed. Jax added one more name. "Mayweather."

The dog's ears raised again and he stared at Jax as if waiting
for something.

"You know her." He was no longer asking a question. He
knew the answer.

CHAPTER ELEVEN

Crossroads

SUNLAN KROWN KNEW she could have driven home in a few hours but she wasn't ready to face her father. Not today. Not tomorrow. Not ever, if she had her way. She needed time to settle into the lie.

Besides, the Franklin sisters had been her security blanket since she was in her late teens. No one from her world in central Texas knew of them or that their little inn was her stopover place when she'd driven home from college.

Even now, when she made the journey from her quiet life on Misty Bend near Denver to her father's spread, she'd stopped at their bed-and-breakfast almost every trip. The sisters had taken her in as if she were their kin, and the time at their inn was always relaxing.

The small Colorado ranch, Misty Bend, had been her mother's home growing up but she'd hated the isolation.

Sunlan, on the other hand, had loved every visit. She'd even gone to college near there so she could spend her weekends learning all about horse breeding from her grandfather. The year she graduated, he'd died, and the ranch went not to his only daughter but to Sunlan.

On her nights in Crossroads, Sunlan and the Franklin sisters would sit up late into the night and talk in what-ifs. Now and then, one of the what-if's would be a real problem she was working her way through.

Rose and Daisy would settle down by the fireplace with their knitting and figure out every possible solution to Sunlan's problem. For the sisters, it was just a game the three of them played. For Sunlan, they were the only sounding board she could trust.

Two weeks ago, the what-if was about how she might marry fast. She'd thought they'd seen the discussion as just a game until two days ago, when they called saying they had the solution to her what-if. The perfect man, if Sunlan wanted him.

She'd jumped. Within hours, she'd hired a private detective out of Denver to do a background check, had a hacker look into all Holloway accounts over the past fifty years and then she'd driven to Crossroads and got the final details from the sisters.

"Griffin has been known to cuss," Rose admitted. "But he took care of first his mother and later his father. By the time most men were living the carefree single life, Griffin had taken over running a huge ranch." He might be only thirty-four, but the load he carried seemed to drive him into middle age.

Sunlan silently put the rest of the pieces together. He'd never committed a crime, never been sued, never lied to anyone on record or even signed up for online dating. The women he'd dated said he'd been honest and kind but never passionate. No sparks. They all claimed that at no point did he seem to be falling in love. Not a romantic bone in his body.

They listed his faults as being predictable, boring and often preoccupied with his work. All pluses in Sunlan's mind, not negatives. She didn't need the man, she only needed his name and his cooperation in playing husband when necessary. Other than that, she planned to live her life and expected him to live his.

By the time she walked into Dorothy's Café to meet him, she knew he was just the man she was looking for. Griffin Holloway was her way out of chaos. The one way, maybe the only way, to escape her father's meddling.

If she told her father the truth about her pregnancy, he'd blame her and chalk it up as just one more time she'd let him down. She might be his only child, but she was a woman, and to Winston Krown, that meant one strike against her from birth. It was always the woman's fault when things went wrong. They were conniving manipulative creatures and Sunlan was no exception. All three of his wives had been, including Sunlan's mother. And now that he was planning to run for public office, he swore he'd disown her if she gave the press any dirt on his family.

Since his family consisted of her, there was no doubt who he was preaching to. The baby coming a few months early might be mentioned, but it wouldn't make the news.

After all, she married a rancher with a good name? Someone born on open land who could talk to her father about the problems ranchers faced? Someone whose ancestors had been in Texas as long as her people had? Someone who would take Winston's bothersome daughter off his hands so he wouldn't have to worry about what nutty thing she'd do next?

Then, if she gave birth to a grandson, who might be worthy of inheriting the Krown Ranch? Maybe her father would calm down. He could run for office, go all the way to Washington if he liked and forget about his daughter.

She'd be free of his bullying. Then she could live her own life in peace.

Sunlan might lie to her father about the reason for the marriage, but not to Holloway. He'd been honest with her about needing money and she'd been honest with him about the pregnancy. She might not have told him all the details of her life, but she'd made a fair bargain. She'd given him exactly what he wanted and he'd agreed to her terms.

She'd checked him out. He was a strong man. An honest man. A rancher who, by all accounts, loved his land. If he lived up to their agreement, if he'd be a good role model to her child, she'd see that his ranch prospered.

If he held true? No man in her life had ever done that. Not even her father.

She needed someone to stand with her. Someone who'd never ask questions. From this day forward, her baby's father was Griffin Holloway.

Two months ago, in the doctor's office, she'd finally grown up when the doctor asked the name of the father. Sunlan didn't know what to say. She felt totally alone. If her father found out, he would find a way to keep her off her own ranch in Colorado and away from everything she loved there. He'd make her pay for embarrassing him. Lately, he was too busy to meddle in her life, but if he lost his dream, he'd make sure her life was a nightmare.

That moment when the doctor handed her prenatal vitamins, she realized she was the problem, not the baby she carried.

She stopped feeling sorry for herself and began to think of a way out of her trouble. Getting rid of the baby was not even on the list.

It took her six weeks but finally, she had her answer. She grinned as that answer walked up the path and opened the Franklins' bed-and-breakfast sunroom door to have breakfast with her.

Griffin looked out of place. From the way he was dressed, she'd guess he'd already been up and working outside in the cold for hours before he came to town to have breakfast.

Sunlan smiled. The cowboy didn't fit in the frilly Victorian room the sisters always overdecorated for every holiday. Before he saw her watching, he thumped the stuffed bear dressed up like a pilgrim for the first Thanksgiving, sending him rolling off the corner table.

Sunlan laughed.

Griffin looked up, caught. "I hate cute decorations. Hell, I hate decorations period. A couple of weeks ago, they had Peanuts characters dressed up like trick-or-treaters."

"I could have guessed how you felt. Any other faults?"

He removed his hat and looked nervous. "Yeah, I cuss. Nothing bad. My mom washed most of the profanity out before I was six, but hells and damns tend to pepper my words on a regular basis." Looking around, he changed the subject. "Am I too early or too late?"

"Neither, Mr. Holloway, you're right on time. The sisters had to leave, so we're alone. I asked them to set our breakfast in the kitchen. I thought it might be warmer there."

He nodded and pulled off his gloves and hat as he followed her through to the kitchen. She didn't miss the chaps and spurs he also wore, along with a worn leather jacket.

"You working today?"

"I've been up since five." He plowed his fingers through sand-colored hair. "We've got a quarter mile of fence down and half a dozen cattle who think they should walk toward town on the road. Snow's coming in so it needed to be taken care of."

"Do you have time for breakfast?"

"Breakfast? I thought it was nearer lunch." When she laughed, he added, "I could use a break. Any meal sounds great."

He stood until she was seated. Polite, she thought.

A silence washed between them while she filled his coffee. As she nibbled on her homemade cinnamon-raisin toast, he cleaned his plate.

"You always so hungry, Mr. Holloway?"

"Call me Griffin," he finally said. "Or Griff, if you like. That's what my brothers call me. And yes, I guess I am hungry. Usually happens three times a day. Does that bother you?" He looked at her, as if fearing she had some kind of food issue.

Laughing, she shook her head. "No."

She laid down her fork and looked directly at him. "Tell me straight out what you're thinking, Griffin. Right now. This minute."

Wintergreen eyes met hers. "I'm thinking you're far too beautiful, too classy, probably too educated for the likes of me. I looked up an article in the Fort Worth *Star Telegram*. Your family comes from royalty in Europe. Mine came over on the coffin ships during the potato famine. Most of my Irish-English ancestors didn't own enough to fill one suitcase when they arrived. I'm thinking before we start this, you have a right to know I'm nothing special. I need the money and I wouldn't mind being married, but I don't want to talk you into anything you might regret."

"You finished?"

"Yep."

"You want to back out of our marriage, Mr. Holloway?"

"Nope."

"Me neither." She fought down a laugh. He'd just confirmed her belief in him. "I've already started planning the wedding. But I have questions." She picked up a notebook. "Will you wear a wedding band?"

"I will. Plain gold suits me fine. Will you?"

She made a note. "I will. Plain gold works for me also. I'll order them online. Preacher or judge to do the ceremony?"

"Either is fine but my folks would probably have wanted me to have a preacher."

"Anything you'd like besides the basic ceremony?"

"No."

"Any preference on kind of cake or colors or flowers?" She didn't miss his blank look, like he'd never given a moment's thought to such things.

He grinned suddenly, as if he'd found an answer rolling around in his head. "Just promise me no cute cartoon characters on top of the cake."

"I promise, but it may not be easy with the sisters helping. They're exploding with ideas."

"I'm sure your choices will be sound. Just as long as you show up, I'll be there."

She smiled, knowing he'd just answered most of her questions.

At the end of her list, she looked up. "Griffin, do you have anything you'd like to add? Now is the time if you've been worried about our agreement. I want it to be a fair bargain." She wanted to know they both understood the rules.

He frowned. "I do have one request, but it's not a deal breaker. If you object, it wouldn't affect anything we've already agreed on."

"What?" Patience was not part of her nature.

"I'd like to have a real wedding night. If this is going to be a real marriage, I want to make it real. One night. Whether we sleep together or not won't change the fact that baby you're carrying is mine. Understand?"

"I'll take your request into consideration."

"Fair enough."

He stood and moved a few feet away as if he didn't want to invade her space. "I'll pick you up at five for dinner tonight at the ranch."

"No," she said, too fast. "I'll drive out. I know the way and there's no reason for you to come get me. I'm not a woman who will need taking care of, Griffin. I'll never allow you to boss, manipulate or threaten me in any way."

"Understood." He picked up his gloves. "Oh, and one other thing. I told my brothers I remembered a friend I'd seen a few times in Dallas and invited her to come up for a visit. We'll tell them tonight that you're pregnant and I'm going to do the right thing."

"You think they'll believe us? You mentioning needing a wife and less than a few weeks later, I show up?"

Griffin shrugged. "They're not deep thinkers. My guess is they'll just think I got a lucky break."

"You think we can pull off acting like we care about each other?"

He picked up his hat. "I think we can. Trust me, Sunlan, if you just smile at me now and then, we can pull this whole wedding off. Folks around here will be happy for us."

Fighting back tears, she moved closer and whispered, "I'll try my best. You're my only solution. There is no plan B."

Griffin leaned over and kissed her cheek. "Don't worry about it. I got a feeling this plan will work."

He disappeared into the sunroom. A few moments later, she heard the door open. Before it closed she caught the blink of a bear, dressed as a pilgrim, flying across the sunlight from the windows.

Sunlan held a laugh just until the sunroom door closed. Then she dropped back into the kitchen chair and decided Holloway might not be polished, but he'd certainly be worth knowing. Suddenly, she realized this crazy plot she'd proposed just might save her. Griffin would add so much that had been missing in her life, not the least of which would be humor.

Before Christmas, she'd be married. She'd be free for the first time, with no one pulling her strings, trying to make her dance to music she didn't hear. Her parents would have no one to play tug-of-war with any longer.

She felt like a high-stakes gambler in Las Vegas. She was betting it all on a man she barely knew. A man whose hair was too long to be stylish. His clothes looked like he actually worked in them. He probably didn't know a thing about art or music or plays, but he believed they might work well together.

That was enough.

There was nothing fancy or polished about Griffin Holloway, but there was strength. He struck her as a man who could stand the storm.

Any storm. Even her father.

CHAPTER TWELVE

The Johnsons

THE LAKE HOUSE was quiet and warm. Wyatt fell asleep twice during the movie. Jamie woke him up both times laughing, which didn't bother him at all.

She was wrapped up in a blanket on one end of the couch and he was on the other. Popcorn and a half-eaten pie he'd bought at the café sat between them.

"How'd you like your first Hallmark movie?" she asked.

Wyatt hadn't noticed the movie was over. "Loved it," he lied. "You want to watch another one?"

It was just nice to sit in her quiet little house and do nothing. The problems and stress of his last assignment seemed a million miles away. The worry about the next assignment haunted his thoughts a bit, but he pushed it aside. He'd had orders that he thought might get him killed before and he'd always made it, though. This one would be well planned, well executed, just like the others. And after it worked, he'd never have to go back to that location again.

He watched the cute little schoolteacher stand. "I can't watch anymore. School tomorrow."

"Right. I'll sleep out here."

"But…"

"No. It's your bed, and believe me, this couch is far more comfortable than most of the places I sleep. If you're still worried about this, I'll be gone before you get home tomorrow. I promise, I'll lock the place up when I leave."

Jamie hugged the blanket. "About that. I was thinking you could take me to school, then use my car to find yours. Around four, you could pick me up before you head out. It wouldn't hurt if a few people see us together so they'll believe there really is a Mr. Johnson."

He was afraid to ask if she might let him stay another day. He'd just let the hand play out, but he'd already figured how it would work in his mind. In truth, he couldn't see much of a downside to staying a little longer. One more day at the lake. One less in a hotel room.

"All right, I'll stay. That sounds like a plan. It couldn't hurt if a few more people saw us together. Make that imaginary husband seem more real."

"Right. Only I have a feeling Mr. Thames will get the word out. He had the oddest look on his face when we walked past him in the parking lot of Dorothy's Café. You'd think, since you went out earlier to introduce yourself, he would have at least nodded a greeting." She moved toward her bedroom.

"I noticed him, too." Wyatt played innocent. "Thought it was strange. Good night, Jamie."

"Good night, Wyatt."

When she closed the door between them, Wyatt fought the urge to yell, *Wait a minute. You're my wife. You fit the fantasy perfectly that I've been carrying around for years. We should play it through until my leave is over.*

The lock on her bedroom door clicked. His fantasy shattered.

He knew a life with a wife in a quiet spot was just his dream. The little house. The peace. The woman who laughed with him. For a moment, he'd almost believed luck would let him have what he longed for so many nights when he was far from home.

But luck didn't work that way. He was a soldier. He didn't have time to build that kind of life.

After lying awake for an hour, he pulled on his sweats and went out back so he could breathe in the cold air and watch the lake. Heaven, he thought. Pure heaven.

He'd enjoy this part of the dream, even if he had to steal the time.

When he finally came inside, he tossed another log on the fire and lay down on the couch, his feet hanging off the end. As he closed his eyes, the dream of home came back to him, but this time his wife had dark blond hair that curled around her face and she wore glasses. She wasn't thin but nicely rounded, and she liked to laugh.

The next morning, neither of them had much to say as they ate the last of the cereal in the tiny kitchen. Their knees kept bumping under the small table until they finally laughed about it without saying a word.

She told him her schedule, like he might remember it all, and he pretended to be interested in every detail of her school routine. He wondered if she was as aware of their time together winding down as he was. Who cared how many students she had in her drama class? All he cared about was how many minutes he had left to share with her.

When he pulled up at the front of the school, he was surprised when she leaned over and kissed him on the cheek.

"See you at four." Her words were light, as if she'd said them every day for years.

"I'll be waiting." He smiled as though there weren't a dozen things he wanted to say, but they all seemed logjammed in his throat. How did he tell someone that she'd been in his dreams for years?

When he drove away, he began prioritizing jobs. Filling her car with gas was definitely on his list. First, though, he'd go to the hardware store for what he'd need to hang that hammock. Then the grocery store. He'd eaten most of the cereal, all her cookies and all the popcorn. Man, he missed carbs when he was out of the States.

If Jamie hadn't made it back Sunday night, he'd been considering gnawing on one of the frozen steaks in her freezer.

No one spoke to him in the hardware store, but the checker in the grocery store called him Captain Johnson like she knew him. Even told him Jamie always bought the whole wheat bread.

On his way back to the lake, he spotted the donut place and stopped in to buy a bag and two cups of coffee. The least he could do was drop them off at the sheriff's office. However, Deputy Thatcher and Sheriff Cline were both out, so he took the coffees and dozen donuts back to Jamie's place, planning to have them for lunch.

Wyatt passed the morning working and munching on the donuts. By lunch, he was starving and decided to drive back into town for a burger. When he'd filled the van up on gas thirty minutes later, the owner of the station addressed him as Captain Johnson. They even discussed how Jamie's van was sounding, and the guy loaned Wyatt the tools he'd need to fix it.

Two hours later when he took the tools back, he stopped by the café and bought a pie. There he ran into the same thing. People knew his name. To his surprise, he was becoming a local.

Just because it sounded so normal, Wyatt spent time talking to Dorothy, the café owner, about what he could cook for supper. She ended up writing a recipe on a sack for him, then filling the bag with all he'd need.

When he tried to pay, she shooed him away. "No charge. Glad you're home, Captain."

By the time he pulled beside the cabin, he almost felt like he lived in Crossroads. Like he belonged.

The afternoon was sunny but cold as he worked outside, mounting the hammock on a sturdy frame. *Strong enough to hold two people*, he thought, even though he knew that was purely fantasy.

He tackled the kitchen cabinet doors that hung off their hinges next. It was almost time to go pick up Jamie when he realized he hadn't checked on the car he'd rented near Wichita Falls, so he dropped back by the sheriff's office on his way to the high school.

The secretary told him the sheriff's report, explained that the car ran off the road and into the fence line about a mile from the Maverick Ranch main entrance. She gave him both the number to the one tow-truck driver in town and the cell of Griffin Holloway, the rancher who'd probably want to talk to him about the fence repairs.

While he waited outside the school, Wyatt called both numbers. The towing service answering machine simply said, "Try again tomorrow, I got all I can handle today." The rancher's phone went directly to voice mail.

He looked up and saw Jamie walking out with the crowd. On impulse, he stepped from the van and rushed toward her. A moment after she saw him, he was lifting her off the ground and swinging her around.

She laughed in surprise, then looked embarrassed when he set her down and they both noticed everyone around them was staring.

Taking her briefcase, he walked beside her. "Sorry," he whispered. "I didn't mean to embarrass you."

"N-no," she stuttered. "It was good."

He opened her door and tossed her case in the back. "I don't think I've ever done that before. It just seemed like something a husband would do."

"Me either. For a moment, I thought I was flying."

As he backed out of his parking place, he asked, "Didn't your father swing you around when you were little?"

"No."

He glanced at her but her head was down. There obviously would not be more information to come. "Mine did." He tried to keep the conversation going. "Once when I was about three or four, he accidentally dropped me. I thought my mom would kill him. Turns out she just divorced him."

"Over an accident?" Her big eyes were staring at him now.

"No, over an affair he was having. But she got over being mad fast. Two months after she filed, she found her 'soul mate' in a counseling class for the newly divorced. After that, Dad was always out reliving his twenties and Mom was home staring into the depths of her soul mate's eyes, where she swore she saw her eternity."

Jamie smiled. "You don't believe in soul mates?"

"Sure. Mom's found three so far. Every time she leaves a husband, she rolls back her age like rewinding the odometer on a car. I've heard husband number three is closer to my age than hers."

"I'm so sorry."

"No. It's fine. The first one lasted ten years. Mom said he was too complicated. Number two had daughters and Mom said they poisoned her chances at happiness. Number three is still with her. But she mentioned something negative about him in her monthly email so he's probably packing as we speak. Now she'll be looking for the next one, promising he'll be sterile, simpleminded and rich. She also added in the note that he'd be too old to pick me up and drop me. Which shows she never forgave my father for that one mistake."

Jamie laughed again.

"I love how you laugh." The words were out before he could stop them.

She looked away and he couldn't help but wonder if Jamie Johnson had had many compliments in her life. She wasn't a woman who'd stand out in a crowd. She was quiet. She loved her students. There was nothing about her that would attract attention.

"What about your father?" She finally broke the silence.

"He's in Berkeley. I don't think he wants to be reminded he even has a son."

They pulled into her drive and parked in the back. He watched her, knowing the exact moment she saw the hammock.

"You fixed it!" She was out of the car almost before he stopped, running toward the back porch. "Now I can swing and watch the sun set over the lake. Oh, thank you, Wyatt."

"No big deal. It was the least I could do."

She jumped in the hammock and began to swing. For a moment, he saw a little girl with a Christmas-morning smile.

When she finally slowed, he added, "I've got some bad news. My car can't be towed until tomorrow. I hate to ask, but I'll need a ride to the nearest hotel."

"You can't. Unless I drive you to Lubbock, everyone will be asking what's wrong."

He scratched his head. "I hadn't thought of that."

Standing, she marched into the lake house. "You'll just have to stay here. We're friends now. It will be all right."

He grinned as he followed her inside.

"What's all this?" she asked when she saw the groceries on the kitchen counter.

"Well, I figured I owed you a load of groceries. I've been eating here. And I thought I'd cook you supper and hoped you'd invite me to join you."

She looked at the chili simmering in a Crock-Pot. "I think you knew I would let you stay, Captain, or you wouldn't have made so much."

"Guilty. Do I stay, or are you kicking me out, Mrs. Johnson? I should mention it's starting to snow outside. But I'll go if you're uncomfortable."

"Stay, of course," she said. "Stay for as long as you like. I'll enjoy the company."

And that was it, pure and simple. They started putting away groceries, and she squealed with happiness every time she found a latch he'd fixed or a door he'd gotten unstuck. They built a fire and had dessert in front of the flames. Then he taught her to play poker and let her win just to hear her laugh when she beat him.

All his life, with all his travels, he'd never thought such a simple evening could be such fun. He felt like he was tucking away memories he'd revisit when he was cold and alone and a million miles from here.

A little after ten, she yawned and said, "Good night, Wyatt."

He watched her walk to the bedroom door. "Good night, Jamie."

Leaning back on the couch, he heard the lock click. The only sound all evening that hadn't been in his dreams.

CHAPTER THIRTEEN

Midnight Crossing

JAXSON O'GRADY COULDN'T believe he was leaving the cabin, not for an emergency or food or anything important, but simply because every time he said the name Mayweather a stray dog raised his head. There was no denying it. Jax even tried mixing the word in with vegetables, with days of the week, with pretty much everyone he'd known in high school. But the dog only reacted to one word. Mayweather.

So, like the idiot he was, Jax started the old Jeep and drove to town with Buddy belted into the seat beside him. The new little hospital was more of a clinic, but if the online paper was right, Mallory Mayweather was still there recovering.

He decided the best time to go would be five minutes before eight at night. Most of the visitors would be gone, but it wouldn't be so late his visit would draw attention. The fewer people he had to come into contact with the better.

The first floor was a wide reception area leading into the clinic. After five, this area usually looked abandoned. The second floor served as a twenty-bed hospital. He knew he could get past the first floor and Jax reasoned that one man probably wouldn't be noticed moving through the hallways upstairs at just about closing time.

But the dog limping beside him might get a few looks. Jax hadn't even tried to put a collar or leash on the animal. Buddy seemed to know that his place was at Jax's side.

He had thought of leaving Buddy back at the cabin, but if the woman did know him, she'd probably be much happier to see the dog than some stranger. If she didn't know Buddy, she'd just think some nut had wandered into her room by accident.

Jax made it through the lobby and up the elevator before some hulk of a man in green scrubs stopped him on the second floor. His name tag flashed silver in the dim lights. Todd Baker, Orderly.

Todd hadn't changed much since grade school, just grown bigger, Jax thought.

"We don't allow dogs," the big man said in a tired voice. He put his fists on his hips, reminding Jax of a broken turnstile.

"Hi, Tiny." Jax tried to relax, but Todd Baker didn't look any friendlier than he had in third grade when everyone called him Tiny because he was a head taller than all of them.

"No dogs allowed, O'Grady."

"But—"

"No buts." The guy spread his feet, as if making the stance he'd used years ago when he'd played fullback. Only most of his muscles had gone south. At over three hundred pounds, Todd could probably flatten Jax by falling on him.

There was no point in further discussion. Jaxson and Buddy turned around and stepped back on the elevator. The collie followed, limping along, his head low. The dog seemed to realize they'd just lost round one.

When the door closed, Jax whispered, "We'll try another door."

Buddy didn't lift his head.

"Mayweather," Jax said and swore the dog smiled as he looked up.

They drove over to the local gas station and Jax bought them both ice-cream sandwiches. With the heater going full blast, he ate his with one hand while he held Buddy's ice cream so the dog's long tongue could lick the ice cream out of the center.

By the time they got back to the hospital, the lobby was empty and the lights in the hallways had been dimmed. No clerk at the front desk. No guard on duty in sight. No one coming in or out except hospital employees now and then. At ten, Todd rushed out without even a jacket and jogged to a junker of a car even older than Jaxson's Jeep.

Buddy and Jax both dozed in the parking lot for a while. With each hour, fewer and fewer employees moved through the doors. By 1:00 a.m., Jaxson figured they'd have a good chance of passing unseen.

"Come on, boy, let's break into this place."

When he headed in, Buddy was right by his side. They were partners in this crime.

The whole building seemed to be sleeping. Most of the patients and staff had settled down for the night. There was no intensive care unit, only a minor emergency area made up of two rooms that stayed open. Any patients with life-threatening issues were transported to Lubbock.

Jax took the stairs to the second floor, thinking the elevator opening might draw some attention. The stairs opened out at the far end of the floor. From the looks of it, several rooms were empty on this end, their doors wide-open as if waiting. He slipped off his boots and walked slowly toward the central desk. Only the light tap of Buddy's splint made any noise, and it seemed to beat in rhythm to the hallway clock.

Moving slowly past the desk heading to the opposite end of the hall, Jax hoped not to be noticed. Two women were in a side office talking. No computer on at the desk. Not even a chart on the wall to help with patient names and locations. That might have given him a clue as to where Mallory Mayweather would be.

When he made it past the desk, he noticed ten rooms remained. Five on each side of the hallway. They moved on. The short wing had numbers posted, but no patient names. Some doors had signs like Oxygen or No Visitors.

Jax felt like he had to be close, but he would have to push every door open. Even if he checked each patient, he had no idea what the woman looked like. Ten rooms. If half had men in them, that would leave five. She'd looked slender. Maybe a few patients would be large. Dark hair, he thought, but that could have been mud in her hair. Not old. If she'd been over sixty, she probably wouldn't be driving a red sports car.

If he figured in all the variables, he might be able to narrow it down to two or three. If the paper was accurate, and she hadn't been released, transported or died.

The closer he got to the first door, the dumber his plan seemed. If they got caught, he decided to blame the whole scheme on Buddy.

The collie suddenly moved ahead of him, taking the lead. At the third room on the right, he pressed his nose against the seam in the door and scratched the metal blocking his way.

Jax rushed forward. "No one is in there, Buddy. The sign says Storage." He tapped the label taped at eye level.

The dog didn't budge. He just scratched again.

"All right, I'll show you." He slowly pushed open the door for Buddy.

The collie rushed in as soon as the opening was wide enough.

Jax followed and was shocked to see a person sleeping quietly as machines surrounded her like silent sentinels. She was slender and young, still in her twenties. A patchwork armor of bandages was all about her. He could see curly brown hair between the stripes wrapping her head.

"I think we just found your Mayweather."

By the time Jax had silently closed the door, Buddy was sitting beside the hospital bed. The dog kept turning his head sideways and making a little sound as if he had questions.

Jax brushed the collie's fur. "Hush, Buddy. She's sleeping."

The pup moved closer and laid his head on the patient's fingers just below where an IV had been poked into her hand.

Jax had no doubt they'd found Buddy's owner. In the silence of the room, with machines beating out the time, he looked at the woman he'd seen from the wreck. She seemed so fragile. Her face was so badly bruised and hidden by bandages that he couldn't tell what she might look like. Nothing personal surrounded her. No cards or pictures. No flowers. Nothing personal on the bedside table.

"Hey, pretty lady," he said, hoping to cheer her up if she could hear him. "The last time I saw you, you were flying in the night sky."

She didn't move.

Jax fought down the urge to make the little sound Buddy kept making, hoping to wake her.

The door swished open and Jax groaned, knowing they were about to be kicked out, again. A nurse dressed in a very proper white lab coat moved silently to the other side of the bed, checking her patient. For a minute, she acted as if she hadn't seen him or the dog.

Jax remained silent. He'd spent so much time being a ghost lately, he thought maybe he'd passed over and become one.

No such luck. The nurse finally looked directly at him. "You're not supposed to be in here," she whispered. "After visiting hours. No dogs allowed."

"I know. But we're family."

The nurse smiled at him. "With all that hair, Jaxson O'Grady, you look more akin to that dog than you do to this girl, but considering the size of the O'Grady clan around here, I'm not surprised she's related to a few of you."

He recognized the nurse now; years ago, she'd been Toni Teague when they'd been in school. They'd grown up in the same church even if she was several years older than him. She'd played Mary in the Christmas play one year and he'd been one of the sheep. At five, he'd thought she was the most beautiful girl he'd ever seen.

"How are you and the kids doing, Toni?" He tried to keep his voice friendly, but he hadn't had much practice lately.

"The twins are in college. Only have one chick left in the nest."

He nodded, not exactly sure what to say. With no children himself, he didn't have any idea if she'd be sad or happy they were gone.

"I'm just checking on how your patient is doing." Jax felt the need to explain. "I thought it might cheer her up to see her dog."

Toni smiled, but her eyes seemed brimming over with sadness. "Mallory is doing better every day. She's having bad headaches, which is expected. She's been given enough sleeping pills tonight to knock her out till dawn. You could come back tomorrow morning. She'll be released soon." She frowned at him. "You might want to shave before you come."

"I have to bring the pup. It's her dog. He was in the wreck, too. I don't think she knows he's alive."

Toni glanced at Buddy. "I guessed that when I saw you two standing by her bed. How about I leave a note for someone to take her out to the sunporch if it's warm late tomorrow morning? You and the pup can sit out there with her. I don't know which one of you is shedding the most hair in here."

"Fair enough. Thanks, Toni," he said as he read her name tag. Charge Nurse was on her coat.

She stared at him. "You're a good man, Jaxson O'Grady. The town misses having you around."

He shook his head. "I see a few of my cousins, and that's enough for now. I just wanted to check on Mallory tonight."

Toni nodded. "I don't know what caused the car accident, but since you're family, you should know that there were several bruises on her body, both old and new that didn't look like they were caused by the wreck. I don't know what she told the sheriff, but he put out a restraining order on her boyfriend. Told us to make sure no one dropped in to visit except family. I failed. I thought the storage sign would fool people."

"It did, but it didn't slow Buddy down. I guess he can't read."

She stared at the pup. "I don't know how you got in here or how you found her unmarked room, but we are watching her and it won't be so easy for anyone to get past us again." Her stare turned to Jax. "Understand."

"Completely. If I come back, I'll stop at the desk first."

Jax decided he should vanish before she could give him another lecture. He turned to Buddy and patted his pant leg.

The dog whined but followed Jax out.

Just before Jax closed the door, Toni whispered, "You're coming back tomorrow?"

"Probably," he said. "If she wakes up tonight, would you tell her I'm taking care of her dog?"

"Tell her yourself. I'll be home asleep before she wakes, and I think it's best I don't tell anyone you were here tonight."

"Thanks." He stared at his first crush, now in her forties. He still saw those sweet Virgin Mary eyes. "I'll be back tomorrow."

"You do that, Jax. Mallory will be glad to have the dog's company."

CHAPTER FOURTEEN

Midnight Crossing

ON THE WAY home from town, Jaxson stopped at the only place open at two o'clock in the morning; the gas station. He bought a cheap razor and a round mirror that would fit in his hand.

It was about time to step back into the world. He couldn't stay lost forever. Someone needed help. "Mallory Mayweather," he mumbled to himself. If ever there was a woman who needed rescuing, it would be the lady behind the gauze mask.

Buddy's ears shot up and the dog looked at Jax. "You love her, don't you, Buddy? I couldn't see much of her face, but she must have a kind heart."

As he checked out, a bored clerk felt the need to issue advice. "About time you shaved, pal. Any longer and you could spray paint that beard and play Santa Claus next month."

Jax was too tired to see the humor. He just groaned.

The clerk looked down at Buddy. "Don't bring that dog in here again unless he's a service animal."

"He's my cousin." Jax figured he might as well claim one more relative.

The clerk laughed. "From the looks of you, he could be."

Jax took his bag and left. He'd talked long enough to a guy who wore a shirt that read Attention Aliens: I am the leader.

The next morning it took Jax an hour to shave and cut four inches off his shaggy hair. When he looked in the mirror, he still didn't recognize himself. Before the accident two years ago, he'd always worn his hair short, almost military style. Now it still looked way too long, but he knew he'd do a terrible job if he hacked off anymore.

"That's as good as I get, Buddy." He patted the dog on the head. "Let's go see Mayweather."

Buddy beat him to the door. For the first time in months, Jax found himself looking forward to something new.

Crossroads Hospital and Clinic

Fifteen miles away, Mallory Mayweather let the chubby nurse's aide in reindeer-print scrubs roll her into the second-floor sunroom. Aide Raelene almost dropped Mallory as she moved her from the wheelchair to a wooden recliner.

"Now be careful, dear," the aide said cheerfully, as if she hadn't been the one at fault. "Mrs. Adams said you should take some sun. And everyone around here always does what Nurse Adams says. She left us a note to tell you there's someone coming this morning that you'll want to see. We can see you from the nurses' desk. If you get tired, just raise your hand and we'll be right out. I'll be doing paperwork right by the window."

Mallory nodded, guessing the visitor would be the Baptist preacher or the sheriff's secretary. Both dropped by every morning and talked without any need to have her respond.

Mallory hadn't said a word since the accident. She hadn't tried. One, her throat hurt, and two, there was nothing to say. That first day when she'd written the sheriff a note about how her boyfriend, Curtis Dayson, had choked her the night of her accident and threatened to kill her dog, she'd known that was all she wanted to say. Letting more details out didn't matter. She knew she'd finally made him mad enough when she wrecked his sports car that he'd find her and make her pay in blood. But first, he'd kill the dog in front of her.

She'd had to turn him in. Had to let someone know who was about to kill her and her pet.

If Charlie was still alive. Each time she thought of her puppy out in the country alone or freezing in some shelter, Mallory had to fight back tears.

Inside her mind, she'd told herself a million times that she was an idiot. Why hadn't she left the first time Curtis hit her? One blow to the cheek he said was an accident. He was only playing around. Hadn't meant to swing so hard. Or the second—he'd laughed off the slaps, saying he'd got a little carried away playing with her. Or the third, harder, faster, madder—he'd been so sorry when he saw the bruises. He'd even bought her the dog three months ago after he'd blacked her eye. *I'll never do it again,* he'd promise every time.

She'd halfway convinced herself it was her fault. After all, he was polished, smooth talking, perfectly built on the outside, but now she knew he was rotten on the inside. He'd been her boss at the agency in Dallas. He'd flattered her constantly ten months ago when she'd been hired on, telling her she was a rising star in the finance world. But once they moved in together, she couldn't seem to do anything right, at the office or at home.

Last Friday, when she saw pure rage as he looked at her puppy, she had to run. The dog had only barked and tried to protect her, but she knew that next time her pet crossed him, Curtis would kill him and her, too, if she tried to stop him.

He'd mentioned once that women turned up dead in alleys all the time, so she'd better be very careful. She'd thought him a bit overprotective. Now she saw the comment as a threat.

In the end, she lost every battle with Curtis. No matter how it started, he had to win. He'd insisted she move in with him. She had to sell her car—after all, he had two. He'd even insisted she give him access to her bank account, saying it only made sense.

When she ran, she knew she was just delaying what would happen. She'd left his hideaway home near Brownwood and raced through the night. Heading nowhere but away. She had no home to go back to in Dallas, and she swore she'd never return to the isolated place in Brownwood. He'd once said he loved the remoteness, but she knew that meant no one would hear her if she screamed.

That first night they'd been alone there, he'd tested her theory. Again and again.

Even when she was hurt, she'd tried to shield Charlie.

Thanks to the wreck, she'd probably lost her collie anyway. Maybe he'd died in the wreck. Maybe he ran. No one had been able to find the dog, and it would be weeks before she'd be well enough to search. Until the wreck, he'd always been by her side; she hadn't thought to put a collar on him.

Mallory leaned back in her chair and let the sun warm her face. Where did she go from here? A year ago, she'd thought she was on top of the world. Now she felt like she'd have to crawl up to even reach bottom. No home. No job. No friends that didn't know or work for Curtis.

She drifted in and out of sleep cocooned in blankets and sheltered from the wind by walls.

Something cold brushed her hand. Charlie, her gentle collie. The cold nose tapped her hand again. Mallory opened one eye. He was there, battered and bandaged, but alive.

Without any thought of the pain or how she'd mess up the bandage left from where they'd removed the IV, she leaned down and brushed her cheek against his soft fur. Tears she hadn't allowed to fall suddenly bubbled over. He'd made it through the wreck. Somehow someone had found him and brought him to her.

"I'm guessing you must be Mayweather." A man's laughing voice came from behind her. "Every time he hears your name, he looks up at me." The man moved into her line of vision. Well built, not too tall, a few years older than her, she'd guess.

"Good to see you without all the tubes running into you today." He offered his hand, but she didn't take it, so he patted the dog instead.

Mallory didn't want to talk to anyone, but this man must have stopped to help her one friend in the world that night of the wreck. She looked up at the stranger again.

When she touched her throat, he seemed to understand.

He knelt beside the dog so she didn't have to look up. "I saw the wreck last week. I was out walking on my land. I tried to get to you, but the ambulance beat me. When I headed back to my place, I heard Buddy whimpering in the tall grass. I took him home and patched him up but it was two, maybe three days, before I thought he had much chance of making it."

She put one hand to the side of the man's face, lightly touching tiny cuts.

It took him a moment, and then he understood. "Oh, no, I wasn't hurt. I cut myself shaving this morning."

She studied him as he talked.

"It turns out shaving isn't like riding a bike. You do forget." He rolled his eyes as if declaring himself crazy.

The corner of her lip lifted. There was nothing to fear from this stranger, who lightly brushed Charlie's back.

She touched her fingers to her chin and held her open hand out to him.

He smiled. "I remember that sign. It means thank you. Well, you are welcome, Mallory Mayweather. I enjoyed Buddy's company, but I knew he was missing you."

She leaned low again and brushed her cheek over the dog's fur. No one who'd been watching could ever doubt that Charlie was hers.

The man pulled up a folding chair. "I'm Jaxson O'Grady. I'm the county hermit. I never talk to anyone much. I live out in a cabin half my own relatives can't find." He laughed. "But apparently I'm rattling on to you. I guess it's because anyone Buddy loves so much couldn't be a bad person. I want you to know I'll take good care of him until you're able to get out of here."

She couldn't stop patting the dog as she watched the stranger. In truth, he kind of looked like her Charlie. O'Grady's hair was shaggy and dark blond, with a brush of auburn mixed in. He had brown eyes almost as dark as her dog's.

Maybe she should judge men not by their clothes or education, but by how much they look like dogs. From the look of Jaxson O'Grady's clothes, she wouldn't be surprised if he'd rolled in dirt before he'd come into town. He'd probably put on his cleanest shirt this morning, but it was wrinkled and looked like it had been washed in river water.

"I'm thinking his name isn't Buddy." Jaxson looked straight at her. "Right."

She nodded as she moved her finger over the blanket covering her legs.

It took her several tries but he finally figured out *c* and *h*.

"Charlie," he said and she nodded. "Charlie. I like that. What do you think of the name Buddy? I thought it fit him."

She shrugged.

"Mind if your Charlie stays with me until you get out of this place and back on your feet? He likes my cooking. It's no trouble to make two plates. I don't have any dog food, but what I cook must be close to what he's used to."

Before she could try to answer, Raelene rushed out in such a hurry the reindeer on her scrubs looked like they were dancing. "We got to get you back to your room, Miss Mayweather. The sheriff's secretary called and said that guy you have the restraining order on showed up at the county offices a few minutes ago. He told everyone in the sheriff's office he's going to find you even if he has to drive the whole state. Claims to be worried sick about you, can't live without you, has to see you or he'll die. He said one small-town sheriff won't keep him away from the woman he loves."

Mallory looked at Jax, and he seemed to read her mind.

"The guy is lying, Raelene. He just wants to find her." Jax never took his gaze from Mallory.

She nodded slightly, knowing he could see the fear in her eyes.

"How'd he know she was here in Crossroads?" Jax asked.

The aide turned to Jax. "Pearly said he tracked her cell. Found it in the wrecked car dropped off in the lot behind the sheriff's office. So he knows she's close, even though Pearly swore she didn't answer a single one of his questions."

The nurse folded up Mallory's blanket as she turned back to her patient. "A nurse is downstairs telling the one guard we got to watch out for anyone showing up with questions about you. When I called the head nurse and told her your kin was up visiting with a dog, she said to ask Jaxson O'Grady to stay with you." Raelene huffed. "I swear, Toni Adams knows everything that goes on in this place, even when she's not here."

Mallory reached for Jaxson's hand and the fear in her gaze must have told this stranger all he needed to know. "I'll stay." He looked over at the dog. "We both will."

Raelene frowned but didn't seem to have time to argue about the mutt. "I'll go get your wheelchair. We need to get you out of sight. That ex-boyfriend of yours could drive by right now and look up. He might not be able to make you out all bandaged and blanketed up, but he'd spot that dog and be heading up here."

Mallory didn't argue. She'd do whatever it took to make sure she never saw Curtis Dayson again.

The shaggy dog of a man beside her, who seemed to have become her kin, stepped forward. "Forget the chair. I'll carry her, if she's willing to risk it."

Mallory raised her arms and he picked her up with ease. But

even as he did, she thought, *Don't trust him. Don't trust any man ever again.*

He must have felt her stiffen because he spoke in a low whisper against her ear. "It's all right, Mallory. I got you. Charlie and I will stand guard. Between the two of us, no one is going to get close to you that you don't want to see."

She relaxed. She might not trust this man, but she trusted her dog.

CHAPTER FIFTEEN

Maverick Ranch

GRIFFIN STOOD AT the huge window framed by logs his grand-father had hauled all the way from East Texas. He barely no-ticed the sunset as he stared out at the road. He could see for miles, his land now winter-white with a dusting of snow, but he couldn't see any movement. No huge truck with a crown on the side. No wife-to-be heading his way.

It was past six. Sunlan Krown was late. Hell, she'd probably wised up and decided not to come. He wouldn't blame her. She obviously thought he was violent, since he punched the pilgrim bear at the Franklins' bed-and-breakfast. Or maybe she hated the way he ate his breakfast so fast, like the food might be pulled away. Double hell—he hadn't even noticed the napkin beside his plate before he was almost finished.

She seemed like the kind of woman who'd notice things like that. Damn, all women were like that. He just hadn't been around them enough to notice. Maybe that was why the sisters tried so hard to teach him.

If he hadn't got the point until now, there was no hope for his brothers. And what had he done tonight?

Invited a lady to dinner.

What kind of sensible woman would want to marry a man without manners? Mamie was right. She'd said she might as well serve meals in the trough the way the Holloway men ate. At least they weren't picky. The housekeeper had cooked the same five meals on the same five nights for so many years, no one in the house ever had to check a calendar to know what day it was. Saturdays one of them drove into town for pizza, and Sundays were fend-for-yourself meals. Cooper lived on cookies and chips. Elliot usually went to town to eat alone, and Griffin made a sandwich out of any leftovers he found.

Griffin looked across the room at his brothers. They'd cleaned up, but as they both yelled at the football game on TV, he realized they wouldn't even know how to talk to a lady like Sunlan. She was ranchland royalty.

He took time to look around the huge old house his grandfather had built. It was starting to look like a vacant lot. In the years since his mother died, things seemed to disappear, and he'd barely noticed. What happened to the curtains that used to hang in every window? Furniture had broken or worn out, and no one ever replaced it. The plants his mother kept wherever sunlight fell inside had vanished so long ago he couldn't even remember what they'd been.

The only thing he could remember ever buying for the house were towels and sheets, because Mamie told him to, and a big-screen TV, because Cooper said they needed it. Somehow, over the years, the Holloway home had started looking like a lobby in the cheapest dorm on a college campus. Cooper used one corner of the wide entryway for his old boot collection, and Elliot had wires crisscrossing the floor.

Inviting Sunlan here was going to be a disaster. The only bright note was that she'd stood him up tonight.

But just then, her big silver pickup pulled into view. He frowned. She was coming down the winding road from the turnoff.

Moving to the porch, he stood watching her. She was driving fast, but it looked like she could handle the truck. She pulled up twenty feet away and climbed out, a basket in each hand.

For a moment, Griffin just stared, hardly believing he was going to marry such a beautiful woman. Tonight she was dressed in dark blue, from her fancy knee-high boots all the way to the wool scarf that covered most of her sunshine hair.

He managed to make it down the steps by the time she reached the porch. He didn't greet her. All he could do was stare.

She handed him one of the baskets. "The Franklin sisters insisted on sending desserts. They spent several minutes informing me that your cook doesn't make desserts fit to sell at a bake sale."

"You're late."

Sunlan met his stare. "I am." No apology apparently.

"I was worried about you."

Her face seemed to harden to stone. "Don't bother. Comments like that seem caring, but they're controlling. I'm not fond of them. Understand?"

"Noted."

He followed her up the steps, thinking they were not off to much of a start, but they'd agreed to be honest and maybe she was just doing that. He introduced her to Elliot and Cooper.

His brothers welcomed her more politely than he'd thought them capable of doing, though Cooper seemed Taser-shot jittery and Elliot kept turning his head from Griffin to Sunlan, as if silently saying, *One of these things doesn't go with the other.*

She had the grace to compliment the home. Lovely view. Beautiful fireplace. So Cooper showed her around while Griffin checked to make sure all the silverware was clean.

As Cooper led her into the wide dining room, his arm crooked so her hand could perch there, Griffin noticed the table was set without a cloth, and Mamie had left bandannas for napkins.

When had that centerpiece of candles disappeared? Years ago, probably. Mamie always set the table at five and left for her home. Since Sunlan was late, the meal would be cold, but that happened most nights around here. Each man filled his plate and ate when they came in. All three of them sitting down at the table was rare.

Over cold pot roast and half-baked potatoes, Cooper told her about his horses and she asked intelligent questions. Elliot asked politely about her father. It was obvious he'd read articles on the great Winston R. Krown.

Sunlan barely touched her food. Griffin thought of telling her she needed to eat, but he had the feeling she'd tell him to mind his own business.

Hell, he decided, he was a bossy man. How had he managed to find a woman who wouldn't take to the idea of being bossed? Griffin mentally thumped himself. No woman liked to be bossed. That right there was probably why he was still single.

He decided to pay attention and stop thinking, period.

Conversation moved from one ranch topic to another. The weather. The price of cattle. The rodeo in Las Vegas. Sunlan seemed comfortable here in this place she'd never been, talking to strangers. She was polished, practiced, perfectly schooled in moving conversation along.

When Cooper stood, explaining that he had horses still saddled that needed tending to, Sunlan rose, as well. "I'll help you," she announced, without asking if he needed any help. "I'd like to see your operation. The old vet in town told me you've modified stalls to accommodate injured horses. I'd like to see just how that's done here in Texas."

Then unexpectedly she leaned over and kissed Griff right on the mouth. "I'll be right back."

He nodded and watched her go. Her long legs keeping up

with Cooper. Her hair moving gracefully past her shoulders and halfway down her back. She was firing questions, and to his surprise, Cooper was answering.

As soon as they heard the back door close, Elliot leaned over. "She's more than just an old friend you bumped into, isn't she, Griff?"

Griffin smiled for the first time. "Yeah, I guess she is. We've gotten together a few times."

Elliot's eyebrows shot up. "It must have been dark. She's not the kind of girl you'd ever be able to pick up, so that means she picked you up. What I can't figure out is why she didn't put you right back down."

Griffin straightened. "I can't figure it out either, but she's crazy about me. She even said I'm the perfect man for her."

"Maybe we should suggest she needs her eyes tested?"

Twenty minutes later, when she walked back inside, her fancy boots were snow-covered and she was shivering. He stood and held out his arm.

She walked right into his embrace and touched her cold nose against his throat. "Warm me up, Griff," she whispered just loud enough for both brothers to hear.

Griffin moved his hands over her back as he kissed her forehead. Elliot and Cooper were staring so hard he played the moment up a little, hoping she didn't slug him for being too friendly.

Without turning loose of her, he said softly against her ear, "Should we tell them, Sunshine?"

"Tell us what?" Cooper shot back. "What's wrong? Oh, Griff, don't tell me she's a doc or a nurse and you've got some incurable disease."

She turned in Griffin's embrace so that her back pressed against his chest. "I think they should be the first to know."

Both brothers looked like they were about to hear horrible news. Griff was dying. They'd lost the ranch.

Griffin cleared his throat. "Sunlan and I have known each other for a while now and today I asked her to marry me."

"What did she say?" Cooper asked.

Sunlan laughed. "I said yes, of course."

"You're kidding!" both brothers said at once.

"We'll be married before Christmas. She has a place in Colorado, so for a while she'll be traveling between her spread and ours." Griffin took over, fearing his two siblings would try to talk her out of joining the family. "Sunlan loves me, but she also loves horses. If I marry her, I'll have to make room for some of them here."

Elliot frowned, as if fearing what Griff said was a joke. Cooper, for once, was speechless.

Griffin pushed on. "Any objections to giving her dad's old white barn for a wedding present? The lady comes with livestock, so she'll need more than an extra closet."

"Are you kidding? We'll give her the headquarters and sleep in tents outside if she's all right with joining the family." Cooper was almost dancing with excitement. "You found a wife who knows more about horses than I do. You wouldn't believe the ideas about improving our breeding stock she was explaining to me. I say marry her tonight before she wakes up and changes her mind."

"She wants a wedding, Coop, a real wedding."

Sunlan nodded, going along with whatever he said.

Griffin might as well get it all out. "You guys remember that horse show in Fort Worth I went to a few months ago? Well, I met up with Sunlan there and it appears we did a little breeding of our own."

His brothers both looked clueless and Griffin feared he might have to go back over the facts of life for them. That was a dumb way to say it anyway. He should at least try to sound romantic.

"What Griff is putting so awkwardly is that I'm carrying the next generation of Holloways." When the brothers continued to stare, she tried again. "I'm having a baby."

Griffin corrected, "She's having my baby."

"No! You two?" Cooper looked so confused Griffin almost felt sorry for him. "You two are pregnant?"

Sunlan circled her hand around Griff's arm. "Well, technically, I'm pregnant. Griff just helped out. I've loved him for a long time, but I never thought he was interested in getting married, so we'd meet now and then and talk about ranching, among other things."

Griff winked at her as he began their story. "To tell the truth, I never thought I'd have a chance with Sunlan. I thought we would always be friends, that's all. We'd see each other at horse auctions a few times a year. Maybe have dinner together, if she wasn't busy."

Elliot frowned. "Sounds like you had a great deal more than dinner."

Griffin knew Elliot would be the hardest to convince. "When I saw her the other day, I realized she mattered to me. I told her I wanted something more than just a friendship before she even mentioned the baby."

"You did? You've never said a word about her." Elliot looked frustrated. "You could have mentioned it to me when you were talking about our problem on the ranch. You go off and asked some woman to marry you without even talking to me."

Sunlan pulled away from Griffin and touched Elliot's arm. "It happened so fast, Elliot, but we're telling you now. Be happy for us. Come spring, you'll be an uncle."

Elliot's pout broke. "I am happy for you. Just surprised. Change isn't something I take to easily, but I have a feeling this is going to be all good."

Griffin watched Sunlan draw them back to the table to taste the sisters' desserts. She knew how to handle people. She could fit into their lives, and for the first time he thought maybe, just maybe, this crazy bargain they'd made between them might work.

He pulled her chair out for her and instead she slipped into the place he'd planned to sit. Griffin almost laughed out loud. Sunlan wasn't a filly who would ever take to a lead rope. In fact, he had a pretty good idea she'd slug him if she knew he'd even made the comparison.

The woman was about to marry him and he had no idea if she even liked him.

CHAPTER SIXTEEN

Crossroads Hospital and Clinic

JAX LEANED AGAINST the hospital window, staring out into the night sky. Now and then a lonely snowflake would fall, sparkling in and out of the parking lot light's glow. It had to be after ten. Mallory had been sleeping for a few hours. The dog, not named Buddy, stood guard at her bedside.

Jax's arms still felt the light weight of her body when he'd carried her inside. He couldn't help but wonder if she'd always been thin or if her loss of weight wasn't another wound she suffered from her boyfriend.

Glancing over at her, Jax could tell little about Mallory Mayweather. She didn't look very tall, maybe five-two at the most. Small build. Her throat was completely wrapped and a bandage covered one side of her face, but he could see her mouth. It was swollen and bruised, so whoever this boyfriend was, he must have hit her pretty much everywhere.

Mallory moved. Her right hand brushed Charlie's head, and Jax added one more point to his assessment. The woman had pretty hands. Long fingers. Clear skin. Artist's hands, he thought, as his gaze moved to her left hand. Bandaged. Also damaged.

"You awake?" he whispered.

She nodded.

"I know this sounds crazy, but when you're feeling up to it, I wouldn't mind if you came home with me and Charlie. Just until you're better. Until you are not afraid to go home.

"I got a little place that only folks who've lived years in the county know about. There's a hill behind my land that shadows the cabin after dark. It's so black out there no one would find the road much less my place."

She was stone still. He couldn't tell if she'd heard him. One swollen eye opened slightly.

"I know a little first aid. I could change your bandages and make sure you get your meds on time. You'd be safe. A few days' rest, or even a few weeks would make it easier for you to travel. You could go far enough that the guy who did this would never find you."

She still didn't move. Maybe she didn't even hear him. It was probably a dumb idea anyway. This woman didn't look like she trusted anyone, except maybe the dog.

Jax jerked as the door tapped closed. He hadn't even heard it open. He braced himself for a fight, then realized if a stranger, or the ex-boyfriend, showed up, Charlie would have reacted.

"I think you may have solved our problem," Nurse Toni Adams said from behind Jax. "She could have been released today if she'd had someone to pick her up but she listed no relative, no friends. If you hadn't shown up, we wouldn't have known she was related to the O'Grady clan."

Toni moved closer, checking her patient. "There's probably a dozen of your aunts or cousins who'd take her in, but whoever takes her home might have to deal with the man who hurt her. He might try to do it again. We don't have enough law to guard her around the clock, and if you found her, Jax, so could the maniac who used her as a punching bag and choked her so badly she hasn't said a word since she came in."

Jax hated hearing details, but if she came home with him he'd be seeing the damage himself. "I could get my cousin Tim to pick up all the supplies we need. He's a writer, so he's probably not doing anything important. Then I could carry her out the back door of the hospital and we'd vanish. No one would see us leave."

"You'd bring her back if any bleeding starts or if she has any signs of internal injuries?"

"I know what to look for."

"You armed at the cabin?"

He smiled. "Isn't everyone who lives in the county?"

Toni smiled. "I guessed you would be, and you do know what to do to doctor her. You were about the best fireman we ever had in this county. I was just a nurse working the clinic when you banged through the door eight years ago with a bloody man on your back. You were shouting orders and we all were jumping." She brushed his arm. "You saved Cap Fuller's life that day."

"It was just a kitchen fire. In his day, when he was teaching the whole county about fire safety, he would have had no problem dealing with it. But age has slowed him down. His arm was burned, but it was the fall he took backward off his porch that caused all the blood. Cap's part of the reason I became a firefighter. I didn't know if we were dealing with a burn, a concussion or heart attack. I just couldn't let him die on my watch."

Jax didn't want to be reminded of what he'd done; he only remembered what he hadn't done. He'd frozen in the line of duty almost two years ago. He'd almost got his men killed.

Two years of taking classes, of learning the chemistry, the forensics, the laws surrounding arson fires hadn't changed the fact that he'd frozen when he should have led his men. The courses, the books, the videos online couldn't tell him why he hadn't acted.

Toni moved to the bedside and brushed a short strand of dirty dark hair back from Mallory's forehead. "If you want to go home with your cousin, dear, I'll call the sheriff and see what he says. Then I'll come out every other morning when my shift is over and check on you. How does that sound? You'll be safe with Jaxson O'Grady. I've known him since he was a little lamb in the Christmas play at church." The very proper head nurse winked at him.

To Jax's surprise, the patient moved her head slightly. Yes!

Toni turned toward Jax. "Call your cousin Tim and have him pull that huge pickup he's got to the back door at midnight. It should hold a bed and all that you'll need. I'll send Todd Baker with him to help set up. That should take about an hour, then Tim can come back, drop my orderly off and make the trip again with you and Mallory as passengers. She'll get worn out from the short trip. I'll make sure Todd leaves everything ready so you can put her right to bed."

Jax handed Toni his keys. "Have Tiny Baker drive my Jeep out if he can get behind the wheel. He better follow closely behind Tim or he'll never see the turnoff. The cabin won't be locked."

The nurse moved toward the door and glanced back. "Jaxson, you may be saving her life, you know. Eventually we'll have to release her. Until she makes a formal statement, the sheriff can't arrest the guy. The crime didn't happen in his county and her ID lists her address in Arlington, but the car was registered in Terry County. The county seat is in Brownfield. There may be a few other sheriffs or police departments who want to go after this guy."

"I'm just helping out a cousin," he said, turning away from the hospital bed and lowering his voice. "And when she's better, whether she files charges or not, I plan to have a talk with whoever did this to her."

"I did not hear that." Toni moved to the door. "But I'd suggest you start carrying a bat. I've seen evidence that he uses one."

Jax turned back to Mallory. Her arm in a cast. Her leg wrapped. The thought that she'd felt the slam of a bat made him sick at his stomach. He'd never been a man given to anger. He'd always wanted to help people. But for once his thoughts were dark.

Life might not always be fair, but this time he planned to even the score.

CHAPTER SEVENTEEN

Maverick Ranch

SUNLAN KROWN HAD only planned to stay at the Holloway head-quarters for an hour. Just long enough to meet the brothers and make sure there were no surprises.

The headquarters was as she'd expected it to be, after years of men growing up alone there. Drafty, unkempt, in great need of updating. But there was a beautiful craftsmanship in its bones that she hadn't expected. A line from a book she once read came to mind: *Look beneath the dust and scraps, for glory often lies dormant in both wood and men.*

Another thing she hadn't expected was how comfortable the ranch itself felt. The rambling land, still half-wild. The barns and corrals well built, well maintained. The main house constructed of solid logs that would withstand any storm. She wouldn't mind spending a few days here from time to time. Maverick Ranch could almost be home.

Her place in Colorado was like that, only smaller, almost home. Sunlan thought if she added just a bit more to Griffin's place, reorganized, redecorated, it would be a perfect place for her to spend time with her child.

She hadn't thought much about how her child would react to Griffin. But now she thought, boy or girl, her child might enjoy the place from time to time and the Holloway men would be kind.

Her father's spread had never been welcoming or safe. It was a fancy train station where people passed through, though no one ever planned to stay. Or more accurately, she'd never wanted to be on what her father constantly reminded her was *his* land, his home.

Some of her earliest memories were of her parents fighting after parties held there. The house would be decorated with all six fireplaces blazing, fine china and crystal and massive furniture. They would be all dressed up, looking like fashion models for a magazine.

Except after they'd told her to go up to bed and the company had left, her mother and father would stand at the bottom of the stairs, yelling at each other. Like Sleeping Beauty's palace, the mansion seemed to decay and crumble before Sunlan's eyes. Sometimes she'd even hear crystal shattering below. Unhappy people tied together by money.

So her mother took her on trips. Shopping in Dallas. Vacationing in Vail in winter, the Caribbean in the fall. Then, as soon as she was old enough, she left for the quiet retreat of school. Most of the girls cried the first few nights when the semester started. Sunlan cried when the semester ended and she knew she'd be going home.

The big house. The parties. The fights. The only thing she looked forward to was the horses. She spent every holiday outside riding or in the barns working with vets and cowboys who knew more about horses than her father ever would.

Her mother complained, but her father said horses were in

her blood. So she was never banned from the barn, but she did become one more topic for them to argue about.

Sunlan noticed, even as a child, that her mother controlled her by keeping a tight rein on Sunlan's money. Sunlan was never allowed any freedom to buy what she wanted or take trips with anyone else but her mother. But when Sunlan inherited Misty Bend in Colorado, her father made sure everything was legally put in only Sunlan's name. He'd given her an independence her mother would never have allowed. Winston Krown continued to give his daughter advice, but they both knew any final decisions concerning her ranch were up to her.

Growing up, a love of horses was the only craving Winston Krown indulged his daughter in without strings. He gave her whatever she wanted in that area of her life, probably more because it angered her mother than because it made Sunlan happy. No matter how loudly Sunlan's mother objected, he sent riding horses to every school she attended. Books on horse breeding packed the shelves of his study, never read by anyone until she came home.

By nineteen, she knew more about the care and breeding of horses than most trainers who circled through the Krown Ranch. Her mother might have insisted she study art in school, but she couldn't smother Sunlan's love for horses.

The idea of having a husband who'd give her free rein to follow her dream was exciting. Sunlan's thoughts danced with possibilities. The more she was around Griffin Holloway, the more she believed she might finally be free of both her parents. At twenty-seven, she'd buy herself a husband and finally live the life she wanted. No one, including her parents, knew how much money she'd inherited from her grandfather. No one would ever know about her bargain with Griffin.

It was almost midnight when Griffin walked her to the door for the third time.

The first time, Elliot had drawn her back from leaving by

asking if she wanted to see a new program he'd developed for managing the ranch's input and output. While they were in the study, Griffin pulled up the records he kept on facts about cattle breeding. She understood finance and horses, but running cattle was something new. Her father never explained anything to her, but Griffin answered every question.

Cooper and Elliot listened in, even asking a few questions. She had a feeling that the brothers kept to their own interests.

When she'd stood to leave the second time, Elliot said they had to have a toast to the engagement. Cooper washed out four wineglasses and Griffin poured milk in each. Elliot lifted his glass and the others followed. "To the first Holloway lady of this generation. To Griffin's bride."

"To my bride," Griffin echoed as their gazes met.

Since they had moved to the dining room to toast, all three men agreed they needed to try another dessert from the selection of pies and cakes the Franklins had sent over. Sunlan laughed out loud when they passed the coconut pie to Cooper. He pushed his plate away and ate the last half of the pie straight from the pan.

His two big brothers kidded him and then broke into telling stories about Cooper. Their kid brother seemed to have had a little trouble accepting that he was a human, and he thought everything that flew, walked or slithered should be a pet around the place.

Sunlan couldn't help but laugh, which pleased all the men. Cooper even started telling crazy stories about himself.

Finally, Griffin said they had to let her get some sleep. She took his hand and waved goodbye to the brothers.

"I had fun tonight," she admitted as they stepped onto the long porch that would be perfect for watching sunsets.

"Next time you come, I'll have you a room made up and ready so you won't have to drive back to town."

She didn't argue, but she didn't plan on moving in before the wedding.

"I could drive you—"

"No." She didn't let him finish. "I can take care of myself."

"I have no doubt." He walked with her down the steps, but he didn't touch her. "When will I see you again?"

"I'd like to come out tomorrow and walk though the white barn. If it won't upset your operation, I plan to have any repairs or adjustments done before we marry so I can begin to move a few horses south."

"Of course. I figured you'd want to paint the rooms that will be yours upstairs, as well. Maybe get new furniture."

"I can't be around fresh paint without throwing up. But I would like to have the rooms redone to fit my taste." She smiled. "Bunk beds are not really my style and the wagon wheel light fixtures won't work either."

"Do whatever you want. We'll help with anything you need done. Just send the bills to me."

"I think I can handle the charges and I will never send a bill to you. You take care of the ranch. I'll take care of me and the baby."

Griffin drew a long breath. "I understand. Hell, I even agree. But it'll take me time, Sunshine. You live your life. I live mine. A marriage of convenience. I got that." He paused. "But there's no reason we can't be friends, is there?"

"No reason at all. I kind of like the idea."

She almost felt sorry for him. This arrangement was new to them both, but she had to make it clear that she would never feel trapped again. Never.

They were at her pickup. Neither seemed to know how to say goodbye. Finally, she broke the silence. "We need to set routines. Things married people do to show the world all is right between them. I want everything settled and in order so there will be no fights, no arguments once we're married."

"What kind of things?" He wasn't looking at her.

"I don't know. My parents usually fought at the end of an

evening. I don't think I'd like that. We may be married but I make all my own decisions. I'll try not to interrupt your world and you stay out of mine. Clear?"

"Perfectly." The one word came fast and hard.

"Good, now back to the routine. We've got until the wedding to figure out how to look like we're in love. I don't think all people will be as easy to fool as your brothers."

"How about we just say good-night and hug when we're together?" He looked like he had no idea what she wanted. "No end-of-the-day disagreements, no lectures. Just a hug. My parents used to do that whenever one of them left the ranch."

"Sounds good." She opened her truck door, then turned to face him.

He put his hands on her waist, but he didn't try to pull her to him. He waited for her to move closer.

She did. They were barely touching. Then she put her arms around his neck and laid her head on his shoulder in an awkward embrace. His hand moved up her back, gently pressing her a fraction closer. She could feel his chest moving in and out and see each breath in the cold air. The warmth of him made it not seem so cold, but his nearness was foreign. She'd developed an invisible shell years ago, and he was getting too close.

She moved her lips against his ear. "You think the brothers are watching?"

"I know they are." He laughed. "You were great tonight, Sunshine. I had a few rough spots, but I'll catch on."

"No one's ever called me Sunshine."

"Then I will, if you have no objection. People about to be married usually have pet names for each other." He pressed his cheek against hers. "See you tomorrow."

Sunlan moved away, barely noticing him trying to help her up into the seat. Then he closed the door and stepped back as she pulled away without saying a word.

He might call her Sunshine, but she didn't plan to play along and give him a nickname. She'd call him Griffin, or maybe Griff like his brothers did.

He still stood on front of the porch, watching her, until she turned onto the county road.

She didn't wave. He was just a solution to her problem. Nothing more. Once they were married, she probably wouldn't see him a dozen times a year.

Friends. That she could be. Nothing more.

CHAPTER EIGHTEEN

LONG AFTER MIDNIGHT, Jaxson carried Mallory Mayweather out the back door of the hospital and climbed into Tim O'Grady's truck. Charlie was already in the cab, nervously leaving muddy footprints on Tim's back seat. The minute the dog saw Mallory, he calmed and pushed his nose between the seats so he could put his head lightly on her bandaged leg.

"I got her, Buddy. I mean Charlie," Jax whispered. "We're heading home."

The dog whined low as if he understood.

Toni fussed over Mallory, blanketing them both as Jax held her in his arms. "You drive slow, Tim O'Grady—" the nurse glared at the redhead "—or I'll find you and thump you so hard short stories will dribble out of your head every time you hiccup."

Tim groaned. "I wonder if New York cab drivers have to put up with as much abuse as I do. I don't guess either of you stopped to think that I might have been busy tonight."

"No," they both answered.

Tim rolled his eyes back. "Even Tiny Baker threatened to sit on me if I didn't take every turn slow. I have a feeling the whole O'Grady clan will disown me if I accidentally hurt this cousin I've never met." He leaned over, trying to see her in the dashboard lights. "She's not even redheaded. Are you sure she's related to us?"

He looked at Jax as Toni closed the passenger door. "How is it possible you, the family recluse, knows this lady, and me, the guy who makes every wedding, reunion and funeral, has never heard of her?"

Jax cradled Mallory carefully and whispered, "You remember, she's Uncle Luther's granddaughter. He was one of your grandmother's brothers who went to California during the depression. Most of them we don't see back in Texas until they retire, then they move around between relatives like they think we're a chain of bed-and-breakfasts, telling us how hard the march to California was back in the Model T days."

"Yeah, I try to avoid them. I read their story in *The Grapes of Wrath*. Which is where most of them got their info from, I'm guessing." Tim pulled slowly away from the hospital and took the back road off the parking lot. "I figure they go back to the sunshine state and tell everyone stories about their hick relatives who still scratch in the dirt like chickens. To date, not one has written me to tell me how much they love my vampire stories. That just shows how uninformed most of my relatives are."

Jax watched the rearview window, making sure no lights followed them.

"Tiny Baker wouldn't tell me anything about what was going on while he was setting up the bed," Tim complained. "You never talk about anything, so I have little chance of getting the facts. Some kind of drama is going on here, and I appear to be playing the getaway driver."

Jax looked down at Mallory. She'd had enough meds to help her sleep through this transport. With luck, she wouldn't even remember the journey.

"Some guy beat the hell out of her," he began, knowing Tim

had a right to know. "We've got to keep her safe. Toni said she didn't think it was the first time the guy beat her up, and if he finds her, the next beating may be the last time because he'll finish killing her. Toni's seen this kind of thing before. Relationships like that don't get better, just worse."

"Wow. That's some backstory. Shouldn't we call the sheriff? The guy should be tracked down."

"All the sheriff has on him right now is a restraining order. Unless she wants to press charges, all the law can do is make sure the guy stays away from her."

"Do you think she'd tell me all about what happened? I'm transporting a victim. We're helping her escape sure death. That's a real plot and a half going here."

"Aren't you worried about her?"

Tim looked guilty for a moment, then admitted, "Of course I am. She's as much kin to me as she is to you, Jaxson. Add to that, she's interesting. I want to help her, but I also have to know how she feels, what she's thinking. It's research. I can't help myself. All writers are miners for emotions. It's who we are, what we do. I just want to talk to her, when she's better, of course."

"Mallory hasn't said a word. I don't know if she's afraid the guy who beat her will find her or afraid the paper will give more information away. The sheriff knows the car she was driving was registered to a Curtis Dayson. Sheriff Cline has probably already called him."

Tim filled in details he'd learned from dropping by the station. "Dayson must be well off, because he's got a place south of here and another in Dallas. Thatcher said the guy went crazy when he saw the wrecked sports car but didn't even ask if the driver was hurt. He just demanded to know where she was. When Thatcher played dumb, the boyfriend left. He was back in the office two days later telling Pearly he was losing his mind because he couldn't find his girlfriend."

"Everyone in town knows Mallory was admitted to the hospital."

"Yeah, and everyone's probably talking about it, but you know locals. They don't tend to give out much information to strangers. Besides, he could claim the injuries are from the wreck."

"Are they?" Tim asked.

"Scratches, maybe a head injury, but the ground was wet, muddy. Toni said she saw new wounds on top of old bruises. But you're right. It would be hard to prove in court."

"I don't care. Our job is to protect her."

"Right," Jax answered.

"That's all I need to know for now." Tim smiled. "I always wanted to be a superhero. So come on, Robin, let's save the lady."

Jax laughed. "I thought I was Batman. You're Robin."

"No. I'm the one driving the Batmobile pickup. Robin never gets to drive."

"But I'm the one holding the damsel in distress." They passed through the sleepy little town of Crossroads, and Jax added, "Make sure we're not followed."

"Will do." Tim turned serious.

As they headed down the lonely county road, Jax relaxed a bit. He could feel Mallory slow breathing against his chest. She was safe.

"Do you know where this cousin of ours lives?"

"Sheriff said she was driving fast on the road coming from the east. Her license had a former address. She hadn't lived there for months, but she hadn't changed her address on her license."

"Which means?"

"Coming from the east…maybe she was running away. She was on the back road, thinking he might be trying to follow. I have no idea why she didn't change her address. Maybe she was living with the guy but saw it too temporary to list."

"Did this guy Dayson take the wrecked car?"

"Nope. He had a tow service pick it up. If he ever shows up again, the sheriff plans to have a long talk with him after Mallory is able to tell him the facts."

"Strange," Tim said after a moment of silence. "Two cars hit that long line of fence running the Maverick Ranch that night. What are the chances of that?"

Jax wanted to say the chance was probably a thousand to one. He'd never seen a wreck out on that road. Of course, the odds were probably even higher that he'd find a near-dead dog and then locate Mallory and bring her home with him.

But the chances were good that she'd be safe with him, and that was what mattered.

CHAPTER NINETEEN

Maverick Ranch

WYATT JOHNSON HATED driving onto a stranger's land, crossing uninvited under someone's gate. It was something that didn't seem to sit right. He'd seen enough Westerns, even modern day ones, to know folks were armed out in the country, but it was time to face what he'd done.

Maverick's grassland had been left wild and open. Beautiful in its colorful breaks and winding streams. The kind of place where movies about the Old West could be filmed. A view a man could look at all his life and never get tired of the untamed beauty.

Wyatt made it to the first step of a forty-foot-wide porch before a man a few years younger than him and looking just as tough opened the massive door and walked outside.

"You lost, stranger?" the cowboy asked with no sign of friendliness in his voice.

"No. You Griffin Holloway?"

"I am, but if you're selling, I'm not buying."

Wyatt smiled. He might be a soldier and this man a rancher, but he had a feeling they understood one another. No nonsense.

"I'm Captain Wyatt Johnson. I'm not from around here, but I was passing by on the county road almost a week ago and—"

"You're the man who took out a quarter mile of my fence."

"Right. I'll be happy to pay for—"

"I'm not interested in your money. How about you help me put it back in place?"

"All right. I'm staying over at—"

"I know who you are, Captain Johnson. The sheriff told me you were on leave from the army. I figure you might help me mend the fence while your wife is in school."

"I wouldn't mind at all, but I got to ask you something first. Do you ever let a man finish a sentence?"

"Not lately." Griffin grinned, looking younger. "You see, I've got fog-snot for brains lately, Captain. I'm getting married and—"

"Enough said," Wyatt interrupted. "What time you want me here tomorrow?"

"How about we have a cup of coffee and we'll talk about it? I think my brother ordered all we'll need, but I'm not sure when it'll be shipped to the hardware store in town. If it's in, I could pick up the supplies and we could work while the weather's clear."

"I'll take you up on the offer for a cup of coffee. My—" he hesitated a moment "—wife is a great cook, but she doesn't drink coffee. I've about had all the tea I can handle. The only good thing about going back on deployment is that the coffee's always hot in the mess tent."

"How long you two been married?"

It was an easy question for a husband, but Wyatt had forgotten to ask Jamie that part of the story. "Three years." He took a guess. "Only I'm home so little we feel like newlyweds. We still haven't learned each other's ways."

Griffin walked him into a big kitchen with breakfast dishes

still in the sink. As he poured coffee, the rancher asked, "You got your wife figured out yet?"

"Nope."

"Me either. I'm pretty much hopeless when it comes to women. I just asked a lady to marry me and the next day the housekeeper turns in her notice. Says she won't work for a woman." Griffin slid Wyatt's cup across the bar. "To tell the truth, I don't think we'll miss her. My dad used to say that since Mamie was hired on here, her main mission in life was to make every day cloudy. By the time I took over the ranch, she'd been here too long to fire."

"Has she ever quit before?"

"Yeah, she quits at least once a year. It's usually her way of asking for a raise, but this time she took most of the pots and pans with her and said she was never coming back."

Wyatt laughed. "Sounds like you got more problems than I do. Half the time I'm home I think I'm just playing like I've got a wife. Sometimes, I almost believe it. Other times it's just a dream."

"I know how you feel. I'm getting married in a little over a month, but I don't know the first thing about *being* married. You ever get the feeling at birth the universe gives every girl the playbook on marriage and forgets about the boys? We start out knowing nothing and they know all the rules."

The two men nodded and drank their coffee. Wyatt almost believed Griffin Holloway might be in a pretend marriage like him. But what were the chances of that? Maybe every husband feels like he doesn't really know his wife.

Only Wyatt *really* didn't know Jamie. He couldn't name her favorite color or her birthday or even her middle name. But he knew she didn't think she was pretty and she must not have many friends, because no one had dropped by the lake house. She never talked of family, and the phone in her place had never rung.

He did have enough sense to know that it wouldn't be fair to

Jamie for him to make a move. He'd be gone in a little over a week. She wasn't his type. Too curvy. Too settled. She'd been sweet to let him stay, though. Too sweet to ever hurt her. When a woman like Jamie fell in love, it would be forever, not a week. He couldn't leave even a crack in her heart. She'd marry some nice guy. They'd have half a dozen kids and never wander out of the state for the rest of their lives.

He had his next assignment waiting for him, and it would take all his concentration. He couldn't allow himself to get involved with Jamie. Once he was back in the field, letting his mind drift even for a moment might put the whole team at risk.

Wyatt tried to concentrate on the rancher's description of how stringing barbed-wire fence worked.

Griffin's brother Elliot joined them for another round of coffee. After they talked about the fence, Elliot asked Wyatt what he did in the army.

"I'm in the Signal Corps working with communications. You know, military intelligence stuff mostly. Basically, I install equipment in places no sane person would ever go. Sounds exciting but believe me, most of it is just work." He almost added that the job he'd been waiting to do had stalled. It would be his most dangerous yet. And if they could get in? Install the equipment and get out alive.

Elliot raised an eyebrow. "You work with computers?"

Wyatt shrugged. "Among other things." He wasn't about to tell anyone the details of his job or how dangerous it was at times.

Elliot hesitated, then asked, "You wouldn't be willing to take a look at my system? My devices don't want to talk to each other."

Griffin butted in. "Elliot, he just stopped by. He doesn't want to fix your computer."

"I could pay you. We can't get any tech support out here and when I call in for help, I get the feeling they're laughing on the other end."

"I got a job. Don't need another," Wyatt said. "But I also got a few hours to kill before I pick up my wife. I've already fixed everything around her house, I might as well give it a try. And the pay is if I'm still here in two hours, you feed me lunch."

He and Elliot refilled their coffee, and Wyatt started to follow him out the kitchen. Griffin stopped him. "One question, Captain, before you two get lost in that mess. How do you like your hamburger?"

"With the works." Wyatt smiled. "Onion rings and fries on the side."

"And beer," Elliot added.

Wyatt laughed. "You men really do need a cook."

An hour later, Wyatt couldn't stop smiling. He loved every minute at the lake house, but it felt good to be around men. Normal. Elliot's system was old, but it had been top of the line a few years ago. He showed the rancher a few tricks and reprogrammed it to run faster.

They ate lunch in front of the screen as they ordered equipment that would streamline his programs. At three thirty, when he stepped off the porch to go pick up Jamie, he saw Griffin coming from the barn.

"Tomorrow okay, Wyatt? I got a call. The fence poles will be in."

"Tomorrow. Nine o'clock. I'll meet you where my car ran off the road."

Wyatt walked back to Jamie's old van. Neither man mentioned that the insurance he'd taken out when he rented the car would have covered the fence repair. Wyatt already had the rental car towed back to an office in Lubbock. Sometime in the next week, he'd figure out how to get another one to drive to the nearest airport. In the meantime, he looked forward to a little physical labor.

Until his leave was up, all he wanted to do was live a normal life, and digging a few fence-pole holes suited him fine. The past three days had been great. He'd fixed everything he could find around Jamie's lake house. Even chopped enough dead wood to keep the fireplace going till spring. But he needed something else to burn up energy.

Every night she came home tired. They'd eaten out twice and he'd cooked one night. They'd played every game she had in the house and watched movies.

But they were still strangers. She hadn't asked much about his job in the army, and Wyatt didn't want to discuss what he did anyway. The next mission haunted him enough already.

She talked about her students at school but never mentioned why she wasn't married. Jamie was the first girl he'd ever met who didn't talk about her old boyfriends.

At ten that night, when she closed the door between them and turned the bedroom door lock, Wyatt spent a few hours staring at the fireplace light and fighting the urge to knock on her door. He wanted more, but she wasn't an "any port in the storm" kind of woman. Casual sex probably wasn't in her vocabulary.

And if he was being honest, it wasn't in his either. Maybe in getting older, he'd realized there was more. Only, with his life, he didn't have time to look for it.

It wouldn't be fair. She was nice, fun to talk to, but neither of them had time to fall in love. Neither one probably ever had, he guessed. She'd said they were friends. She trusted him. He was lucky she was letting him stay. Best leave he'd ever had and it had just started.

He rationally went through every reason why her bedroom door would stay closed. Instead of counting sheep, he went over it again and again until he finally fell asleep.

And when he did, he dreamed of home. A little house. A curly-haired wife with glasses.

CHAPTER TWENTY

Midnight Crossing

MALLORY MAYWEATHER DIDN'T move any other part of her body as she slowly opened her eyes. She'd come awake one sense at a time. First, she was aware of the warmth. Then the silence. No traffic. No sounds of people around. Nothing moving or beeping or rattling.

Bone deep, she knew she wasn't in the hospital.

Slowly, she registered the sound of a fireplace crackling. Then smells drifted over to her. The light hint of mesquite wood burning. She'd smelled it at a few steakhouses in Fort Worth. The waxy smell of a candle. The aroma of coffee brewing.

She breathed deeper. Clean air. Fresh air. None of the antiseptic smell of the hospital.

The night before came back to her. She remembered the stranger who took care of Charlie, explaining that she was moving locations as the sleeping pill had blanketed over her mind.

The stranger, Jax O'Grady. He'd said he was a hermit, but he seemed to talk to her. And Charlie liked him, she could tell.

Very slowly, her eyes opened wider. The room was in shadows. Her vision moved inch by inch outward. The hospital bed. A blanket, also hospital issue. Charlie sleeping on the floor between her and a low-burning fireplace in a room framed with logs.

Mallory closed her eyes once more and breathed in. A calmness surrounded her. Maybe she'd died and gone to purgatory.

She'd take one more peek, then go back to sleep. Her gaze drifted across the space. The room was maybe twelve feet wide and maybe thirty feet long. One end had a tiny kitchen all done in natural wood. The other end looked to be a library with one desk, one chair, one computer and what appeared to be at least a hundred books. No pictures; the walls were basically made of shelves. No table, no couch and no chairs, except the one by the desk.

The windows had no curtains, and she could see the first rose color of dawn. She didn't miss an old rifle propped up by the front door, and a worn coat on a single peg above it.

She turned her head slowly, taking in the whole room. Front door. Back door. Maybe bedroom door.

A rattle came from the bedroom and she realized she wasn't alone. For a moment, she tensed, then relaxed. Charlie would have reacted if there was danger. The dog hadn't roused.

A man appeared from the bedroom. Jax O'Grady, the county recluse. The one who'd said he was her cousin, or maybe he hadn't, maybe the nurse had said that.

Mallory narrowed her eyes almost closed.

He moved around her bed, tucking her blanket in. Then he put another log on the fire and patted Charlie on the head. Strange nurse, she thought. His hair was wild, his shirt unbuttoned and worn. Levis were tucked into his boots.

The stranger patted his jeans and Charlie stood beside him. Silently they moved to the door. The man pulled on his coat and grabbed the rifle before he slipped outside. A few minutes later, they rushed back in.

Charlie followed the man to the kitchen area, as if planning to help with breakfast. It was light enough to see a dusting of snow on his shoulders. He wasn't a big man, but he seemed well balanced.

Mallory gave up any pretense of sleep and watched them. As the sun brightened, the man seemed less careful about being silent. When he had eggs frying, he turned to her, caught her watching and grinned.

"Morning," he said, almost shyly. "You hungry?"

She tried a little smile and found it not as painful today. She pointed to the plate he carried and then her mouth.

He shook his head. "Oh, these aren't your eggs, they're Charlie's. He's always starving in the morning, and I've noticed he likes eggs better than bacon. Might be because I usually burn the bacon."

Jax lifted the coffeepot. "Want a cup of coffee while I fry your breakfast?"

She nodded and reached for the button to raise the top of her bed.

When she took her first sip of his strong coffee, she swore she felt it run the length of her body. She was alive and safe, and most of all, healing.

She'd survive. Curtis hadn't won. Not this time.

As the morning passed, her only entertainment was watching Jax. He talked a bit, telling her his routine, asking if she was all right. But he didn't insist on walking her to the bathroom or hover over her with questions. He was sitting in his desk chair reading when she took her morning nap, and still reading when she woke up.

When she began unwrapping her hand, he turned from his computer and stood close to watch. The skin was wrinkled and bruised but scabbing over.

Handing Mallory the analgesic cream, he let her rub it into

her skin. Then he studied her hand, carefully turning it in his gentle grip. "You want me to rewrap it?"

Shaking her head, Mallory was relieved he didn't insist. One of the terrible things about being in a hospital was that you lost control over your own body. Others decided everything for you. Jax wasn't doing that.

She slept for a while again, then woke to a sandwich lunch made from the eggs she hadn't eaten for breakfast.

When she made no effort to eat them, he frowned. "You don't like eggs all that much, do you?"

She shook her head.

Jax took the plate away and handed her a pen and paper. "What sounds good to you? You got to eat."

She glanced at the kitchen that wasn't big enough to stock much. Pizza was all she could think of, so she wrote it down. Salad. Ice cream. She wrote both down.

Jax frowned and moved to his computer. A minute later, he leaned back in his chair. "Ordered."

It couldn't have been an hour later that she saw the pickup she'd ridden in last night pull up to the cabin. Her new red-headed cousin jumped out.

He didn't bother to knock. He just walked in carrying a big pizza box, a bag of lettuce and a tub of Neapolitan ice cream.

Tim O'Grady winked at her. "Good afternoon, beautiful. My brain-dead cousin didn't tell me what kind of pizza so I got half meat lovers and half veggie. Did the same with ice cream—part vanilla, part chocolate, part strawberry—but I should warn you, I'm eating the chocolate third."

"Close the door. I'm trying to keep the place the same temperature," Jax ordered.

Tim shrugged. "She's not a baby, Jax." He dropped the food in the kitchen, walked directly toward her and sat on the end of her bed. "How you feeling today, M&M?"

"She doesn't talk," Jax answered from the kitchen.

"Can't or doesn't?" Tim asked. Both men waited for the answer.

She touched her bandaged throat. Slowly, as they watched, she unwrapped the gauze. She saw the shock in Tim's face before he hid his reaction.

Mallory closed her eyes but held her head high. She would not hide away from what had happened. Not this time. Not ever again.

Jax moved closer and looked straight on at her throat. "You've got a few scratches. One long and deep enough to leave a scar, but it's not bleeding." He turned his head as he continued his examination. "And bruises. Deep bruises."

Tim found his voice. "In the shape of a handprint. You were choked."

She nodded.

Jax leaned over her. "You want me to bandage it back up?"

She shook her head. They'd already seen the damage. As she looked into the sorrow in Jax's eyes, she heard Tim say, "Well, the good news is it's got nowhere to go but better."

She tried to smile, then almost laughed when Jax told his cousin to shut up.

While Jax chopped the lettuce, Tim went back to his truck and brought in three folding chairs and a folding table. He started talking while he was still on the porch.

"I know you're a minimalist, Jax, but company has to have a place to sit. Every time I visit, we always sit on the porch. Now I'm inside, I see why. Squirrels have more furnishings in their nest than you do. It's obvious you've been stealing books from every library in the state for years. You could have made a few of them into furniture. You've got a shed full of lumber and all you make is shelves. So much for Uncle Darrell's hope you'd become a carpenter."

Jax frowned. "I order the books from a university bookstore and have the bookstore mail them direct to my PO box. Every few weeks, I drive in and pick new ones up after dark."

"Then why didn't you say anything? I've been getting your mail at my house and delivering it every month. You could have just changed your address to the PO box and saved me a trip."

Jax smiled. "I like seeing you now and then."

Tim looked as if he didn't know whether to be mad or flattered. He smiled at Mallory. "You do know that you are living with a crazy man. If he stays out here by himself much longer, he'll be more myth than man. Some folks have already forgotten I have a cousin named Jaxson. Griffin Holloway, Jaxson's nearest neighbor, says he sees a shadow walking the hills now and then."

Tim paced the bookshelf-covered walls of the room, letting his hand glide over the spines of thick books. "All this time I thought you were just whittling on all the wood your uncle sent you and turns out you've been reading—no, studying. These books are tagged, dog-eared, written in, I'll bet. Most of these look like textbooks." He slowed, reading the titles aloud. *"Forensics, Fire Science, Burn Patterns, Criminal Justice, Chemistry, Investigative Interviewing."*

"That's enough, Tim." Jax's words came low. "I'll bet Mallory would rather you serve the pizza than read book titles."

"Right," he said and he lifted the pizza box and opened it.

Mallory picked up the plate Jax had set on her blankets and reached for a slice. After three days of hospital food, the pizza, even cold, was perfect.

As she ate slowly, feeling tiny bites slip down her sore throat, Jax and Tim entertained her. Tim did most of the talking, but Jax added a dry kind of humor that never failed to make her smile.

In the sunlight, she watched the hard lines of Jaxson's face soften. Something very deep about him drew her. There was far more to the man than he let people see. A sort of kindness she decided. He lived a very simple life, but he was aware of every detail of his surroundings.

When Tim finally stood to leave, he handed her the pen and

paper. "Write down what you want and, if I can find it in Cross-roads, I'll bring it tomorrow for lunch."

She wrote. Fruit. Vegetables. Cookies.

"I can handle that with all the fixin's." He leaned over and kissed her cheek. "So long, cousin. I'll bring you puzzles to-morrow and maybe a few games. The Christmas puzzles are in at the gas station. You want one with puppies under the tree or horses running across snow?"

She shrugged and waved as Jax walked him out. A few min-utes later when Jax walked back in, she was almost asleep, barely aware that he was tending to the fire and doing the dishes and folding away the chairs and table.

A complicated man who liked a simple kind of order.

"Thanks," she whispered, but her voice was too weak for him to hear.

CHAPTER TWENTY-ONE

Maverick Ranch

GRIFFIN WALKED THE rooms on the third floor of his home trying to figure out if what he'd committed to would slowly drive
him insane. His future bride had dropped by every morning
with updated plans for the wedding and revised charts for her
rooms upstairs. After almost a week, the entire third floor of the
headquarters looked like some modern art project called *Chaos
in shades of earth tones*.

The second morning, she'd brought a contractor and two
cleaning ladies.

On day three, she'd added a truckload of carpenters, two elec-
tricians, a design consultant and an old hippie who looked like
he hadn't changed clothes or shaved since the sixties. He said
he was the tile guy. She introduced them by their occupations
as they stormed the stairs.

Finally, when no one showed up on the fifth day, Griffin relaxed, deciding she was finished fixing up what was now her
suite of rooms, her space. Only when he climbed the stairs, the
mess was still there. Yesterday they must have knocked out a

whole wall, making her bedroom bigger. A set of windows had been removed to add a huge round hole on the east wall, big enough for a man to walk through. It had been covered with thick plastic that rattled and popped.

He walked slowly back downstairs. If the wedding didn't happen, he'd never be able to pay for the un-makeover. Griffin poured cold cereal in a mixing bowl and grabbed a half-empty gallon of milk. Then he sat out on the porch to enjoy the first warm day in weeks.

Before he was half finished with breakfast, trucks started pulling up. People he'd never seen followed the stuck-up decorator into the house as if Griffin were invisible. Like ants, they circled back to the trucks for more stuff. Pillows, curtains, chairs, mirrors, furniture, couches, rugs. It all went up.

Their footsteps on the stairs sounded like buffalo on the move.

Elliot finally gave up working in the study and joined Griffin on the porch. "What is going on?" he asked. He sloshed his coffee when he leaned against the porch railing.

"Sunlan is redecorating."

"Seems more like a hostile takeover. Maybe we should start locking the doors. Do you know even one of those strangers tromping up and down our stairs?"

"Nope. I said howdy to one guy, and he stopped long enough to stare at me and say he didn't speak cowboy. But since they're bringing things in, I don't think they came to rob us."

Elliot thought about it for a moment, then nodded. "We paying for any of the repairs or rebuilding going on? We're beyond tight this month."

"Nope."

Elliot relaxed. "Then I think we should let your future wife make herself comfortable if it makes her happy."

Griffin had no idea what would make Sunlan happy, but he had a feeling it wouldn't be wise to cross her. His future wife was a woman who knew her own mind and he had no doubt, if he let her, she'd drive him out of his.

A few hours later, she drove up with trays of food and the Franklin sisters. Both of the old ladies looked at him like he was the yard dog.

The shorter one of the sisters stopped long enough to greet Griffin. "We're lending a hand to Sunlan. She's so busy, you know. So Rose and I are being professional caterers today." Daisy giggled. "We padded the number so there will be plenty for you boys. We've heard you still haven't found a cook willing to drive out here."

"Thank you for the delivery." Griffin had been about to go for hamburgers, but these people didn't look like the burgers-and-fries crowd. "Elliot and I are much obliged, but Cooper rarely makes it back in for lunch."

"Then what does he do?" Daisy looked truly concerned.

"I think he just grazes with the cows."

Daisy ticktocked her head. "We're here to help, Griffin. Sunlan asked if we'd assist in the selection of a new cook for the place. I've got a few ideas. You'll want someone who can cook the basics, right?"

"Right. Nothing fancy."

"I'll send out people for interviews on Friday. You'll have to hire someone else to come once a week to do the cleaning."

"You got a list of people who might be willing to do that? Really clean, I mean." He had no idea what to tell a housekeeper. Mamie usually ran the vacuum a few times a month but never dusted anything. The only time the windows were cleaned was when it rained, and she'd wash towels and sheets only when one of the men delivered and picked them up from the laundry room.

"I know a few folks who could use the work." Daisy grinned and hurried off behind her sister.

Griffin sat back down in the porch chair. He had no idea

what was going on. He wasn't sure he wanted to know. Elliot hated change, Cooper ignored it and Griffin had a feeling it was washing over him.

His new bride might not want any advice or help, but Griffin needed all anyone would give him. Maybe he should offer to drop by the bed-and-breakfast once a week for lessons again. One beautiful woman, who didn't look like she even weighed a hundred and thirty pounds, was complicating his life.

Maybe it would all settle down after the wedding. She'd get on with her life. He'd run the ranch. They'd see each other now and then. No drama. No changes. No joint bank accounts. Sounded like a happy marriage.

Sunlan rushed out the front door and froze when she saw him. Griffin wasn't sure she'd noticed him when she came in.

"Griff?"

"Sunshine," he said, thinking a better name for the lady might be Stormy. "We going to introduce ourselves every time we see each other?"

"No, of course not." She moved closer and awkwardly put her hand on his shoulder. "The sisters and Elliot are eating in the study if you want to join them. I'm afraid the people I sent out to work filled both the dining room, the kitchen table and the bar."

Sunlan shifted. "I didn't realize I'd sent out so many. I just wanted it done before I head back to Denver tomorrow. Now I've got people asking me questions from every direction. I feel like I'm on a quiz show and there's never a commercial break."

"When you planning on coming back here?" He almost said *home.* "All of this can wait, you know. The house and I aren't going anywhere."

She smiled. "You're right. I'll be back before the wedding. I've got new stock coming in and need to be at Misty Bend. Remember at the café, our first meeting, I said I'd always let you know where I was."

"I remember. But tell me, are you leaving all these people here?"

"And if I am?"

"Then you'd better come back soon. I'm not sure we speak the same language. Some guy in tight pants rushed down a while ago and asked me if I'd seen a sangria pillow. When I looked blank, he added real slow, 'Sangria-colored pillow.' I thought that was a drink, not a color. I told him I saw it riding off on a whiskey horse with a brandy mane toward a tequila sunset."

She relaxed a little, letting her hip brush his shoulder. "I'll make it a short trip." He heard laughter in her voice.

"It doesn't matter. There's no hurry. I can handle any problem that comes up about the wedding." Griffin had seen horses that were jumpy like her: uncertain, afraid, ready to run. "No storm's coming. It's all going to work out." She didn't need to know his fears right now. She had a bucket load of her own.

Sunlan smiled slightly. "It will. The sisters were right. We'll fit together as a couple."

He took her hand as he rose out of the chair. "Any food left? We should eat with the sisters."

She followed him back into the house. The moment they were within sight of the crowd in the dining room, she moved against his side, her arm across his back.

Griffin smiled. Waved at the crowd, then turned and kissed Sunny on the forehead. Part of him felt like a fool pretending, but it was what he'd agreed to do. He'd get his ranch and she'd get her freedom. A fair enough swap. From what he'd gathered from bits of conversation, Sunlan's parents took turns trying to run her life. Whatever she did to please one only angered the other.

As they filled their plates, he asked, "Have you been to the white barn?"

"Not yet. I thought I'd go there after lunch."

"Mind if I tag along?"

She hesitated.

"If I know what you want, maybe I could get started on some of the changes while you're in Denver."

"You'd do that?"

"Sure. This is winter, our slow season. If I have any questions, I could call and check in with you." *If I had your cell number,* he almost added.

An hour later when she'd told him all her plans to upgrade a barn that had already been built to impress, she reached for his cell and typed in her number. The contact name was simply Sunshine.

"I'll hire the men who know how to update this barn and put them up at the B & B while they're working," she said. "They shouldn't bother you much with questions."

He took her hand as they walked out into a cool afternoon sun. People could see them now. "We've got a bunkhouse that could house them. It's not used this time of year. That would save them an hour in travel every day."

She agreed. "You sure you wouldn't mind?"

"Not at all. There's a small kitchen out there. I'll stock it with sandwich makings and the cabinet with soups. I'll check up on them and if I find a cook, I'll make sure they have a hot dinner every night."

Her eyes glared at him. "What do you want in return, Griff?"

"Nothing. Just helping out."

"No. We're not just neighbors or friends. We made a bargain. You ask for something and we trade."

Man, this woman was cold. About the time he thought it would be nice to cuddle up with her, she porcupined up. "You're right. The bargain. Everything fair and square. When you come back, I'll try to have that runway packed so you can land your plane on that long stretch about a half mile behind the barn. I'll have an ATV parked out there so you can drive in. But, in exchange, you consider spending the nights in your rooms...here on the ranch but not with me. I want us to spend at least a little time together before the wedding." He caught a bit of fear in her glance. "You have my word you'll be safe here. None of us is going to try to run your life, Sunshine. Hell, we have enough trouble running our own."

"But the sisters? They'll expect me."

"I think they'll understand. Once all the workmen are gone, you may want to move into town with them for a few days to plan the last details of our wedding. We've got a hell of a lot to do in only a few weeks. It'll work smoother, faster, if we're close."

"Anything else?"

"Yes. I've been thinking about it. We need to go tell your dad about the wedding in person."

She shook her head. "I don't think it's necessary."

"A man shouldn't find out about his only child's wedding when he gets the invitation." Griffin swore he saw worry in those blue eyes. "I'll be right beside you. And no matter what he does or says, nothing changes between us, right?"

"Right." She kissed his cheek and smiled. "I'm going to like being married to you. I love the way you lay the cards on the table and don't try to manipulate me. Would you have gone alone to talk to my father if I'd said no?"

"I would have and I swear I will never tell anyone about our bargain. Some things are only between us and they always will be."

"Till death do us part?"

"Till death do us part."

They walked back to the headquarters holding hands. He was trying his best to get used to the touching that was just for show. In truth, unless a girl tended to wander off or was drunk, he'd never held hands. It seemed something kids would do. But with Sunlan, it felt right. Her stride matched his. Her fingers laced comfortably in his hand. A give-and-take union. A bargain. No manipulating. All fair between them. It sounded like the perfect marriage.

Except for one thing. No sex. No love. And it crossed his mind like a will-o'-the-wisp over still water that they were going to be nothing more than polite strangers for a lifetime.

Polite strangers.

CHAPTER TWENTY-TWO

Maverick Ranch

A FEW DAYS after Sunlan went back to Denver, the decorating began to spill down the stairs into the dining room, then the kitchen and finally the great room. First, the new housekeeper removed Cooper's collection of old boots he'd kept in the corner of the entryway for years. Then the couch and TV got moved to face away from the fireplace, and end tables were added. Next, ten-foot-long curtains were hung over the huge window and pulled back on the sides.

The scarred dining table disappeared and another twice as big was brought in from Dallas in a truck that also carried rugs so big it took three men to carry them in. Next came a massive sculpture of cattle crossing the Red River that sat on the new table.

The three brothers took time to stare at each change.

"It's like this bronze has always been missing on our table." Cooper spoke first. "Anyone can see it belongs there. I just didn't know it until I saw it."

"I agree," Elliot voted. "I've heard about a woman's touch in a room, but our Sunlan isn't just putting her stamp on our place. Somehow she knows what our tastes are, and she's making it look like the Holloway headquarters should have always looked. No frilly curtains, no furry pillows lying around. No ashtrays that look like you can't drop ashes into 'em."

"I, for one, wouldn't mind a few furry pillows." Cooper wiggled his eyebrows. "You know, just in case I come in drunk and crash on the couch. I'd have something to cuddle with. Tell our Sunlan to add that to the next shipment, would you, Griff?"

Griffin glared at both his brothers. "She's not our Sunlan. She's mine. You two are going to have to find your own wives, because this is one thing we're not sharing."

"But where are we going to put wives, Griff? She's got the third floor. Our bedrooms are on the second, and everything downstairs is public space."

Elliot looked bored. "I asked that very question, and she told me we could build two wings on. Make the place U-shaped in back. Then she said she'd have an outdoor kitchen built and seating for thirty. She even hinted she'd like a pool for the kids someday."

"I thought the fire pit was our outdoor kitchen." Cooper shrugged. "A pool would sure be nicer than the pond. Last time I went for a swim I came up for air, and a cow licked my ear so hard I didn't get the snot out for a week."

As they sat down to eat, Cooper complained about missing the Wednesday night meat loaf. But he ate two plates of tortellini with grilled mushrooms and chicken on top.

The new cook wouldn't talk to them and she hadn't cooked the same thing twice. When she started serving desserts, Cooper asked her to marry him. She didn't answer, but she raised her wooden spoon like a weapon when he stepped into her kitchen space.

Griffin picked at his food. The cook who came the day after Sunlan left was good, quiet and professional, but it wasn't the same as having his almost-wife there. The house felt empty.

Like a piece of their family had been missing and no one noticed until Sunlan came. He missed her laughter. She made the old house seem more like a home somehow.

Sunlan was flying in tonight. He had other things on his mind besides food. Details they needed to talk over. Plans to make. The wedding was fast approaching and after that, there would be the actual marriage.

Griffin had got the new runway ready on the Maverick Ranch, even though Sunlan said she didn't mind landing on the airstrip one ranch over until he finished.

She'd even met Staten Kirkland and his wife's niece, Madison O'Grady-Weathers, the day she'd taken her first look at Griffin's ranch. Madison's long name fit her and she and Sunlan had bonded at once, talking about planes and their love for flying.

Griffin liked the idea of Sunlan finding a friend. Maybe after the wedding, they'd invite Fifth Weathers and his wife, Madison, over for dinner. The women had a great deal in common and Griffin guessed Fifth would fit in with him and his brothers—after all, he was the fifth boy born into the Weathers family. His mother had been so upset she didn't have a girl she'd just given him a number and moved on.

Couple friends. Griffin laughed. Sounded strange.

This was the first time Sunlan would be trying out the runway Griffin had overseen. It was smaller than Kirkland's. Not as well lit. He'd followed her design she'd emailed, and made sure it was just the way she wanted it.

He had no doubt if Sunlan wasn't happy with it, she'd let him know.

Halfway through the meal, he heard the roar of the ATV and stood. All three men met her at the door. Cooper and Elliot both hugged her as they talked at once about how much they missed her. She'd brought bottles of wine for Elliot, and Cooper seemed just as happy to get a six-pack of beer from a new brewery in Denver.

As Elliot and Cooper took their gifts to the kitchen to open, she turned to Griffin but didn't hug him. He hesitated, never knowing exactly how to act.

"You made good time," he said. She'd kept her word and notified him just before she took off. "I wasn't expecting you for another hour or so."

"I did. How did you like the things I sent for the house?"

"I thought they were great."

"The sculpture?"

"It looks like it belongs there."

"I knew it would the minute I saw it."

Griffin nodded, acting like he cared. "It fits the house, the ranch." He couldn't bring himself to ask if she was staying. What would he do or say if she said no? She was her own woman. He had no right to make any demands.

As she turned toward a stack of plates on a sideboard that hadn't been in the dining room a week ago, she asked, "Would you mind getting my bags? I'm starving."

"You're staying?"

"Of course, and I'm so hungry I'd even eat cold roast beef. I've finally figured out I'm eating for two." She didn't look up.

He wasn't sure what to say. This was her first reference to the baby since they'd told his brothers she was expecting. Was it okay to talk about it now? Six months seemed a long way off.

After a minute of silence, she changed the subject. "The first of my horses will be arriving here tomorrow. They'll get used to the new place a few at a time. I want to be here to calm them as they learn their new home. They're young stallions that are too rowdy to be around my mares right now."

"Everything is ready for them. The men finished work last night." He guessed he was telling her what she already knew. "That round pen you had built looks strong enough to hold a herd of elephants."

Halfway to the ATV to get her luggage, it registered that she'd said she was starving. He'd never seen her eat more than two bites. But she was hungry. That had to be a good sign. Griffin grabbed her three bags and walked back to the house.

He sat down beside her, eating his own meal as she talked to Cooper about horses and Elliot about the stock market. And she ate. Something else had changed, too, besides her appetite. There were no dark shadows under her light blue eyes.

Somehow, this crazy bargain they'd made seemed to have settled her. The few times they'd talked had been all business, but their conversations were growing easier, more comfortable.

When they were all lingering over dessert, Griffin put his hand on her back as she leaned forward to make a point.

He let his fingers slowly slide over the silk of her sweater. A gentle touch. Not the start of anything.

She tensed but didn't make any attempt to move away. All it would have taken was one look and he'd have lifted his hand. But she didn't seem to mind. Maybe she thought he was doing it for show.

He lightly stroked her again, feeling her bow slightly toward his touch. Part of him reasoned she'd obviously known the touch of a man before; after all, she was pregnant. But the way she responded made him feel as if this was a first for her.

The baby was his, she'd said, making it plain they'd never talk of the lover or boyfriend or the one-night stand who had been with her.

When the brothers offered to take the plates to the kitchen, she turned into him. He leaned back in his chair and held her for a moment.

"I'm exhausted," she whispered.

"How about I walk you up to your room?"

"Great. If I stay here much longer, you'll have to carry me up the stairs."

He took her suitcases and slowly followed her. "These feel like lead."

"I know. There were things I wanted to bring to leave here." She reached the third floor and smiled. "Looks like my room's finished and they've moved on to my study and sitting room, which will turn into the nursery next year." She looked around as he turned on lights.

He thought of asking how the baby was, how big, was it moving, but they weren't to that point. After the wedding, they'd have six months to work out details of what was okay to talk about and what was off-limits.

"I don't spend much time checking on your workers up here. I figure they have their orders and I'd just be in the way." He set the cases down by the closet. "Two or three of the carpenters come in early every morning, but except for them, I'm gone before the others arrive. All of them are usually gone before I make it in at night. They're like the housekeeper and the cook. Shadows. I know they're here, but I don't really see them."

He watched her hang up her coat and put her shoes neatly in the empty closet. "Elliot is the only one they'll talk to." Griffin knew he was rattling but he wasn't ready to leave. "One of the decorators told Cooper he only ate vegan, and Cooper asked him to point out the critter and he'd shoot him one for supper. Ever since that conversation, the decorators go back to town for lunch."

Sunlan stretched as she walked toward him. Her sweater lifted enough to show a few inches of skin at her trim waist. "One hug and I'm off to bed."

Closing his arms around her, Griffin finally got his hug. Gentle. Lingering. Warm.

"Good night, Griff," she said, and she moved to the bed.

"Good night, Sunshine. See you at dawn."

"Dawn," she whispered as she pulled the blankets back and crawled into bed.

He turned out the light and silently closed the door. Her world might be dark tonight, but come sunup, thanks to that huge window she'd had installed, Sunlan was about to meet sunshine in its full glory.

The next morning, he wasn't surprised to find that she was up and dressed before he came down. Like the men, she grabbed a biscuit sandwich and went to work.

Griffin wanted to follow her, but he had a full schedule this morning. When they reached the porch, he nodded in her direction and said simply, "See you at supper."

She nodded back and headed toward the white barn. The eyesore had never looked better. An army of workers had come out in trucks loaded down with supplies. They not only rebuilt stalls and corrals, they'd painted a sky blue strip three feet wide near the bottom of the building. The structure that had cost his family almost a million dollars now looked like it belonged on the ranch.

Griffin knew his father would have liked that. He'd been a dreamer. A good father. A loving husband to the end. But he hadn't had a head for business. Griff smiled. Maybe if you have to drop one card in life, in the end, that one mattered least of all.

Only for Griffin, losing the ranch mattered. This wasn't just where he grew up, it was where he belonged. Maybe he fought so hard every day to keep it because he couldn't see himself anywhere else. He was bone and blood a piece of this land. He wasn't sure his heart would beat if he left for long.

If anyone understood that, it might be Sunlan. Maybe they were a better match than he'd first thought?

Griffin circled by the headquarters every few hours on horseback while he worked cattle in a nearby pasture.

The sun melted away most of the dusting of snow, making the prairie look less like a Christmas card. A carpenter's work van was pulled up close to the porch, but there was no sign of the horse trailer that Sunlan had mentioned coming in from her place in Colorado.

About noon, two other small trucks pulled up. One held plants and another belonged to a flooring company out of Lubbock.

Finally, at about two, a long silver trailer arrived. This one didn't have the Krown branding on the side, just a light blue strip running near the bottom. The same color as her eyes, he thought. Sunlan's brand.

By the time Griffin reached the yard, Sunlan was right in the middle of helping to unload the horses.

Griffin fought the urge to rush in and pull her back from any danger. She was pregnant, after all, and loading or unloading was always a tricky job. But he knew he'd be breaking the rules if he ordered her away. She probably knew the danger and maybe knew she could handle it.

Cooper was right beside her, taking half the load. He had a way with horses. If one acted up, Griffin had no doubt his brother would step between trouble and Sunlan.

Moving to the corral gate, Griffin joined in the work. Within thirty minutes, they had the first six of Sunlan's new stock home. She leaned against the railing and introduced each one. There was no doubt how much she loved them. Griffin might call horses by their color, but his wife seemed to think they needed to be addressed by their proper names.

"I'll bring more next month, after we're married."

Two hands from her ranch walked the mares. They looked to be in their early twenties and seemed more like college boys than ranch hands. "Andy and Dave plan to stay a few days until the horses are settled in," Sunlan announced. "They're both taking a year off from school to decide what to major in. I think the hard work is convincing them to go back to pre-law, it'd be easier." She looked at Griffin. "I know you wouldn't mind them staying in the bunkhouse, but I thought I'd put them up at the Franklins' place. The ladies will love feeding them and the guys promised to help Rose and Daisy decorate for Christmas as well as the wedding. With all the excitement no one had time to decorate for Thanksgiving." She grinned. "They've got so many ideas. I think the ladies think they're my fairy godmothers. Don't be surprised if you see a pumpkin carriage."

Griffin fought down a groan. "They may need to stay longer than a few days. I'll hire on a few more day hands and let these boys show them exactly what you want done with the horses. Cooper will make sure they stay in line with how you like things."

She bumped her shoulder against his. "You know, Griffin, you're starting to grow on me. I need the guys back with me as soon as possible, though. We've got our hands full at Misty Bend and soon I'll have to leave long enough to get married." She kissed his cheek. "A man whose only fear seems to be cartoon characters should be easy to get along with. I think I'll snatch you up fast."

"I'm not afraid of them." He doubted she even heard him. Sunlan was busy nuzzling her face into a hay-colored Morgan's neck. Her love for the animal was obvious. Griffin realized just how much these horses meant to her. They were her life, her family. He knew she'd do anything to protect them, even marry a stranger.

When she turned the horse loose, the two-year-old took off in a run around the corral. Sunlan turned back to Griffin and patted his arm. "I'll have to go into town a few mornings while I'm here to see how the wedding plans are coming along but I thought it might be fun to see some of your ranch on horseback this afternoon. Have you got the time?"

"I'll make the time."

He thought of reminding her that they needed to drive down and see her father, but it could wait a week. With her staying here nights and moving horses to his land, the possibility of the wedding really happening seemed to be growing.

Something had changed about her, and he had a feeling it was more than just having the horses here. She'd relaxed since she'd left. She might not be to the point of liking him, but she no longer seemed afraid of him. She hadn't lectured him on the rules of their agreement for a few days, and she was touching him, almost as much as she was touching the horses. That had be a step up in rank for him.

The days were dropping off the calendar and there was still a great deal to do, but he could see life calming in the future. She'd float in and out of his life, and he'd build his ranch thanks to her giving him the chance.

As they saddled their horses, he watched her straighten. He waited, knowing she had something else she needed to say.

"I thought we'd show up at the Krown for a party. My father always invites lots of people for a big dinner. Sometimes my mother even puts in an appearance. That will probably be a great time to tell him about us."

"When people are around? I guessed him to be a yeller."

"He is, but he'll keep it down with people around."

"Will we have to stay the night?"

"No. If the weather's clear, we can fly in, have the talk and fly home." She swung into the saddle and he did also.

As they crossed the yard and headed out, he said, "I'd like that but I wouldn't mind staying long enough to have dinner. Around here, Thanksgiving is pretty much just football, beer and frozen pizzas. When my mom was around, she'd have us all hanging wreaths after dinner. When she died, Dad took all the decorations up to the attic. All the holidays left when Mom passed away. I think his heart died then, too. It just took a while for the doctors to notice."

Sunlan reached over and touched his arm in an almost-caress. "I'm not sure my dad even has a heart, but maybe you're right. He does need to know I'm marrying. I'll text him and tell him we're coming for dinner. I'll tell him I'm bringing someone very special. He'll be surprised, maybe suspicious."

"What about your mom?"

"She'll be angry I'm not letting her plan the wedding. She'll pout. Then she'll fly off to some spa somewhere and send pictures. Dad has a picture on his dresser of me when I was eight. Mom has a picture of herself.

"The first time I went away to school, she forgot to come get me. Dad had to charter a flight. Man, was he mad. But it worked out. He got a pilot's license so he could always pick me up, and as soon as I could, he made sure I was licensed, as well. He'll be surprised I'm bringing someone home."

Griffin took the lead as he moved into a gallop. "Why?" he called back.

"Because," she said as she caught up with him. "I've never brought a *plus one* home."

With her by his side, they rode straight toward a little place he wanted to show her. Mistletoe Canyon.

The wind stilled as the canyon walls began to climb on either side of them. Here, trees were sheltered and could grow tall and straight. Griffin's father had been fascinated with trees as a boy and mail-ordered dozens that weren't supposed to survive in the dry Texas climate. Hardwoods, evergreens, tall pines, colorful oak and even a circle of magnolia trees thirty feet high. He'd blown money he didn't have to spare on wells to keep them watered. This was his boxed canyon valley. His slice of heaven on earth.

"My dad loved trees almost as much as he loved this land. I think he would have been happy living in the mountains, but his home, his land, was here. Not all he planted in the canyon survived, but most did. He liked seeing all the colors of leaves in the fall."

She rode closer to an oak, raised her hand to touch the last dying red leaves. "They're beautiful. What did he use this place for?"

"Nothing really. I guess it was his church. In this part of the state, the land looks pretty lonely in winter, but Dad liked to ride out here. He used to say he could hear nature sleeping in this canyon."

She slid down from her horse and picked up an armful of leaves, tossing them up. Making a rainbow waterfall. Her laughter was light and free now.

Griffin couldn't hide his smile. This Sunlan he could learn to love. Not the one who was bossy and had to run her own life. Not the one who was successful. But this one.

He joined her in the almost knee-deep leaves. They walked among the forest of sheltered trees. He took her hand and wondered if she felt the same peace here as he did.

She deserved more than a business agreement for a marriage, but he had a feeling that was all she'd accept. Maybe here, where mistletoe hung green on winter branches and nature's colors blanketed the ground, she could relax. Maybe let her guard down just enough for him to get to know her.

"I have trees surrounding my place in Colorado. We could ride through them when you visit. Up in the mountains the seasons change so much that I never get tired of watching the show."

She'd said visit, not live. "I'd like that. Maybe someday I will visit."

He stopped under an old live oak that had probably grown next to the stream for over a hundred years. It always reminded him of an old man, bent over, thin but still alive. The roots crawled out like arthritic fingers as if hanging on to life.

She circled among the low branches.

"Somehow, maybe when some tree was shipped, we got a bit of mistletoe," he said. "It grows here because the canyons block a bit of the cold." Slices of sunshine flickered in her hair as he came closer.

She looked up and saw a green ball on one of the branches. "Nature's Christmas ornament. You don't mind them, do you, Griffin?"

"Not at all." He could only see her. If possible, she grew more beautiful each time he saw her. "You mind if I kiss you under the mistletoe? For tradition's sake."

"For tradition's sake." She leaned forward, offering her cheek. He waited. "A real kiss, Sunshine."

She turned slightly. "Why not?"

For once Griffin didn't give her a light pretend kiss, and to his surprise, she kissed him back. One long kiss, flavored with caring, mixed with a bit of passion.

When she broke the kiss, she didn't pull away and he held her against him.

"For tradition's sake," she whispered, "would you kiss me like that at our wedding and every Christmas, just to remind me I'm still alive?"

He wanted to say he'd kiss her every night like that, but he didn't think that was what she wanted. Sunlan was a woman who had to be in control and if she was going to allow herself to slip now and then, he'd be there to catch her.

When they rode back at sundown, there was a peace, an acceptance of each other that hadn't been between them before.

Elliot and Cooper were sitting on the porch waiting for him.

"We're going out to dinner," Cooper announced before Griffin and Sunlan reached the steps.

Griffin fought down a string of swear words. He'd be happy with a beer and chips for supper. "All right," was all he could muster. "I'll wash up."

To his surprise, Sunlan followed him to his bedroom door.

"I have a few things to discuss while you're getting ready. Do you mind? I'd rather not talk in front of your brothers." She stepped into his room as if she'd been invited.

"No. I don't mind." He waved his hand to the only chair. Hell, he should be happy she'd walked into his room, but in truth he did mind. No woman he'd ever dated had been in his room. This one place in the house was his private space. The brothers had agreed on that for as long as he could remember. Every other room in the house was common space.

He looked around. No underwear on the floor. The bed made. Most of his books in order. After living like a pig his freshman year of college, Griffin had decided to keep command over his living space.

She also looked from one corner of the room to the other. "You like everything in its place?"

"Yes." Somehow he feared she was asking a trick question, but his brain was too tired to figure it out.

"That why you wanted me here at Maverick Ranch? Everything in its place?"

"You are not a thing, Sunlan." He was too tired to argue.

"Good answer." She sat down on his bed.

Griffin stepped into the small bathroom but didn't bother to close the door. As she talked, he pulled off his shirt and began to wash the dirt off his hands and face. She hadn't mentioned his idea about having a real wedding night, so he guessed that was off the table.

Her very proper tone shattered his thoughts that had nothing to do with being proper. "The local preacher can only marry us on the twenty-third of December. He has services on Christmas Eve."

"That suits me." He leaned back enough to smile at her.

"About who comes?" She pulled out a piece of paper from her vest pocket.

She paused so long he asked, "Everything all right?"

"My father hates weddings, but he'll probably come just to pout and tell anyone who will listen about how much he hated all his weddings."

"All right," Griffin said slowly. The idea didn't sound fun, but he'd play along. If Winston Krown wanted to gripe, it wasn't Griffin's problem. "What about your mother?"

"She's in Spain, and she told me last July that she wouldn't step foot in the States until my father died. But she always says that. Then she makes a scene when she shows up as if she'd planned all along to surprise everyone. They have a big fight and she leaves again."

"So you are inviting one to the wedding. Your dad. Maybe your mother?"

"No, I've a few friends from Misty Bend who might make the trip. I told them about you before I left. Lloyd, my caretaker, said he was happy you were a cowboy, but couldn't I find one that wasn't from Texas." She smiled. "I told him I tried, but they grow them strong here in Texas."

"I'm not sure I'm going to like Lloyd."

She ignored him. "The Franklins think they can put them all up for a few nights. Knowing my dad, he'll come in just in time to walk me down the aisle and leave before the cake is cut."

"That's fine." He decided he'd better shave while she was talking. Who knows, she might decide to kiss him again.

Surlan moved to the bathroom door, leaned against the frame and crossed her arms. He watched her slow smile in the mirror. "The Franklins plan to invite the whole town to sit on your side."

"What?" He nicked his chin.

She moved in and started trying to help him dab away the blood. "Don't worry. I convinced them you only wanted family."

Griffin relaxed and simply enjoyed her being so close. "Good. That makes two on my side, a few on yours and us."

"Sounds like the perfect number." She kissed his chin and moved away.

He washed off the leftover cream and combed his hair. By the time he pulled on a shirt and sweater, she was on to the topic of their honeymoon.

"We're going to take a honeymoon?"

"Sure. I could fly you up to Misty Bend. It's beautiful this time of year. We can relax for a few days."

"So… I'm definitely invited to your place?"

"Of course. Any time you want to come. I have a guesthouse no one ever stays in."

He heard what she wasn't saying. The honeymoon wouldn't change anything about their agreement. That's what she wanted. That's what he'd agreed to.

He offered his hand and her fingers laced in his. "Come on, Sunshine, I'll take you to the finest restaurant in Crossroads."

She acted like she was dusting off her jeans. Even working in the barn most of the day, she still looked like a model stepping out of the pages of a catalog.

"You look great."

"Then let's go to Dorothy's. I'm starving."

CHAPTER TWENTY-THREE

The Johnsons

A WEEK BEFORE THANKSGIVING, Jamie mentioned she'd never cooked a Thanksgiving dinner, and Wyatt said he couldn't remember having one, except at the mess hall.

"Since I'll be back to work on Thanksgiving Day, I'll miss it all around." Just a statement, he thought. Not asking for any sympathy. He'd picked his life, and he didn't have any regrets. He'd enlisted at eighteen and credited the man he'd become to the army, not his parents.

In a few more months, he'd have his twenty in. If he decided to get out of the army, he'd saved enough money to start a little computer repair business. Or maybe he'd find a job with a big tech company. He planned to settle down somewhere quiet and just enjoy life. On weekends, he'd learn to fish, or maybe take up surfing. Maybe he'd re-up with a bonus and wait another ten years to relax. He might buy a bike and see the country, or he might come back here and build his own place at this very lake.

Jamie pointed her finger at him and announced, "I've got an

idea. Let's have Thanksgiving early. We could do it this weekend and then when you're flying back to work, you'll be stuffed."

He shrugged as if it didn't matter, but in truth he liked the idea. Growing up, his mother's idea of Thanksgiving was takeout in front of a football game. "Sure, we can look up recipes. How hard could it be? We could spend the next few nights planning."

When he picked her up after school on Friday, they went shopping in Lubbock, then stayed to eat dinner and walk around the mall. After spending his days at the lake and helping out at the Maverick Ranch, all the people in the mall seemed loud and bothersome, but Jamie wanted to shop.

"I have to have a new dress to wear to Thanksgiving dinner." She laughed. "And of course, we have to find you an apron."

She rushed in to explore one of the women's stores, and he wandered into the shop next door. The teashop was giving away samples. He thought he'd try them all until he found one he could tolerate. If she liked tea so much, the least he could do every evening was join her for a cup.

Twenty minutes later, when she came out with a dress in a bag, he also carried a bag. "What did you buy?" she asked.

"Tea," he said, proud of himself for finding one he liked. "You?"

Jamie pointed to the dress in the window. "I found that one in my size."

"I'll show you later what else I got, if you'll model your dress." He glanced at the mannequin in the window. "I'm betting you'll look great in that one."

She blushed and seemed to forget about his bag. "I hope so."

He thought of commenting that with her curves she'd look better in any dress than some stick of a mannequin ever could, but he didn't want her to think he'd been staring at her body. They had an easy friendship going. The quiet nights on the lake were quickly becoming his favorite leave ever.

The heartwarming movies she watched took his mind off the

mission to come. The slow pace of his days gave his heart a rest and almost left the nagging fears behind. He'd been lucky. He'd been hurt a few times, but he'd always walked away. On this next mission, they'd be planting communications that would save many lives if they all worked. This time, the risk to him and the team would be greater. The odds of them all coming back weren't good. All the team knew it, but they didn't talk about it.

He smiled at Jamie, pushing his dark thoughts behind him and he studied her.

The idea of a woman having curves was growing on him. They said men had types of women they liked—with long legs or big breasts—but Wyatt knew his type was shifting.

On the drive home, Jamie held their two takeout peach cobblers in her lap as she planned the big holiday dinner. She claimed she wanted every side dish that she'd ever heard might be served on Thanksgiving. He swore he'd be the assistant cook to whatever she thought sounded good.

Like two kids playing house, they took on the challenge at dawn Saturday morning. He'd warned her that his cooking skills were weak. Within an hour, she'd declared them nonexistent.

They dedicated three hours to making pies. Two out of three turned out and he admitted he really didn't like pumpkin anyway. All afternoon they worked on what she called prep, and the next morning the serious cooking began.

With both of them in the small kitchen, they bumped into each other so frequently it finally became routine. She'd tap her hip against him to move him out of the way. He'd circle his arms around her, hands over hers, as he learned each step of kneading dough.

Wyatt recognized the dance they were playing. The casual touching. The laughter. The easy conversation. She even agreed to take a break while the winter sun flooded the back porch.

Both carefully climbed into the big hammock and relaxed on their backs, touching from shoulder to knees. He said he planned to sleep, but she never stopped talking. He finally shifted and offered his arm for a pillow. She cuddled close, saying she was cold.

Progression of the game, he thought. Getting to know the other's touch, nearness. He liked the feel of her so close, but he knew it would never go any further.

The only problem was, he wasn't sure she knew the game. She was just having fun. Just getting warm. To her, they were buddies, pals, friends, like all the study partners she talked about in college. He wondered if those guys in college had thought she wasn't interested in being more than friends. Maybe that was why they all finally walked away.

Something told him she'd never lowered her voice in invitation or given a look with those big eyes of hers steeped in passion.

When he finally pulled them out of the hammock and back into the kitchen, she gave him a quick hug. A friend's hug. Another touch. Nothing more.

"Time to go back to work." She laughed when he frowned.

While the turkey baked, they drank spiced cider and talked about growing up. She told him about her college days when money was tight and panic came at the end of every semester. He told her about the army's training and how he'd picked up a degree online, a few classes at a time. But neither mentioned old lovers or broken hearts. Something about being with her made him feel like a newborn. Neither seemed to have any old relationship scars.

Again and again, he reminded himself to keep it light. He'd be gone in three days. He couldn't give her forever and anything less seemed a cheap gift.

When the table was set, he dressed in his uniform and she changed into her pretty blue dress. He almost wished they'd gone out. It would have been fun to show her off. But then he realized it was just fine if they were alone. She was all the company he wanted today.

He cut the turkey as she leaned against his side and read the instructions.

As the sun brushed the lake, they sat down to the perfect Thanksgiving dinner. All the dishes lined the counter and a single candle sparkled on the tiny table.

Wyatt tasted everything and swore each dish was perfect. He'd never had corn bread dressing before, but pour enough gravy on it, and he'd have two helpings.

The night grew cold, but the house was warm with smells drifting thick as gauze though the room. He took in everything, building a memory that would last forever. Finally, he leaned back and declared he couldn't eat another bite. "Best meal I ever had," he bragged.

"Me, too."

He thought of saying something like *why don't we do it again next year*, but he might not be in the States next year, much less Texas. She might be married. The last thing he wanted was to have her waiting for him, even as a friend, and him not be able to show up.

They left the dishes on the table and moved to the couch. Jamie on one end. He on the other.

For once they didn't turn on the TV or reach for a game. They just talked about how much fun cooking together had been and how they should have tried something a little simpler.

"Like turkey sandwiches," he suggested.

"Oh, no. Next time we should put the names of all our favorite foods in a bag, shake it up and pull out three." She laughed. "We'll cook only those three, even if they don't go together."

"Sounds like a plan," he said, knowing that there would be no next time.

"What if we get sick eating chili, ice cream and sardines?"

"Nobody likes sardines."

She didn't argue but he could almost hear her brain trying to think of things that would never go together.

"So this is what it's like to be married, wife," he finally said. "We cook all day, eat dinner and collapse."

"We make a good team, Wyatt. It doesn't really feel like pretend."

"I agree. Sometimes it seems more real than any part of my life has ever been. It's like my dreams and my reality traded places."

Curling her legs up on the couch, she faced him. "You dream of being married?"

"I dream of coming home. I picture the peace of it. The calmness."

"Is that what you want, Wyatt? Home? Peace? Calmness?"

"Isn't that pretty much what everyone wants?"

She made a face that caused him to grin. "Not me," she announced. "I've had calm and peace at home since I left college. I've had a job since the week after I graduated high school, sometimes two. I always saved as much of my money as I could. Lived cheap. Then once I had a few thousand dollars cash and a steady teaching job, I spent weeks looking for the perfect place to live. The place always had to be peaceful. Quiet. Each time I transferred schools, I did the same thing."

"And now you're tired of it?"

"Not tired, I just want more. I want an adventure. I'd give anything if I was like you and could travel the world."

"Believe me, most of the places I go you'd be lucky to miss." He was not going to talk about his world. The real world. The one he had to go back to in three days. He couldn't bring any part of it into this perfection.

"Why don't you try adventure, Jamie? There are Americans teaching all over the planet. There is nothing tying you down. You could go to Europe in the summers."

She shrugged. "I'm not brave. Plus I could never pack up my things and store them. I know people probably think the yard art is just junk, but I've collected one piece from every town I've ever lived in. And my Precious Moments figurines remind me of students I've had. My mice tea sets are my heirlooms. I bought them at garage sales and antiques shops but treasure them as if a relative passed them down to me."

Silence stretched between them. Finally, he risked a personal question. "Where did you grow up, Jamie?"

He didn't think she would answer the simple question, but finally she said, "In foster homes and children's homes across Texas. I had parents, they were just never around. At fourteen, I ended up in a children's home in Amarillo. It was nice. The people were kind. When I graduated from high school, they encouraged me to start college and it wasn't all that hard to work and study while I lived in the dorm. After all, I'd kind of lived in a dorm all my life. But when I started teaching, I knew I'd have to find a place alone where there was silence. Where I could live all by myself and not have to wake up to someone else's alarm going off.

"I never had much growing up. When I moved, everything I owned usually fit in a suitcase and a box. So I started finding things to keep. Each serves as a memory, or a dream of a memory." She shrugged. "I had a pretend life even before you came along."

"What are you going to buy to remember the first Thanksgiving you've cooked?"

She lifted a stuffed turkey he'd picked up at the gas station, claiming that if the cooking didn't work out, they could set the toy on the table and pretend as they ate cereal.

"Oh, no. That's my turkey." He reached for it.

The stuffed toy started gobbling and she quickly hid it behind her back. "Possession is nine-tenths of the law, remember. He's telling you in turkey talk that he wants to stay with me."

He circled her in a hug, but he didn't pull the toy away from her. "Name your price. This memory is very special to me. I've got to have that turkey."

They were so close he could feel the warmth of her. The soft-

ness of her. The adult game they now played was far more serious than the silly child's game they were pretending to play.

"Okay." She giggled. "I'll let you have the turkey, but you
have to give me another memory to keep."

He moved away a few inches so he could see her face clearly.
"Name it."

"Kiss me, Wyatt. Kiss me like you're not playing."

He shoved off the couch. "I... I can't."

She moved back, curling into her corner. "I understand. You
don't want to. It's all right. It was a dumb request. I'm sorry I
asked."

Wyatt stared at her. Hating that he'd hurt her. Hating himself for not stopping earlier.

Making up some reason why he couldn't kiss her wouldn't be
easy. But he had to think up something. She'd know it wasn't
real, but maybe they'd both pretend it was. After all, they were
getting very good at pretending.

But he had to be honest with her. She meant too much to
him to be anything less. The whole reason he was here in her
house might be a lie, but he couldn't lie to Jamie. Not about this.

Anger boiled in him. The truth would change things.

"It's not that I don't want to kiss you." His words came fast
and hard. "I stay up hours after you close that damn bedroom
door thinking about how I'd like to do a hell of a lot more than
just kiss you. But, Jamie, it wouldn't be right. You deserve more
than a pretend husband."

He turned to stare into the fireplace, not wanting to see the
pain in her eyes. "If I leave with us being friends, I won't have
to think about you crying every night because some jerk, me,
broke your heart."

He was ruining what they had. He should have laughed it
off or kissed her lightly and continued their pretending. He was
shattering the fairy tale they'd been living for a week. "I don't
belong here. I live fifty weeks a year in a place where staying

alive is my only goal. Two weeks a year I'm in the States, and a few of those times I've spent all my leave drunk."

He was telling her too much. His life was not her problem. It wasn't broken. She couldn't fix it. Every woman he'd gotten close to had tried and failed.

But right now their pretend life was all he wanted. He'd do anything. Say anything to have them be friends until he had to leave.

But he'd ruined it all.

When he turned around to apologize, she was gone.

CHAPTER TWENTY-FOUR

Midnight Crossing

THE SEVENTH DAY Mallory woke in Jax's cabin, she no longer felt any fear. Jax still carried the rifle when he went outside, but the peace surrounding her slowly settled her mind. She had no doubt he was a kind man, a rare man.

As before, she was awake just before dawn and pretended to still be sleeping when he stumbled in half-asleep. He checked her blankets and put more wood on the fire. He had to be well into his thirties, but with his hair wild and his clothes tossed on, he looked almost like a kid.

She knew when he returned, twenty minutes later, he'd be showered and dressed, but it was touching that he checked on her welfare first.

After drifting off, Mallory woke again to the sounds of him cooking breakfast. She raised the head of her bed and watched as he burned the toast, as always. She couldn't tell if he was talking to himself or Charlie, but his mumbling as he cooked made her smile.

This morning he brought his plate as well as hers and sat on the end of her bed so they could eat together.

"You like the bacon?" he asked when she'd finished her third slice.

She nodded.

Jax turned to the dog. "You see, Charlie, I told you that you have no taste in bacon."

Handing him back an empty plate, she proved him right. Her appetite was back. She was recovering. His cooking wasn't, but she'd learned to adjust. Once she covered the toast in butter and jelly, she barely tasted the burned side.

As he moved away, she began unwrapping the bandages on her leg, but it was hard to reach past her knee.

"I'll help," he said, moving toward her. "If you don't mind and you're sure you want to see what's beneath? A few days ago it didn't look near healed."

She handed him the end of the bandage she'd been rolling up and he took over. Slowly, carefully, he lifted her leg, set it on his bended knee and removed the dressing.

For a moment, after he finished, she couldn't look.

Mallory hadn't seen the damage the first few times Nurse Toni cleaned the wounds. She'd only known that it must have been bad, because every inch seemed to hurt. When Jax changed it yesterday, she'd glanced but couldn't bear to do more. His expression told her all she needed to know.

Now, holding her breath, she forced herself to look. Mallory couldn't fight back the tears. Places looked skinned, so raw they were almost bloody. Other parts were black with deep bruises. They'd take weeks to heal. Now and then, there were breaks in the skin as if it had been torn and pulled so tight it just gave way in tiny jagged strips.

"It will heal," he said as he reached for the cream the hospital had sent with her. "Okay if I put some of this on? It'll help with the healing and decrease the chance of infection."

Nodding, she leaned back on her pillow, thinking that nothing would help. Even after the wounds and bruises healed, she'd still be broken inside. She'd never trust anyone again.

She watched him through her tears as he gently applied the cream. His hands were caring, almost a caress.

Mallory tried to forget the night she'd felt the blows. Curtis had meant to cripple her. His words kept echoing in her mind. *You'll be sorry you ever thought of walking out on me.*

Jax began unwrapping the other leg.

She didn't move. It was too late to be embarrassed. He'd already seen the damage.

Tenderly he let the cream slide over her skin. She was almost asleep when he said, "If you'll roll over, I'll make sure the back of your legs are covered with cream."

Slowly, awkwardly, she shifted, trying to keep the gown in place as she rolled to her stomach.

After a few minutes, he added, "Anywhere else?"

"My back," she whispered in a rough voice that sounded like it came from someone else.

Her legs already seemed better after the cream had been applied. It was working.

She felt him untying the strings that held her gown together across her back. He would see all her wounds, now. The nurses had seen them, the doctor, even the sheriff, when he'd taken a few pictures for her file. And now Jax. Her almost-cousin.

"You want to know how your back looks?" His voice was calm, matter-of-fact.

She closed her eyes and waited.

"Toni said he used a bat. I see two long outlines of that and a few round bruises. I'm guessing that was where he poked you hard enough with the end of the bat to leave a bruise. That's all. No other cuts or bruises."

He'd guessed right. The last poke was when she'd lain still on the floor, too weak to fight anymore. She hadn't even reacted when the tip of the bat tested to see if she would still re-coil from the blows.

She'd been a limp rag doll after that, her brain barely register-ing the slaps and kicks. He'd grabbed her by the hair once and shoved her hard against the coffee table, trying to wake her up so he could continue what he'd called the lecture.

"Your back's not as bad as I feared it might be," Jax said as he retied the gown from her waist to the back of her neck. "You're lucky he didn't break your back."

He helped her roll back over, then covered her with the blan-ket. "The cast on your arm will have to stay on, but I'll wrap it in a plastic bag if you feel like taking a shower on one of the days that Toni isn't dropping by."

She thanked him with a touch to her chin.

The next morning, Mallory was ready for Toni when she ar-rived complaining about how hard the cabin was to find. The nurse helped her shower and wash her hair. The bruises on her face made her look like a monster, but she couldn't stand the thought of hiding behind bandages any longer. Both her eyes were swollen but open. She was making progress.

Toni combed her hair and helped her into warm flannel pa-jamas two sizes too big. "You'll feel a little better each day from now on. By the time you come in to have the cast taken off, the bruises will be little more than shadows."

Mallory nodded and kissed the nurse's hand.

Toni looked like she wanted to hug her but didn't try. "I'll be back in two days with a change of clothes. Jax and I are staying in touch with email. He'll let me know if you run low on meds."

Mallory nodded. She'd never worn flannel pajamas in her life, but they felt so soft against her skin she decided, from now on, they would be her only nightclothes.

That afternoon when Tim dropped by with groceries, she heard the writer whisper to Jax that they needed to talk outside. Tim barely looked at her.

Something was wrong, she decided. Something they didn't want her to hear. When they came back in, she pretended to be asleep. Tim didn't stay long.

Trouble whispered through the quiet cabin for the first time.

Jax worked at his computer as always, seemingly keeping a close eye on her, but fear built in her. If Curtis found her, he'd be furious. The first thing he'd do when he found her was hurt her so she'd be too afraid to move, then he'd kill Charlie.

Fear shivered through her. If anyone tried to stop Curtis, he'd hurt them, too. His mood would turn as black as midnight.

She remembered crawling to the back door after Curtis went to bed that night. He hadn't even checked to see if she had been still breathing. He hadn't cared.

She'd heard Charlie whining outside in the cold and had to move. All she'd planned to do was let her dog in before he froze, but once the cold air greeted her, Mallory's survival instincts woke up.

Charlie stayed right by her side as she grabbed Curtis's keys and stumbled to his car, her eyes almost swollen closed, her heart pounding in fear of another blow hitting her from behind as she ran.

All she'd been thinking about was getting as far away as possible. One more hit, one more kick, might end her life. Or the dog's.

They'd made it to the car. Charlie barked as she fumbled for the right key. As the engine roared, she slammed the car door and raced out of the drive, afraid to look back.

Ten miles. Twenty. A hundred. Mallory had just kept driving. She'd felt one eye swelling closed. She'd lost the use of one arm, but she kept going. She didn't even remember missing the curve on the road. She only remembered flying for a moment before the world went black.

CHAPTER TWENTY-FIVE

Maverick Ranch

A FEW DAYS before Thanksgiving, Griffin's cell rang when he stepped out of the shower. He grabbed a towel and ran the length of his bedroom to catch it in time.

The name Sunshine flashed across the screen. She'd said she'd call before she took off from Misty Bend, but he hadn't expected her to leave before dawn.

"Hello," he greeted her. "I'm about ready to see you again, Sunshine. Dinner with the brothers is no fun without you." In truth, he'd been working so hard it hadn't seemed like a week had passed since she'd left.

"Griff, I'm not coming." Her voice came fast, panicked. Her words choppy as if she were running while she shouted into the phone. "The barn where we keep the mares ready to foal caught fire during the storm before dawn. We thought we had it contained but we didn't… Several of the mares are hurt. I can't leave. I can't talk now. There's too much to do. I'll call you later."

The phone went dead.

Griffin grabbed his clothes, opened his door and yelled for Cooper as he dressed.

"Yeah, I'm coming." From the thud's echo on the other side of Cooper's bedroom door, it sounded more like he fell out of bed.

"Elliot, you up?" Griffin shouted.

"No." Elliot calmly opened his door down the hallway. He was fully dressed.

Griffin wondered if his brother slept in his clothes, or even if he'd left his computer long enough to sleep.

Buttoning his shirt, Griffin faced them. "Sunlan's barn is on fire. She's got a mess up at her place. Hurt horses. Possibly premature dropping of foals. I'm calling in that favor from Kirkland. His new plane should get me there fast. Elliot, pull up my truck. You're driving me over. Cooper, load all the medical supplies that might be helpful. I'll be dealing with burns, birthing and blizzard conditions."

Neither brother moved.

"Well?"

Cooper faced his older brother. "I'll load everything we got, but I'm going with you. She'll need men who can handle horses."

"I'm going, too," Elliot stated. "Cooper's right, she'll need help. She told me her place is so isolated some months a plane is the only way in."

"Hell," Griffin mumbled as he reached for his jeans and boots. "Layer for the cold if you're coming. We may be dealing with heavy snow tonight."

A few minutes later, Griffin wasn't surprised Kirkland answered the phone on the first ring. It was almost sunup, and his neighbor was usually in the saddle by dawn. He told Staten Kirkland what had happened.

"I'll have the plane ready by the time you boys get here. My wife's niece and her husband are staying with us through the holiday. No one better to fly you out than Madison. I'll also send boxes of supplies. From what Sunlan said, the last time she

used my strip to land, she had no trouble flying in and out of
her place, but one mountain pass near her place sometimes stops
traffic. With the snow, she may not be able to get in medicine
fast enough to be of help."

"Thanks."

"No problem. We'll be waiting for you."

As the sun cleared the horizon, all three men were in Griffin's truck headed toward Kirkland's place. Griffin's mind raced.
They'd deal with the horses but it was Sunlan he was worried
about. He'd seen how she loved her animals. They were her
family.

He'd also been reading online about pregnancy since she came
into his life already expecting. It was early yet, but all this excitement couldn't be good for his wife-to-be or the baby.

His baby, he reminded himself. He'd sworn from the day they
agreed to marry that the baby was his.

Elliot checked the weather on his cell. "Storm's raging over
her area. They're expecting another inch or two this afternoon
and more tonight. It's moving south. Should hit our place in
another two days, but they're forecasting no more than a few
inches once the storm reaches Texas."

Griffin's logical mind put facts together. "She told me she
always has the strip cleared the night before she takes off. It's
dusted an hour before she leaves if there is any chance of ice. We
should be able to land, but I'm not sure how long it will take
before we can get out to come home."

Elliot was already ahead of Griffin. "I texted Hank and his
sons. This time of year, there's not a lot of work for cowboys
who hire out by the day. I'll tell them to move into the bunkhouse as soon as possible and be ready to work. They should be
able to keep everything running."

Griffin agreed. "Tell Hank we'll pay them double. All they
have to do is keep the place running till we get back. He's
worked for me long enough to know what has to be done."

"Will do."

Cooper broke in. "Did Sunlan tell you about her place? We only talked about the horse operation she's got going."

"Only that it's small. Her grandfather loved raising horses and made good money doing it. As he grew older, she went to school in Colorado just so she could be near to help. Besides the two boys who drove some of her stock to our barn last week, she said she has a married couple who live a few miles north. They watch over the place when she's not there. They hire help as they need it."

"How many horses are we dealing with?" Cooper's tone was tight with worry.

"Thirty, I'm guessing, maybe more. I don't know how many were hurt." Griffin swore if he could get out and push the pickup to go faster, he would. Kirkland was his closest neighbor and it still took ten minutes to get from one headquarters to the other.

Staten Kirkland and the pilot, Madison O'Grady-Weathers, were waiting by the plane when Elliot raced onto the runway. Also standing ready were a half dozen cowhands to help load. Supplies in the cargo bay, medicine in the copilot's seat, blanketed and belted in.

"Sorry we're pulling you away, Madison," Griffin managed to say as they climbed into the back of the small plane.

"No problem. I'll miss the big shopping trip to Lubbock and if I'm lucky I'll miss a few hours of cooking, too. I'd much rather fly than cook. Between the Kirklands and the O'Gradys, almost every day in December will be a mob scene. Aunt Quinn was in the kitchen starting the pies for the party after the school's Christmas play when Uncle Staten and I passed through."

She handed each of the Holloway men a small bag. "Breakfast bread and juice. Use the bag if you think you have to throw up. Do not throw up in my uncle's new plane. It took me two years to convince him that he needed the bird and one bad smell would probably be all it would take to change his mind."

All three brothers nodded. At over six feet, Madison was not a woman many men would argue with.

By full light, they were loaded and taxiing down the runway. Kirkland's niece was a military pilot who was married to the sheriff a few counties over. As they took off, she said that she'd get them there fast and safe, but she couldn't stay.

Griffin understood. If she stayed even a few hours, the chances of her getting snowed in went up. Madison wanted to be with her family.

"My wife will fly us home when the snow clears," Griffin yelled back over the engine. The idea of flying in a little plane *once* bothered him. *Twice* downright scared him.

When he leaned back between his brothers, Cooper slugged him on the shoulder. "She's not your wife yet, Griff. In fact, even if she is older than me, I'm thinking I might ask her to marry me. I'm better-looking than you and we've got horses in common. If she's picking from the Holloway basket, I'm naturally the best choice. I'll live longer. Better investment all around." Cooper nodded once as if to end with *enough said*.

"Not a chance, I saw her first."

"What about me?" Elliot interrupted. "I'm obviously the smartest. If she gets to choose, I'd win out over both of you. When this crisis is over, I'm asking her. You didn't even buy her a ring, Griff. I'll get down on one knee and do it right. Women like that."

"How do you know, Elliot? The only women you talk to are online." Cooper leaned across Griffin and took a swing at Elliot.

Griffin considered tossing them both out. The plane wasn't all that high yet. They'd bounce.

"I'm marrying Sunlan," he yelled. "And you two are staying out of it."

To his shock, they both burst out laughing, and Griffin realized they were simply cracking the tension. Distracting him until they were in the clouds.

Madison laughed. "Relax, gentlemen. It'll be smooth sailing from here. You might want to get some sleep. You can fight over the lady after you save her horses."

"There will be no fight. The lady is mine." Griffin surprised himself by wishing it were true.

CHAPTER TWENTY-SIX

Midnight Crossing

JAX TURNED OFF his computer and stared at the woman sleeping in the hospital bed a few feet away. She looked so small, so fragile, so alone. But she was a fighter. He'd watched her slowly climb out of the pain. Mallory Mayweather was pushing herself.

Each time she got up to go to the bathroom, she walked a few extra steps. Her body might be stiff and hurting, but she stood up straight.

He grinned. In those too-big pajamas, she looked almost like a clown. Her hands and feet seemed to disappear.

But tonight, curled up holding one of her pillows against her chest, she reminded him of a sleeping angel. Her dark hair covered most of the bruises on her face, and the shadows let him see the line of her jaw without seeing the marks.

How could a man, any man, for any reason, do that to a woman?

An anger built in him unlike any he'd ever known. All he'd ever wanted to do was help people. That's why he became a fireman. It fit him. He'd loved his job and had been so wrapped up in it that he'd put off getting married and starting a family. There would always be time, he'd told himself. When the time was right, the right woman would come along. But the time had never appeared and now it was too late. He'd morphed into a hermit no woman would want.

Just the thought of leaving his cabin to step back in with the living bothered him. When he'd first moved in at Midnight Crossing, he'd thought he'd stay a few months, maybe a year. Now when Tim mentioned going back, only one word crossed Jax's mind. Never.

He'd stay here a few more years, maybe even until he was forty. By then he'd be too set in his ways, he'd be lost to the world. In the end, he'd grow old here, never going back among people.

It seemed a quiet life. A world he could handle.

He was so used to staying alone to heal that he was rotting. Even the constant studying and taking classes online and writing articles and blogs hadn't made him want to step back among people.

Since Mallory had arrived, something dark was boiling in Jax's mind. For the first time ever, he wanted to hurt someone. The man who'd done this to her deserved it. He should have to live with the same pain he'd caused her.

Jax knew he'd have to learn to deal with his anger before it ate him up inside. But the feeling kept growing like a cancer, eating away at his peace.

Slowly, he stood, stretched and walked over to Mallory. Gently he pulled the cover over her shoulder. Tonight would be colder than usual. He'd get up every few hours and make sure the fire kept going. Silently, he made her one promise: she'd never see the anger inside him. It would only cause her more pain.

Tim's news this afternoon still bothered Jax. His cousin had told him that Curtis Dayson had put an ad in the Crossroads paper offering a reward to anyone who had any knowledge to the whereabouts of one Mallory Mayweather. He'd said that her family was in a near panic looking for her and he was simply helping them out.

Only Mallory had listed no family when she'd checked in at the hospital and she'd never mentioned wanting to call someone to let them know she was all right.

Tim said that even with a restraining order, the sheriff couldn't stop Curtis from seeking information, as long as he didn't come near Mallory. The guy was slick. He had all the right answers when the sheriff questioned him. Cline said he swore he saw tears in the guy's eyes when he told of how worry was eating Mallory's parents alive.

Sheriff said Curtis kept saying over and over. "I just want to know she's safe, that's all. Her parents have a right to know that, at least."

Then he went on to recite his story as if the sheriff didn't know the facts. The bruises must have been caused during the wreck, he claimed. She was just mad at him and blaming him for everything. She always overreacted when she didn't get her way, ask anyone at the office. Curtis even admitted he'd been about to fire her as well as break up with her when she'd stolen his car. This whole show was just a way to get back at him.

Then, like a chameleon, Curtis shifted. He told the sheriff he really did love Mallory, and if she'd just grow up a little, he could put up with the mood swings.

Jax asked Tim if the sheriff bought any of Curtis's story.

Tim said, "Not a drop."

But if the ad went out, even for one day, someone who saw something might want to earn a little of the reward. A thousand dollars was enough to have anyone at least think about talking. They might think they were doing the family a favor, helping them locate their relative.

Only Jax knew if the boyfriend learned anything, it would only mean trouble.

Trouble coming right toward Mallory…right toward Midnight Crossing.

CHAPTER TWENTY-SEVEN

Misty Bend

THEY SAW THE fire from the air as they neared Sunlan's ranch.

"Holy cow, it's still burning!" Cooper's announcement bounced off the cabin's walls. "I thought we'd be dealing with the aftermath."

"Nope, looks like you're going right into the fury." Madison circled around the wide valley nestled between the lower hills of the Rockies. The breathtaking beauty of aspen and evergreen trees across a blanket of snow was shadowed by a dark cloud that seemed to climb its way to heaven. "I'll come in from the south, with the wind but out of the smoke. Buckle in tight, boys. This isn't going to be a smooth landing."

Elliot slipped his laptop into his padded jacket, zipped up and crossed his arms.

Cooper yelled like he was riding a bronc.

Griffin closed his eyes. If they were going to crash, he didn't want to see an action video of it for the rest of eternity.

He could feel the winds rocking the plane and swore he could hear his heart pounding over the roar of the engine. He mentally tossed his planned to-do list and began a new one. If Sun-lan was dealing with both injured horses and a fire, one would be neglected, as there were probably only five or six people to help. It was evident which one. She'd let her barn burn while she fought to save the horses.

The horses would have to be his first priority, as well. She'd said she had an old hay barn on the place and a hangar to pro-tect her plane. She'd mentioned she stored horse trailers in the hangar, so there would be extra room. Both places could be used as temporary barns.

He'd start setting up. They'd move the horses. If any were still alive.

The plane bumped against the runway with a few quick jolts. Griffin forced his muscles to relax. They'd made it to her. By the time the plane stopped, all three brothers were piling out. Griffin thanked Madison and said he owed her one.

She saluted. "Anytime."

Cooper ran for a tractor with a front-end loader already at-tached.

Griffin knew Cooper guessed the keys would be in the igni-tion, and he was right. By the time Cooper drove back to the plane, snow was falling. Huge flakes whirling in the wind al-most big enough to bat away.

Turning the tractor's bucket toward the cloudy sky, they began working as a team. Elliot and Griffin loaded the supplies while Cooper hopped out and carefully moved the medicine. Between their stash and the Kirklands', they'd be able to run a clinic for a few days.

Elliot climbed on one side of the tractor. Griffin turned to watch Madison taxi around and take off toward home, the wind now at her back. Cooper was already moving toward the fire as Griffin jumped on the tractor.

He had expected chaos, and that's exactly what he found. A dozen horses that didn't look burned or hurt were running wild in the corral near the burning barn. No one had time to move them. No one would dare let them out.

So far the gates were holding, but if the herd knocked one down, there was a good chance the horses would run right back to their stalls in the burning barn. Horses born on the land might run away, but he guessed all of Sunlan's horses were born in stalls, and that was where they were fed and housed. Their safe place. They'd run to that home, even if the barn was burning.

Dave and Andy, the two young hands who'd delivered Sunlan's horses to Maverich Ranch then stayed around long enough to train cowhands to take over, welcomed Griffin with a wave.

Sunlan's college boy hands had bandannas around their noses and mouths as they pulled a horse slowly from the barn. Fear and insanity flickered in the mare's eyes as she fought the handlers. Burns slashed her beautiful back like claw marks.

The roof must be burning.

"She's broken free twice and made it back inside," Andy yelled. "The barn is about to tumble. If she goes in again, we may not be able to get her out. We got one more still locked in the stall. She's hurt and afraid. Won't let us near."

Shouting above the noise, Cooper broke into a run. "I'll get her."

Both boys yelled, "Wait!" but Cooper was already running full out. There was no time for discussion.

Griffin saw worry reflected in Elliot's gaze. "He can take care of himself," Griffin shouted.

Nodding, Elliot took over driving the tractor. Cooper was a man, old enough to make his own way, and both his big brothers had to respect that.

"Dave! Where is Sunlan?" Griffin had to know she was safe first.

The taller of the two hands glanced back. "She's in the hay barn, but it's bedlam in there. We've got horses down and others crazy scared. The local vet and Lloyd, her foreman, are with her."

Griffin jumped on the tractor so he could give Elliot directions. Between the bucket loaded with supplies and the snow making visibility almost impossible, his brother would be driving blind. They headed toward an old barn a quarter mile from the fire, praying there was nothing beneath the half foot of snow that would slow them down.

"Are we even on a road?" Elliot yelled.

"I don't think so." Griffin's entire focus was on the closed doors of the hay barn. As they neared, he could hear the sound of screaming horses and prayed Sunlan was all right. For her, madness must be hearing her animals cry out.

Thirty feet from the door, Griffin yelled, "Stop!" and jumped from the tractor while it was still moving.

Elliot slid a few feet before stopping. "What is it?"

Griffin moved toward something dark lying on the snow, almost covered in newly fallen flakes. Leaning down, Griffin picked up the black foal, stiff with cold. "It's a newborn. Barely alive. I'll carry him in. You get as close as you can to the barn and start unloading."

Elliot hit the gas as he drove the last few feet. Then, he jumped out and opened the door only wide enough to let Griffin inside. If there were untied horses in the barn, there would be a danger of them getting out. The snow was coming down so thick now that no one would be able to follow a runaway.

The scent of blood and smoke and burned hide hit Griffin like a blow. He'd helped put out a barn fire once, but no animals had been involved. He'd smelled burning hides a few times, and everyone living knew the smell of blood. But put the three together, and Griffin felt like he'd just filled his lungs with the odor of hell.

He moved through the dusty barn, barely hearing the horses screaming or stomping in fear. A middle-aged couple worked to his right. They were stacking hay bales against one wall, making room for more horses. They only took the time to nod at him.

He looked around. All the horses that were standing had leather halters and were tied. Those on the ground didn't look like they had enough life left in them to stand, much less run.

The man in his fifties left the woman's side and stepped forward. Without introducing himself, he brushed the last of the birthing sack off the colt Griffin carried.

"Get him dry and warmed or he won't make it."

"Doc?"

Tired eyes seemed to focus on him for the first time. "I am. I was on my way here when the fire broke out. Another hour and I don't think I could have made it through the pass with this new snow. Whoever you men are, we're glad you're here."

"We brought supplies. Medicine." Names weren't important right now. "My brother is waiting for you to tell him where you want them."

Elliot banged through the barn door with the first box.

"We'll need them. Most of our supplies were burned before we could get to them. Stack them over there." The veterinarian was already moving to help Elliot.

Griffin had planned to hand the newborn colt over to the doc, but he rushed away too fast. Griff moved deeper into the barn, shifting his hold on the colt as he looked for Sunlan. Horses burned, horses hurt, horses dying. If he'd brought ten brothers, that still wouldn't be enough to handle all that needed to be done.

He found Sunlan curled up beside a beautiful bay. She was hanging on to the animal's neck and crying. The horse's eyes were lifeless.

Griffin wanted to pull her up and take her away from all this pain. She loved horses, probably more than she'd ever love anyone. But taking her away wouldn't stop this kind of bone-deep grief. He had to step into the sorrow with her.

Carefully laying the black colt down beside the dead horse,

he whispered, "Easy now, fellow." The mare was still warm. She'd offer some warmth for the colt.

Elliot appeared behind him and handed Griffin a couple of blankets. "I'll help the doc. I might not be great with horses, but I can take orders." He disappeared before Griffin could answer.

Rubbing the blanket over the colt, Griffin wiped him dry. The baby horse jerked as he pushed his hand hard over the colt's mouth and nose covered in ice. He had to make sure the tiny horse could breathe. The ice might block his airways as well as keep him from being able to suck.

He worked with the colt, fully aware that Sunlan was watching him. "We can't do anything for this bay, but we got to try to save this colt."

Straightening, she placed her hand over his glove. He met her eyes, which were still rimmed in tears. Dear God, even when she was exhausted and covered in mud and blood, she was still the most beautiful creature he'd ever seen. Somehow, he had to find a way to help her.

"We'll make it through this, Sunlan. We'll save as many as we can. I'm with you in this until it's finished."

She nodded and began to rub the colt's legs.

"I'll get the other blanket." When he stood, he had to touch her. Pulling off his glove, he ran his hand over her wild hair. "I'm here," he said softly. "I always will be if you need me."

He wasn't sure she heard him. All her energy was with the colt that lay cuddled against the dead horse.

The next several hours were a blur. Griffin circled by Sunlan whenever he could, but there was more work than they could do. Cooper found saddles in one of the horse trailers and saddled up on a half-wild stallion the boys called Thumper. He handed both of his brothers mounts, as well. Griffin's gelding was a workhorse, a cowboy's horse, steady and well trained. All three brothers could cover ground between the buildings faster now.

Cooper rode hard through the snow, back and forth from the

crumbling barn. He pulled the horses from the corral a few at a time, still too close to what remained of the barn. As the last flames played out across black remains, the sun slipped behind the hills, but the work didn't slow. Lights came on along the walkways between the barn and the house. Lanterns were hung in the old barn, and slowly the panic of the day settled.

The animals that needed doctoring were brought to the hay barn, and those that were merely frightened were taken to the cool shadows of the hangar. It was made of metal and creaked and popped in the wind, but the horses could easily be tied to trailers lining the low sides. They were used to being transported in the trailers and seemed to calm.

On his third round, Cooper stopped in to check on Sunlan. Griffin watched his little brother walk up to her and give her a bear hug. Cooper didn't say a word. He just put his hat back on and stepped out into the wind.

As the day aged, a few of the neighbors showed up on snowmobiles. They helped with the care and feeding. Those who didn't know horses worked with the foreman's wife to pass out coffee and sandwiches. No one was hungry, but they ate, knowing they'd need fuel to continue.

Griffin felt like he'd drunk a gallon of strong coffee trying to get warm from the inside out. Every time he slowed to take a long breath, he saw another dozen things that needed doing.

Ten horses dead in the fire. Eight were hurt. One had died trying to deliver her foal. But with luck, thirty-six would live. It could have been a lot worse if Sunlan's caretaker hadn't been up, watching a mare about to deliver her baby. He'd called the doc before he spotted the fire in the tack room.

Just after sunset, Cooper brought in one more mare. She was young and must have delivered her first baby amid all the excitement. Cooper talked low and calming to the mare as he walked her to the back where the tiny colt cuddled against a now cold horse.

He talked to the mare as if she understood every word he said. "Now don't you be frightened, girl. I just want to introduce you to your baby. He might not look like much, but he'll grow."

Everyone in the barn stood and stared as the horse lowered her head and smelled the sleeping colt. Then she pushed him with her nose. Once, twice. All the time making sounds as if she were waking him up.

The colt looked up, then slowly tried to stand.

For the first time in a dozen hours, Sunlan smiled as the colt finally waddled over to the mare and discovered there was a meal waiting.

Griffin and his brothers were all watching, too. Somehow this one new life made the horror of the day bearable.

Sunlan turned and moved into Griffin's arms, hugging him hard as she cried.

Griffin held her against him and looked up at his brothers. "Thanks," was the only word he could get out. They'd fought as hard as he had.

The world seemed to settle a bit after that. The neighbors headed home, promising to come back tomorrow. Cooper, Andy and Dave finally stopped long enough to grab coffee and a few sandwiches each. They talked of the day like young soldiers who'd just survived their first battle, and the hands invited Cooper to sleep on the extra bunk in the loft of the hangar.

"It's dry and warm, and we got HBO, if you can stay awake long enough to watch it."

Cooper shook his head. "I'm sound asleep on my feet right now. Just point me to a bed and yell timber!"

Before they could leave, the vet informed them that they'd be doing shift work starting at midnight. "Figure it out, boys. I want one of you watching over this barn while I sleep a few hours."

All three nodded and darted out before the doc thought of something else that needed to be done. Sunlan's foreman and his wife left, too, saying they'd be back before dawn to cook breakfast and begin the cleanup. On a clear day, their cabin was within sight of Sunlan's ranch, and his four-wheeler could make the short journey even in a blizzard.

Griffin kept working. Organizing supplies. Checking on each horse. Making sure all were safe and fed. He'd made up his mind. He would not stop until Sunlan did.

Long after dark, the embers of the barn had cooled beneath a thick layer of snow, and all the horses were treated and resting. The doc bedded down in the loft of the hay barn, which everyone was now calling the horse hospital.

Elliot accepted Sunlan's offer of the guesthouse when she told him she had internet set up there.

"Andy told me he wanted to be a vet." Elliot gave her a polite hug. "I thought I'd look up the closest school. He said he might go back to college next semester and work for you on the weekends if he can find a college within driving distance."

She shrugged. "He's been 'about to go back to school' for a year. Maybe you can help him get there."

Griffin knew his brother just might be able to help. He'd missed his chance to go away to college, but thanks to online classes, Elliot had never stopped learning.

Finally, the world settled. Even the light snow still falling was silent. Taking one look at Sunlan, Griffin saw she was barely standing. He picked her up and headed toward a little two-story house that looked like it belonged in California, not Colorado.

Surprisingly, she didn't protest. She just wrapped her arms around his neck and melted against him. By the time he reached the porch, he had no doubt she was sound asleep. Carefully, he turned the doorknob and carried her inside. The house was warm, inviting, with only the porch light shining though the windows to offer him direction. Someone had lit a fire in a small fireplace, and the smell of coffee still lingered.

Holding her close, he gently leaned back on a couch and let

his muscles relax. He felt like a prizefighter who'd gone a hundred rounds. Worn out. But he was exactly where he'd needed to be. With Sunlan. As he closed his eyes, Griffin smiled. She was safe.

It occurred to him that having a wife might not be as easy as he thought it might be, but then again, being married to Sunlan would never be boring.

CHAPTER TWENTY-EIGHT

The Johnsons

WYATT HAD DONE the dishes Sunday night, thinking Jamie would come back. She'd taken her van but forgotten her coat. She was probably just driving around. He wished he could say that she was like that, but he wasn't sure what she was like when someone—no, not someone, him—hurt her feelings.

He didn't know her well enough to predict. He knew the games and movies she loved. She talked nonstop when she was nervous or happy. He knew she was kind. She had a huge imagination. She had no family to spend Thanksgiving with. No family to run to if she was upset.

He knew little things about her. But not what counted.

His backing away when she'd asked him to kiss her must have hurt her feelings, and she'd ran. Add one more fact. He hadn't even recognized how insensitive he must have been before she was out the door. He should have guessed she'd be a runner. When the creep kept bothering her last weekend, she should have flattened him, not simply turned away. He needed to teach her how to do that.

He walked out on the porch and for once he didn't see the beauty of the place. All he saw was the memory of the hurt he'd seen in her eyes.

The minute she felt uncomfortable, she wouldn't want to argue. She'd just walk away. That probably explained why no boyfriends or lovers hung around.

Wyatt closed his eyes. He was standing in the most peaceful spot he'd ever found in this world, and he felt like he was taking hits straight to the chest.

She ran because he hurt her. She should have kicked him out that first day. If he'd thought he'd ever hurt Jamie, he would have stepped out of her life when they met. Thinking about how she was the one who started the last conversation didn't help. She'd just said aloud something he'd thought of doing almost since the day he met her.

He'd even had a few dreams about what would happen if he didn't hear the click of the lock one night. Or better yet, if she'd just left the door open.

Around eleven, he walked out to the edge of the lake and watched the lonely moon dance by itself across the water. He wanted to tell her how much this place, her company, had meant to him. He had a feeling he'd dream of her and the little lake house for months. He'd remember the way they laughed and cooked and touched. Hell, he'd probably start watching the Hallmark Channel just so he could close his eyes and drift back, pretending to be on her old couch.

When she came back, he'd say he was sorry. He'd just had the greatest day he'd had in years, and he'd ruined it by getting serious. Hell! He should have kissed her. What if it did lead to them sleeping together? At least he'd leave her with a memory. That might be all she wanted anyway. Not him so much, just the memory.

After all, that's what she collected. The mice tea sets, the Precious Moments figurines, the junky yard art. Memories of where she'd lived or who she'd taught. Jamie even had memories of ancestors she wished she had. A family, friends, a home.

It was so cold by the lake, he could see his breath, but he didn't walk back. The midnight water reminded him of sifting sand, always moving, like a living thing. In a week, he'd be back, probably staring out at the desert and thinking about this lake.

The next mission that always lurked in the back of his mind came full force, front screen now. His team had been talking about it for months, dreading it, putting it off until closer to the end of their tour. Everything would have to go like clockwork. They'd have to go in with the equipment on their backs. The mission would take days. Nights without sleep. Little food. They'd only have room to carry water. Any delay, the loss of one tool, a sandstorm, one guy getting hurt…

Wyatt shoved the details back. He'd deal with it all when he got back. Right now he need to think about Jamie. If he couldn't help her, couldn't promise her time, the least thing he could do was cause no more hurt.

The wind finally kicked up and clouds shadowed the moon. Wyatt didn't go back to the little lake house. Not when he started to shiver. Not when he thought he heard her car.

There were a dozen possibilities he'd thought he might do when he faced her, but Wyatt knew there was also the chance that he'd simply make a bigger fool of himself. They'd kept their friendship light until tonight, and he doubted either one could go back to the way it was.

He watched the lights go out in the kitchen of her home, the living room, then finally her bedroom. She was closing up, calling it a night. He might not hear her bedroom door closing, the lock clicking, but he felt it all the way to his heart.

Why hadn't he kissed her? In play, a light kiss, and then they could have both laughed. Or deep, completely, like he'd thought of doing every night.

She wasn't his type. He didn't have time for a relationship. He didn't want to hurt her.

So, why did it matter so much? Why did *she* matter so much? Why did being with her make him feel like he was living in double time? Stacking up memories, feelings. Growing. Learning.

He noticed she'd left the porch light on. She'd probably seen him standing out by the lake. She was being considerate, even in her anger. The porch light had been the last light he'd left on every night. He liked having one last look at the lake.

Slowly, he walked back to the house. He'd pack tonight and be gone before she woke. It wasn't that far to walk into town. He'd have breakfast at the café, then leave on the first bus passing through town. He'd even tell Dorothy that he couldn't bear to say goodbye to Jamie, so he'd left her sleeping.

Which was true. He couldn't.

When he slipped back in the house, he picked up the box he'd bought at the mall and unwrapped an eight-inch teapot with tiny porcelain mice having Thanksgiving dinner in a circle around the pot. The detail was beautiful. It would fit perfectly beside her other tiny teapots with dancing mice.

Wyatt shoved it into place on her shelf. "A memory from your pretend husband," he said. One forever memory that might make her smile as time passed.

When he stretched out on the couch, he thought about how he'd failed. Not in just being her friend or her pretend husband, but in making her believe that she was pretty. He should have told her that at least once.

And a dozen more things. How special she was as a person. How her students loved her. How when she smiled his whole world brightened.

He remembered how he'd thought she was nice, how she wasn't the kind of woman he was usually interested in. He'd fought never to show her anything but friendship, and now he'd somehow let her believe she wasn't the kind of woman he'd ever be interested in. He'd backed away when she'd asked for one kiss.

Every day, he'd noticed things about her that were beautiful. The way she smiled. The way she moved. The graceful way she curled up on her corner of the couch.

When her alarm went off behind her bedroom door, he was still wide-awake. He heard the bathroom door close. By the time the shower came on, Wyatt was lacing up his boots. Almost daylight. Time to go.

He stood, shoved the toy turkey in his pack and walked out. She had the teapot. He wanted something to keep. Something to hold a memory.

Before Jamie had time to turn off the water, he was heading up the hill toward town. For once, he didn't notice the sunrise or the clouds promising snow to the north. He just marched.

When he reached the sleepy little town, Wyatt stepped into the empty café, which was just opening. He ordered a breakfast he didn't have the appetite to eat.

He sat in the first booth, waiting for a bus to pull up across the street in front of the post office. The town slowly began to move outside the window. Mostly just cars and trucks passing through, barely noticing the little spot in the road with its one stoplight.

He ordered more coffee. On previous mornings, he'd swear buses passed often, heading different directions. But not this morning. It didn't matter which way they were heading; he planned to catch the first one. He just needed to get out of town before anyone noticed. He'd ride to the nearest city that had an airport, take a cab to the terminal and catch the first flight to DC. He would spend his last two days of leave in a hotel watching football and ordering room service. Then he'd go back where he belonged.

The next leave, Jamie Johnson would be just a memory.

He grinned. He did love her big imagination and the way she

grinned when she was about to tell him something funny. She'd think of something to tell people back in Crossroads. He might even send her flowers at school. His last act as a pretend husband.

He pictured her going to school alone for the first time in over a week. Her eyes would probably be red from crying. Maybe people wouldn't ask too many questions. Then she wouldn't have to make up too many lies. All she'd have to say was that he was gone, and they'd comfort her.

Maybe he'd sign the card on the three dozen roses he'd send, *Love, Wyatt.*

The idea. The word, felt right. Love. Real love, not pretend. That was all he could think of to say. No other word fit.

He stared into the coffee. He couldn't see his future. He never had been able to. But he could see tomorrow and the next day. And he had to live it, even if that's all he'd ever have. He could do it alone. He didn't need family or friends outside his buddies in the army.

That ache in his chest came again. He was taking invisible fire. He couldn't bring himself to say that he was fine without her. He needed more than the dumb toy turkey. He needed more memories for once. This time, a few days of peace wasn't enough. He needed her.

"Hell," he mumbled as he stood and grabbed his pack. Now he had to make it back to the lake before she left for school. He dropped a twenty and marched.

CHAPTER TWENTY-NINE

Misty Bend

GRIFFIN WOKE, ONE slow muscle at a time. During the night, he'd managed to pull off his boots and coat. His hat lay on the floor where it must have fallen.

He remembered helping Sunlan with her boots, then she'd pulled a throw over them both and cuddled down beside him. He vaguely remembered her telling him to be still and hold her. Even while half asleep, she was still giving orders.

Griffin looked around as if he'd accidentally misplaced her. His foggy brain saw her boots, her coat, the throw, but no fiancée. Like the snow, she appeared to have melted off him during the night.

Scrubbing his face, Griff felt a day's stubble as yesterday came back to him. The flight. The fight to save her horses. The fire. They'd all worked until they were about to drop in the cold and snow.

Then he'd carried her home.

Slowly the room came into view. He wasn't surprised by what he saw: the place was neat, organized, planned. Decorated in a blend of Western style mixed with Santa Fe, but it wasn't big and rambling like a ranch house. He knew without asking, this place was her refuge, her lair, her hideaway.

Smells drew him to his feet. Coffee, breakfast.

Griffin raked his hand through dirty hair and followed his nose down a hallway to a small dining room that widened into a U-shaped kitchen. The middle-aged woman who'd helped all day yesterday was standing in a kitchen.

"Morning, Mrs. Norman," he managed in a voice that sounded rougher than usual.

"Morning, Mr. Holloway. You can call me Kendra—everyone does. I fed the others an hour ago, but Sunlan told me to let you sleep in. Would you like some breakfast?"

Griffin glanced out the window. The sun wasn't full up, and he'd apparently overslept. "No breakfast, but I could use a shower."

She nodded. "Your brother brought in your bag. I put it in the guest room. Up the stairs. First room on the left."

"Thank you." He had to think for a second before he remembered the name she'd just told him. "Kendra?"

"Yes, sir?"

"Call me Griffin. I feel like we fought the storm and the fire last night. We should be friends by now."

"All right, Griffin. I'll fix a breakfast roll with sausage and have it ready for you by the time you've showered. Got a feeling you'll want to head out."

"You're right." He managed a quick smile and walked back through the house, hoping he'd come across the staircase before he had to go back and ask directions. He'd noticed the smell of smoke and lathered horses filled the house, then he realized the odor was following him.

Hell. I'm the one who smells.

Ten minutes later, his sore muscles had relaxed under a hot shower and he felt ready to face the day. He pulled on the only change of clothes he'd brought, didn't bother to shave and picked up his takeout breakfast on his way out of the house.

If everyone was already up and working, he needed to join the crowd.

The sight that met him was breathtaking. The snow had stopped and now sparkled across the land like scattered diamonds. Mountains were on his left and rolling hills on his right. Huge evergreens, their branches heavy with snow, ran along what might have been a fence line. The scene reminded him how close to Christmas it was. How close to his wedding.

He shaded his eyes and studied the land. Even the scar on perfection, the burned remains of the horse barn, seemed to sleep now under a blanket of new snow. The back of the once-big barn still stood, like one last soldier refusing to fall.

Griffin understood why Sunlan loved this place. She'd said once that this little ranch was as close to a home as she'd ever had. The very place her mother had hated and run from was now Sunlan's paradise.

The memory of her sleeping next to him on the couch came back to him. They weren't even friends, but it had felt right having her close. For once, she hadn't been distant and all business.

Cooper rode up with a mount for Griffin. "Don't you just love this place? I vote we sell Maverick Ranch and move here. I could so get used to having something besides buffalo grass and tumbleweeds to look at."

"No doubt it's beautiful." Griffin took the reins from Cooper. "Where is everyone?"

"Elliot is at the burn site with a deputy sheriff who came out from some small town. He claims he's an expert because he took a course on fires." Cooper shook his head. "I read one sheet of paper Elliot printed off from the internet last night on the ten most common causes of barn fires, and I think I outrank the deputy in knowledge."

"Where is everyone else?"

"Elliot and Andy are trying to identify the horses who died in the fire. A few were trapped beneath the barn. Andy's helping dig them out. The vet had to put down one more this morning. He's got men coming in to handle the disposal."

"Did you run everything by Sunlan?"

"Yep. She knows about it, but I don't think she wanted to see it." Cooper lowered his voice. "Our Sunlan is really taking this hard."

Griffin wanted to remind Cooper that Sunlan wasn't theirs, but he felt that considering how long his brothers had worked last night, they'd proved just how much they cared. "What are you up to?"

"I've been out circling the pastures. There is still one horse unaccounted for. He was new, only came in last week. A high-priced stallion. He may have been hurt, so there's a good chance I'll find him down. But if he's alive, he can't be too far. This place isn't all that big."

"Where's Sunlan?" Griffin swung up into the saddle.

"Over with the doc, taking care of that colt you brought in last night. She's mothering him like that baby is the future of her ranch. He might very well be."

Griffin turned his horse toward the hay barn. He didn't bother to say goodbye to Cooper. He'd be bumping into him all day. Five minutes later, he found her just where Cooper said she'd be.

"Morning, Sunshine," Griffin said in a low voice as he stood behind her.

She didn't smile when she glanced back and answered, "Morning, sleepyhead."

Griffin stepped into the makeshift stall and began to help. He wanted to talk about how they'd slept together last night, but there were too many people around. They were engaged; everyone probably assumed they slept together, so advertising it wouldn't be any news.

"Thanks for your help last night." Her voice was calm as she brushed the mare. "I couldn't ask you to come, but I'm glad you did."

"Happy to help. We'll stay till we get this cleaned up. I have a family of cowhands watching over my spread. You can use us here for a few days."

She agreed. "As soon as I can, I'd like to move as many horses as possible south to your place. The few mares I have to leave here will have the doc and Lloyd to look after them. But with more snow coming soon, it'll be easier to handle most of the herd at your place."

He agreed. "I noticed three horse trailers in the hangar. Two could carry six. The third looked a little battered, but if it is road ready, we could put a few of the wounded horses in it and load in extra equipment."

"Sounds good, but that won't take care of half of those who could be moved." She looked a bit broken. "Without my big barn, I can't keep many here."

He leaned down as she knelt to brush the colt. His low words were only for her. "I'll call home and have a couple of my men start driving this direction. I've got a six trailer, and I know where I can borrow another. My men can leave within the hour and be here by dark if you think the pass will be clear to get over today." His light touch on her shoulder silently told her she wasn't alone. Not anymore.

"I checked." She nodded, her strength coming back into her eyes. "They're plowing now. But your men need to get here by sundown. There are spots on the pass that freeze over as soon as the sun sets."

"If Andy and Dave can drive one each, Cooper could handle the third one pulling out from here. If they leave by noon, they should have no problem. They'll be out of the bad weather by the time they cross the Oklahoma panhandle. I'll have Elliot order more feed delivered to our place so we'll be ready for them when they arrive. If the snow holds off, my rigs can be here, loaded and leave again tomorrow morning." Griffin looked down at the colt. "He'll need to stay here with his mother for a few weeks."

She rubbed her cheek against the colt's neck. "I know, but I'll miss him."

Her comment told him the one thing he'd hesitated asking. She was going back to the ranch with him. "We'll get through this, Sunshine. It may not be till spring, but we'll rebuild."

She nodded. "If it's okay, I'll stable as many as I can in your barns until I'm operational here."

"The white barn on my place is yours," he corrected. "I gave it to you, remember? If I can put up with half a dozen decorators in my house, I can easily handle thirty or so horses in the barn."

"I forgot about the decorators. They're supposed to be finishing by now."

Griffin growled as he fought down laughter. "They probably are. I didn't lock the door. They won't even notice we're gone. Elliot hides in his study from them. They run when they see Cooper, and I'm usually gone before they drive under our gate."

She laughed and an ounce of sadness left her. "You men hated them, didn't you?"

"No. We like what you told them to do, and we wanted you to have your rooms the way you wanted them."

A bit of distrust echoed in her tone. "Why?"

"Because, Sunlan Krown Holloway, whether you stay a few nights or all year, I want you to know that you'll always have a home at Maverick Ranch."

She took his offered hand. "I think, in less than a month, I'll be dropping the Krown part of that name. I think just Holloway will suit me fine."

He closed his fingers around hers, and she let him help her stand. They might have a mountain of chores to do before tomorrow when, weather permitting, they moved her stock south, but he felt like they were working together.

Cramming his hat on, Griff winked at her. "How about we divide and conquer? You and the doc take care of the horses in here. Lloyd and I will take care of the deputy sheriff and the cleanup." He leaned slightly and kissed her cheek. "We'll talk at supper. Deal?"

"Deal."

Halfway through the day of dirty jobs and bad smells, Misty Bend's caretaker, Lloyd, finally turned to Griffin and said his first sentence that wasn't about the work. "Me and the missus are mighty glad you finally got here, Holloway. We've been wondering how long it would take you to find our Sunlan."

"What makes you think I found her? Maybe she found me."

Lloyd shook his head. "No, not possible. She may talk all strong and bossy, but when it gets down to it, she's afraid of men. Her daddy tries to run her life, and I think she's afraid any man she comes across would do the same."

"I don't want to boss her around, Lloyd. I never will."

The older man grinned. "I know. I noticed that. That's why she must have let you close." He scratched his bald head. "Something else I noticed, Holloway. Now and then, she looks at you the same way she looks at that colt. Over the years, when she was here visiting her grandfather, I've seen her sleep next to a sick or dying horse many a time, but until last night, I never saw her sleep next to a man."

"Are you telling me you've never seen her with a man? No boyfriends or lovers?"

"Oh, sure, her father tried to match her up with some rich dandy every now and then. A few even come out here determined to win her over. But I had a feeling she'd never settle for anything but a real cowboy."

Griffin walked away smiling. Lloyd obviously didn't know as much about Sunlan as he thought he did. She'd found him, and before that, some other guy who didn't use protection.

She'd still be her own person when they were married, and

he'd have his ranch after the wedding. But things were getting a bit mixed up.

They were becoming friends.

CHAPTER THIRTY

The Johnsons

JAMIE JOHNSON SAT on the couch holding the teapot Wyatt had left on her shelf. She was dressed for school, but she couldn't make herself go. She needed a bit of time to think.

She'd gotten up early. Planning to say she was sorry for leaving Wyatt last night. She'd mend fences, and they'd laugh about it. If he just wanted to be friends, she should treasure that and not ask for more. *Never* ask for more. He might have admitted he thought of more between them, but he obviously wasn't willing to risk it. Like the tiny mice on her teapots, she should just be happy with what she had.

But when she walked out of her bedroom, Wyatt had already left. Without sharing breakfast. Without saying goodbye. All signs of him ever being in her life had disappeared.

She'd thought they'd have one more day, maybe two. She'd intended to say she could drive him to wherever he needed to report. She could take a few days off. Her principal would understand. After all, her husband was in the army.

Jamie swallowed a cry. Captain Wyatt Johnson was not her

husband. She'd had so much fun pretending that for a moment, she'd almost believed it herself.

But last night something had shattered their little make-believe world. She wasn't sure what woke them up at the same time. Asking for a kiss? Wyatt afraid to step over some invisible line?

She'd been dumb to ask him to kiss her. She'd embarrassed him, and he'd rattled on, trying not to hurt her feelings. He'd said he couldn't go halfway. Did he think one kiss was an invitation to join her for the night?

She knew he cared about her. She saw it in his eyes. Felt it in his gentle touch. Or at least she thought he did. How could her signals be so off?

Slowly she stood and placed her new treasure back in its place. She had a memory of almost being married. If that's all she got, she wouldn't complain.

She stood tall. All her life she'd learned to appreciate the little things she had, and she'd do that now. She had a job she loved. Everyone believed she was married, so hopefully there would be no more harassment or efforts to hook her up with unmarried relatives. Half the town had seen her husband. Wyatt had done her a great favor.

That was enough. He didn't have to kiss her. That hadn't been part of their bargain. She had nothing to complain about, she repeated. No one got all they wanted in life.

She laced her shoes and picked up her bag. Maybe she'd write Wyatt and send it general delivery to the army. Surely they could find him. She'd thank him for the great time. Today she'd teach her class. Maybe she'd get out her tiny Christmas tree and plug it in by the window. Then she'd order her one gift and pay the extra to have it come wrapped.

She could tell herself all would go back to being the same, but she knew it never would. Wyatt had left a big hole inside her. Now her real life would seem to be the pretend one.

Pretending to be happy. Pretending nothing was missing. Pretending she hadn't fallen in love.

She stepped onto the porch and for once didn't see the beauty around her. Wyatt wouldn't be taking her to work today. She wouldn't be kissing him on the cheek for everyone to see. She loved that part of their game. People who'd noticed them would smile at her when she climbed out of the car.

But not today. They'd probably only look at her with sad eyes. Mrs. Johnson's husband had gone back to the army.

Snowflakes pirouetted in the early morning air, thick and heavy, wet on her cheeks. She smiled, remembering how he'd swung her around that first day as if she were made of air. Memories, she thought. *I'll collect all the good memories and leave the broken ones on the floor. I'll think of how we began, how we pretended, how we laughed. I'll forget how it ended.*

As she pulled out of her lane and headed up the long incline to the main road, Jamie fought back tears. She'd known the game wouldn't last long; after all, they were only playing house. Nothing was real about the time they'd pretended.

But she'd hoped for a few more days. You'd think she'd learn. Those days of packing her one suitcase and one box drifted in her mind. *Don't expect more. Never expect more. Be happy with what you have in life.*

She blinked into the morning sun as a figure appeared directly in front of her. He was walking down the center of the road as if it were a mountain trail and not the only way out of the lake community. He was big with a pack on his back. A soldier. A warrior. Wyatt!

Jamie barely hit the brakes in time. He stood ten feet in front of her, just staring. He looked carved in stone. If she'd hit him with her van, the van probably would have taken all damage.

She held her breath. The man glared at her as if the road belonged to him and she was trespassing.

Like a tornado coming straight toward her, he marched to

Jamie and jerked the door of her old van open so hard she feared the entire piece of metal and glass might give way.

"Get out of the van, Jamie." An order, nothing more.

She remained frozen. If he was planning to steal her car, he'd have to take her with him. She clicked off the engine. Wyatt taking her van made no sense; he could have driven away with it any day or night for over a week.

He dropped his pack, reached across to unbuckle her seat belt, then grabbed her around the waist. In one jerk, he pulled her out of the van and stood her directly in front of him.

His wintergreen eyes, full of anger and doubt, stared down at her.

She realized she wasn't afraid of him. Not one bit. Wyatt Johnson might be a soldier, but he would never hurt her. If he'd come back to tell her how she'd ruined his leave, then so be it. She'd face him. Running last night had not been not about him but her. She'd tried to outrun her hurt, not him.

He didn't say a word. He just kept staring at her like she was the third little pig and he was still starving.

"Is there something you forgot to say?" She took a step toward him.

"No."

"Then don't you think you should step out of the center of the road so I can get to work?"

"No. I don't want to move." Confusion seemed to make him blink.

She had the feeling he was arguing with himself.

"Did you forget something, Wyatt?"

"Yes."

"Oh, well, let's go get it." She started to move, but this boulder in a uniform stood in her way. "I have to be at school in fifteen minutes." She took one step more and prepared to push him aside. Like that could happen.

"I don't care if you're late."

Frustration made her jumpy. "Then do what you need to do or say what you plan to say because I'm not waiting all morning for you to make up your mind."

To her shock, he leaned in and kissed her. A light brush of his lips against hers, as if he were testing to see if she'd bite.

When she didn't react, he did it again. A slight kiss, nothing more.

The tenderness of this big, hard soldier surprised her. When she didn't move, he kissed her again, harder. A real kiss.

Not bad, she thought, for a man who'd refused to even try last night.

With one tug at her waist, he pulled her against him. The next kiss was full out, nothing held back, and she couldn't help but respond. This was the kind of kiss she'd dreamed of… The more-than-a-movie kiss. A kiss she felt all the way to her toes.

She wrapped her arms around him and kissed him back as he lifted her off the ground.

When he finally broke the kiss, he whispered against her ear, "That's all I have to say."

"Well, I have something to say!" a male voice shouted from ten feet away. "You two Johnsons need to take it back to the house. There are folks who want to use the road this morning."

Wyatt didn't let go of her, but he turned to face the sheriff. "You planning to arrest a man for kissing his wife?"

Sheriff Cline grinned. "Since I probably wouldn't be able to pry you two apart, I'd have to put you in the same cell. Not worth my time to do the paperwork. So go back home. I'll drop by the school and tell them to find a substitute for your wife. You're both obviously sick. I can tell you've got a fever from a car length away. If they can't find someone to take your classes, Mrs. Johnson, I'll send Thatcher to teach those kids the law. He's been studying it long enough to carry a lecture for an hour."

"We're going home?" Wyatt whispered against her ear. "You ready for that, Mrs. Johnson?"

She nodded.

Wyatt let go of her long enough to toss his pack in the back, then they climbed into the van like Bonnie and Clyde on the run. Neither said goodbye to the sheriff, but when Wyatt glanced back in the rearview mirror, Cline was laughing.

Three minutes later, they were stumbling into the lake house, trying to kiss each other and walk at the same time.

As soon as he closed the door, Wyatt swung her around. "I couldn't leave you, not like that. You have to know how crazy I am about you." He dug his hand into her hair and destroyed the bun she'd tied back. "There were a hundred things I needed to tell you. How pretty you are. How sexy. How I love everything you say and the way your mind works and how you hold on to things as if they're treasures. But all I can think to do right now is kiss you senseless."

Like wild kids, they began undressing each other, laughing, bumping heads, kissing whenever possible.

Finally, he picked her up and walked to the bedroom door. "Are you sure about this, Jamie? If I step into your bedroom, there will be no halfway, no pretend. I plan on making love to you for real."

She kissed his cheek. "I've been waiting for you to do just that since I saw you step from the shower wearing only a towel."

He shoved the door open, and they fell into bed.

As he held her against him, she didn't have to close her eyes and dream of what might be. This time he was real and he was all hers, if only for a few days.

CHAPTER THIRTY-ONE

Midnight Crossing

THE COLD CAM in on a forty-mile-an-hour wind as the end of November neared. Jax O'Grady watched Mallory grow stronger each day. Her bruises were fading to browns and purples, and the swelling on her face was almost gone.

Some mornings he felt like he was watching her turn into a swan. The awkward moves she'd made the first few days were gone. There was a grace about her movements now. She'd started a habit of pushing her body almost as if she were a dancer warming up.

He liked watching. Appreciating how hard she tried.

She might be small in build, but when she smiled, he felt like she lit up the room. She'd gotten into the habit of setting the table and chairs out at each meal, and he'd folded them up thirty minutes later. He hadn't complained; after all, it was good exercise.

During the second week, she'd managed to say thank-you in a low whisper. Slowly, a few more words a day, she begin to carry on a short conversation without having to touch her throat. Slowly, she was talking.

Not that she had much practice. When Tim came over, he did most of the talking and loved saying things that made her laugh. Sometimes he spent an hour telling her how hard it was to be a writer. Then he'd spend another hour helping her work on a puzzle as if the deadline he'd been complaining about was a million days away.

Jax wasn't much help with conversation either. He talked to Charlie more than he did to Mallory. He'd lived alone too long; he'd forgotten how to just visit with people.

Tim brought her a new puzzle every time he came, and she spent one whole day working on one that pictured kittens under a Christmas tree. Jax decided the puzzles must have been from the retirement home because most were pictures of animals or winter wonderland scenes. But they seemed to help her pass the afternoons in a kind of simple peace and he figured that was exactly what she needed.

"We should hang this as our only Christmas decoration," she whispered as she put the last piece in.

Jax stood up from his desk and walked over to the card table he'd placed by the window. "You think so?"

"I think so." She smiled at him as if she saw all his flaws and liked him anyway. "I know change isn't easy for you, but what can I say? You're the one who brought me home."

"So I asked for it?"

"Yep. First me, then Christmas decorations."

He nodded. "I'll build a frame for our one decoration. Anything else you'd like?"

"Yes." She patted the second folding chair. "Talk to me, Jax."

"All right."

At first their conversations were awkward. She was learning to trust again an ounce at a time and he was remembering how to open up to someone.

At dusk every night, he'd wrap her in a blanket and they'd sit on the porch for a while, then he'd cook supper. Most meal preparation consisted of opening a can. Each night, they'd linger a little longer at the small table talking.

She was taking long showers by herself now. He guessed the heat helped relax her muscles. And just before bedtime, he'd rub cream on her bruised legs and rewrap the one place just above her knee that hadn't healed.

"I can do this myself, Jax," she'd said one night. "I don't mean to be such a bother."

"I know. I don't mind. I can see the healing every day but I want to make sure this one wound doesn't get infected. You're going to make it through this, Mallory, and I'd like to think that I helped."

"You do, Jax. Maybe we help each other?" she whispered and they both knew what she was talking about. His wounds were deeper than hers. "When we're both well, can we still be friends?"

He taped the bandage. "I think I'd like that."

"You know, Curtis was a jerk. Probably a criminal. Sometimes, late at night I wake thinking I hear him coming to hurt me. Then I remember you're just ten feet away and Charlie is on his rug by the fireplace. Part of me wants to hide out here forever. Would you mind, Jax?"

"No. But you've got a life to get back to, I'm guessing. I'm just a guy that was around when you needed somewhere to hide out."

She looked up at him. "You're much more than that, Jax, and someday when the time is right, I plan to talk about that."

"With the number of hours we seem to spend talking, I'm sure we'll get around to that. Once you're on your feet, I'll just be a memory. Soon we'll start planning how you're going to get back into your life that's waiting for you."

"Nothing is waiting. I have no job. No apartment. I've been thinking I should move somewhere else, maybe as far away from

Curtis as I can. Make a fresh start. My folks lived in Georgia. I grew up there but nothing remains for me to return to but their graves. The town they loved seems too small for me to move home and find a job. I don't think I could ever go back to Dallas either."

"Because of Curtis?"

"He'll probably move on to his next victim. I could try to press charges, but it'd be my word against his. He could claim all the damage to my body was because of the wreck. He could even claim I stole his car, which I did."

"Give it time, Mallory. A few more days. A week. After all, once you leave, Tim will have to go back to writing."

She smiled at Jax. "I love your humor. Hermit humor."

"Where are your things, your clothes? You can't go looking for a new job wearing those pajamas."

"All my stuff, clothes and all, is probably in the trash. When I left, I didn't think about packing a bag. I do have a storage spot Curtis doesn't know about, mainly because he couldn't be bothered to help me stash my furniture. When we moved in together, he said he didn't want any of my things cluttering up his home."

"What about money?"

"I've got savings in an old account back in Georgia. I can pull from that to last me a few months. When I stop scaring people with my face, I could probably travel down to Galveston. An old roommate would put me up there until I find a new job."

Jax turned away. "You're already figuring it out."

She touched his arm. "That's just it. I don't. I feel like I just made a mistake. A big mistake. I could have gotten myself killed. Right now I'm in a place where I not only lost my trust in people, I've lost trust in myself."

He looked at her. "Then stay awhile. This cabin should be branded the figure-it-out hideout."

"And you're one of the inmates, I'm thinking."

"Yep."

"Want to talk about it?"

He shook his head. "Nope."

She grinned at him. "You're not getting off that easy."

He groaned. "I was afraid of that."

CHAPTER THIRTY-TWO

Misty Bend, Colorado

SUNLAN WOKE EARLY, as always, and was in the kitchen when Griffin joined her. He wore the same jeans and shirt he'd had on last night. She guessed they were the cleanest of his dirty clothes.

Yesterday they'd shipped the first fourteen horses, and today they'd ship another dozen. Ten would remain on her ranch because the journey would be too hard for them with their wounds or they were too close to foaling.

"Morning." Griffin awkwardly kissed her head.

"Morning." She handed him a cup of coffee. They'd worked together for two days, slept together on the couch wrapped up in the same blanket, and he still didn't seem comfortable around her. He was a man who'd been raised around hard men. A woman in his life was obviously new.

But then, having him in her life was new for Sunlan, too.

Griffin would never be polished like her father, but he wasn't demanding either. He took pride in being honest. He and his brothers had shown up to help when she needed them. They were hardworking ranchers who didn't back down from a fight.

They knew what to do and had the stamina to see the job through.

"We'll load the horses in about an hour." Griffin sat down across from her. "Then I'd like to walk through all the injured stock with the doc."

"I agree. I don't think I can leave if there's more we could have done. Lloyd is good with the animals, but he'll have his hands full with Andy and Dave at your place, at least until my mares settle down."

"Elliot says he'd like to stay here and help out for a few days. Cooper, since he's driving one of the trailers, will be back home tonight, so he can handle things at our place." Griffin stood and refilled his cup. "Elliot says your computer is better than his, and if he can get a friend, Wyatt Johnson, to set up his home connections, he can handle our ranch accounts from here."

Sunlan didn't like the idea of a stranger being on her place, but Elliot was almost family at this point. "He can help the doc, I guess. Kendra cooks meals here for herself and Lloyd anyway, so I'm sure she could feed him, too. It would be no problem for him to stay."

Griffin watched her. He always studied her as if testing the waters. "If it bothers you, he could ride back with Cooper in one of the trailers."

"No. It doesn't bother me," she lied. In truth, she had far more to worry about. "By noon, the last two trailers should be gone, and we'll be flying toward the Krown Ranch. My father's big dinner is in a couple nights."

"I forgot about that. I didn't even bring clothes. In fact, everything I brought is well-worn and smells of smoke. I could tell Cooper to grab my suit when he gets in tonight and drop it in the overnight mail. It might get there in time for the party."

"You're worrying about what you're wearing, Griff? You surprise me."

He laughed. "Clothes don't make the man. I guess I could

pick something up at the nearest store to your home. There is bound to be a Western store or a Walmart near."

"Krown Ranch is not my home. It hasn't been since I was twelve. And the nearest clothing store is over fifty miles away. I doubt they'd have anything that would be appropriate. Live chickens roam their aisles."

He shrugged and dusted off his worn jacket. "Well, how do you like my evening duds?"

"Oh, no. You can't go like that." She shoved a paper napkin over. "Write down your sizes. I'll take care of it."

He didn't look like he believed her. "We could go later in the week. You could tell him you had an emergency and we couldn't leave. Then I could pick up my black suit. It's almost new. I've only worn it to two funerals."

"Write down your sizes. Everything. Every size, including shoes. I have a friend coming from Dallas tonight. I'll call my order in and have her pick it up on her way out of town." She gave in a bit. "If you don't like the clothes, you don't have to wear them. I'll just tell everyone you've got the flu or something."

"Fair enough." He frowned. "Everyone will think you're marrying a sickly man."

Kendra and Lloyd came into the kitchen, and Griffin moved to the chair next to Sunlan. He looped his arm around her shoulder. They were back to pretending to be a loving couple.

While Kendra pulled a breakfast casserole from the oven, Elliot joined them. Everyone seemed to be talking at once. For the first time since the fire, Sunlan had the feeling that everything was going to be all right.

She'd tell her father she was marrying Griffin tomorrow during the party. He wouldn't yell in front of all his friends. He'd probably pout the rest of the night because he hadn't been consulted earlier, but they'd be gone before he sobered up the next morning.

Griffin was probably right. It would work out. They'd handled the fire. Surely they could handle Winston Krown.

Twenty minutes later, she linked her hand in his as they headed out to help with the loading of the remaining horses traveling south to Texas. Griffin's trailers weren't as fancy as hers, but they'd handle the long ride with six horses in each.

The sun broke through the clouds as they loaded the last of the animals. A gray mare bolted when she heard the clank of the gate hit the ground. Panic flashed in her eyes, her ears went back and her front legs rose.

Trying to hold the lead, Sunlan screamed as the damp rope slipped in her hands. It happened so fast, she didn't have time to think, much less react. Wide-eyed, she saw the frightened horse head straight toward her. The only way out for the mare seemed to be through her.

Griffin had been balanced on the trailer gate. When he saw the mare's only route to freedom, he jumped, grabbing Sunlan in midflight. A moment later, the mare raised and kicked, first at the gate and then at them. Griffin turned so that he hit the ground first and cushioned Sunlan's landing. With her cocooned in his arms, they rolled out of danger.

It had all happened in a heartbeat.

Elliot and the doc ran after the animal, but Griffin didn't move. He just held her tight against him. She could feel his rapid breathing. If possible, he seemed even more panicked than she was. But he'd reacted. She'd just stood there.

"You all right?" he asked as he lifted her off him.

She found her footing but couldn't catch her breath. "I think so." She touched her forehead where the gate latch had banged against her as they fell. Blood.

Griffin saw it at the same moment. "You're hurt."

"No. It's only a scratch." She couldn't miss the worry in his stare.

Sunlan was still repeating her words ten minutes later as Doc, Lloyd and Elliot all stood over her arguing.

"We need to take her to the hospital." Lloyd sounded like an overprotective father.

"She's only got a scratch," Doc added for the third time.

"What do you know, Doc?" Elliot shouted. "She's not an animal. I say we slip into some emergency room and get an MD to take a look at it."

Sunlan noticed Griffin hadn't let go of her.

Kendra finally ended the discussion by announcing that it was indeed a scratch, but it would leave a bruise. She gave Sunlan two aspirin and sent her off to pack while the men finished up the loading.

Sunlan felt fully recovered an hour later as she waved goodbye to the two trailers, knowing she wouldn't be seeing her horses for three days. She already missed them. Now, with her horses divided between Colorado and Texas, no matter where she was, she'd still be missing some of them.

By midafternoon, she and Griffin were climbing into the plane. She'd purposely planned the trip so that she'd arrive at Krown Ranch too late to have dinner with her father, if he was even on the property. Lately, he was spending most of his time in town. The ranch, which was run by a foreman, was simply a retreat to Winston Krown.

Sunlan glanced over at her cowboy in the copilot's seat. He'd been so brave saving her life, but now he looked like he might panic and run, just like the mare had.

"Don't worry," she said. "I've been making this journey since I was eighteen, and today, I'm taking no chances with the man who saved my life on board."

"I just pulled you out of the way. I was up higher. I saw the horse's reaction before you did." Griffin seemed to want no part of being a hero. He took a deep breath and closed his eyes. They were in the air before he opened them again.

As they leveled off, she took his hand. "It's going to be all right," she said, grinning at him. "I won't tell anyone you're afraid of flying."

Griffin shrugged. "Everyone pretty much knows it."

CHAPTER THIRTY-THREE

The Johnsons

THE AFTERNOON SUN sliced across the covers, but Wyatt didn't move. He looked around at Jamie's bedroom. When he'd first woken up in it, he'd thought the place dull, boring, nothing special. But now that he knew Jamie, he could see touches of her throughout the room. Calendars tacked behind the door. A whole year of dates sliced between pictures of London and Paris and ten other capitals of the world. Her days off were circled in red. Winter Holiday. Spring Break. A few Mondays off.

He'd bet she'd never been to any of those capitals, but she looked at them every day.

One corner of her room had a pile of quilts stacked with the biggest on the bottom and the smallest on top. A colorful patchwork Christmas tree of almost-heirlooms.

She'd made bookshelves using rough boards and big rocks she must have found by the lake. Shakespeare's plays, classic children's books and romance novels filled the shelves.

He moved his hand lightly over the bedcovers, gliding along the curve of her body. They'd made love in a playful way, with her laughing and him feeling awkward for the first time. It hadn't been that X-rated passionate love scene that he'd thought about, but more a delightful bonding of new lovers.

He'd never had so much fun in bed. For the first time in years, he remembered that he was still young. The army had aged him.

After they'd made love, they'd talked and held each other close. He'd finally drifted to sleep with her head on his shoulder and her warm body pressed against his side.

Wyatt closed his eyes as he relived the moments they'd shared. Funny how it seemed he'd lived a lifetime with her. He drifted into sleep as the real world and his dreams blended.

When he woke to her kissing him, neither said a word. In the silence of late morning, they made love again. This time there was no awkwardness, no hesitance, no playing. There was only a hunger. He saw it in her eyes. In the way she touched him. In the way she made love.

When they were both exhausted, they lay side by side, not touching, as their breathing and their hearts slowed.

"Are you all right?" he asked.

She laughed softly. "I think I went to heaven there for a moment."

He smiled. "Me, too."

Then, without another word, he lay his hand over hers, and she drifted into sleep. As he listened to her slow deep breaths, he kissed her gently so she wouldn't wake and whispered, "I think I'd forgotten how to feel. Thanks for waking me up."

They slept the day away. He figured neither had gotten much sleep the night before; the bedroom door had been between them. That, and a mountain of words that should have been said.

Much later, he shifted, and she cuddled back against his side. Tugging on a strand of her hair, he pressed his lips against her ear. "We have to get up."

"No. I'm asleep."

He tugged again. "Well, I'm starving."

She finally opened one eye. "Food?"

"It's already cooked. I say we raid the refrigerator."

"Sounds like a plan." She grabbed his shirt while he tugged on his trousers, and they ran to the kitchen.

As they ate leftovers at the tiny table, they watched the sun lower near the lake. He grabbed the blanket from the couch, wrapped her in it and carried her out to the hammock so they could watch the sunset.

She was wrapped and warm, resting on his chest as the hammock rocked them gently. For once she didn't talk, and he wondered if she felt like he did. They'd had their one more day.

He didn't want to shatter the perfection.

Finally, when it was dark, they hurried back to the warmth of their blanket on the couch. Neither brought up the dying day or the fact that he had only a part of one day more, if he took a late flight. In two days, he'd be thousands of miles away. Their time would be over with no promise of ever sharing another day.

Wyatt felt like he was already stealing time. He'd never had this kind of peace. This kind of happiness.

There were probably things he should be saying. Maybe tell her how he felt or ask what she was thinking. But for once in his life, all he wanted to do was feel alive. He wanted to memorize every part of her body. He wanted to hold her so close he'd be able to feel her against him for days, maybe months, to come.

He wanted to take her to heaven one more time.

Finally, long after midnight, when the fire had grown low, she stood and took his hand. Silently, they walked to the bedroom, and she pulled him down into the covers.

Logic told him he should slow down. He didn't have the time to make a life with her, and a woman like Jamie deserved a life. A real marriage. Children. Someone to grow old with.

He had none of that to give. Not with the mission he'd already signed on to do as soon as he got back.

But he couldn't leave without letting her know how he felt.

He could give her that much before he vanished. She needed to understand that for a few days she was his world. She was all he needed. All he wanted.

She'd never be just the affair he had one time when he was on leave. She was the one time he'd lived a normal life. He'd had a wife. He'd known peace. He'd loved one woman with all the love he had in him. She'd given him a lifetime in less than two weeks and he had to tell her.

Tomorrow they'd talk about how he felt. Maybe she'd drive him to Lubbock or Wichita Falls. They could spend the night in a hotel, eat out at some fancy restaurant. Then he'd tell her just how much this time had meant to him.

Then...he'd leave.

She'd get over him. She'd go on with her life. And he'd always hold her memory close. The one time his dream of home had come true, if only for a few weeks.

CHAPTER THIRTY-FOUR

Krown Ranch

GRIFFIN WASN'T PREPARED for the view or the size of Krown Ranch. Hell, he could see the huge Krown brand over the main gate from the air. Winston must have truly thought himself a king.

Sunlan circled the plane over the land, showing him the headquarters that looked more like a country club estate than a ranch. Griffin thought he saw golf carts lined up next to the barn, and a swimming pool that should belong to a fancy hotel.

The ranch was farther south than Maverick, so everything still had a hint of green to it.

He stared out the window. "Sunlan, I swear that grass looks mowed."

"It is."

Griffin studied her as if he thought she was kidding. "What kind of idiot mows grass on a cattle ranch?"

"Your future father-in-law."

"Oh." He turned back to the window. "Hope it's not a hereditary defect."

When she began heading down to land the plane, he closed his eyes. She did her best to keep from laughing, but she failed.

Griffin didn't open his eyes, he just growled at her.

The landing was smooth, but he didn't look until she patted him on the leg.

"You all right, cowboy?"

"Yeah, just resting," he lied, deciding he liked flying, after all. It was just the takeoffs and landings that bothered him. "Why'd you learn to fly?"

"My father insisted. If I was going to keep checking up on my grandfather in Colorado, I needed to be able to get there and back when I wanted to. Since I ended up going to school near Granddad, it worked out. He put me in private lessons before I was eighteen and turned a deaf ear to my mother's screaming. I often wondered if he would have pushed me so hard to learn if she hadn't been so against the idea."

When Griffin looked toward the house, he saw a cowhand in one of the golf carts pulling up beside the plane. Griffin was sure she heard him growl again.

Sunlan cut the engine and unbuckled. "Time to meet my father, if he's here. I've known him to be the last person to step into a party."

"Good," was all he said.

They climbed out and walked the half mile to the house. The cowhand followed in the cart with her two bags and Griffin's one backpack full of dirty clothes.

"Is there anything I need to know before I meet the great Winston Krown?"

"No. He'll like you, I think. You're taking his bothersome daughter off his hands. After he finishes complaining that he wasn't clued in to the idea earlier, he'll probably ask you why you're willing to take me on."

"And I'll answer that you're smart and beautiful and fool enough to agree to marry me."

She laughed. "He'll probably have you declared insane. That is not at all how he sees me. My mother told me once that he wanted a boy, and as the years went by and he didn't get one, she claims he resented me more and more. In truth, I never noticed any change. Everything I did, he expected the best."

"Sounds like a hell of a guy."

Her smile didn't reach her eyes. "Now and then he brings some suit home and tells me he thinks of the stranger like a son. I get the feeling he wishes I'd marry the guy just so my father could have him in the family. They're usually lawyers climbing the political ladder."

"You ever tempted?"

"No."

"Why?"

She grinned. "They weren't you, Griffin. I think I've always had in my mind what I'd like in a man. I knew if you lived up to the sisters' bragging about you, you were the one for me."

He knew she was lying, but it felt good to hear anyway.

They reached the house, and Sunlan was greeted by a house-keeper who obviously didn't know her. The middle-aged woman wasn't friendly, but did tell Sunlan to call her Mrs. S. "Your father told me to expect you and a plus one. He also said he wouldn't be able to make it in before tomorrow afternoon."

"That's fine," Sunlan answered politely, showing no emotion. "This is Griffin Holloway. I told my father he was coming so there is no need to refer to him as the plus one."

"I got the library suite ready for you and... Mr. Holloway." Mrs. S. glared at Griffin as if he were a pet Sunlan had brought along. "You do know where it is, Miss Sunlan?"

"I know." She smiled that smile he'd seen before. It had no warmth. "And, Mrs. S., please ask the cook to prepare a tray. We haven't had lunch or dinner. I assume the fridge in the suite is stocked?"

"Of course." Mrs. S. looked bothered. Griffin thought about

borrowing one of the golf carts and driving until he found a Dairy Queen. But this was Sunlan's call. He was only the *plus one*.

While Mrs. S. yelled for the cowhand in the golf cart to set their luggage on the porch, Sunlan whispered to Griffin, "I had so many housekeepers growing up that I started calling them by their number. I think we were on about twenty-three by the time I was in college." She smiled. "They must be working through the alphabet now. The ones my father doesn't run off, my mother fires when she flies by on her broom now and then."

"Did you ever come back here after college?" Griffin followed her down a long hallway lined in Western artwork that looked like it belonged in a gallery somewhere.

"Only for a night now and then. Father wants me here when he's throwing big parties, and sometimes in Austin, if he wants everyone to believe he has a family. I haven't had my own room here in years. He just puts me up in one of the guest rooms, usually the one he calls the library suite. I told him that the one he calls the library was my favorite. I'm surprised he remembers."

They reached a double door, and Sunlan opened the right half. "This is usually my hideout when I visit. Two rooms really, with a small library in between. I used to think he put me here in case my mother dropped by, which she hasn't done lately. She wouldn't want to share even a suite. They're still married. He doesn't want to split his land with her. It's cheaper to simply pay her bills."

Griffin suddenly understood Sunlan a bit better. This arranged marriage of theirs was nothing new to her. For Sunlan, it must seem normal.

She closed the door to their apartment. "I'll take the right bedroom. You can have that one. It's got a nice view. I prefer the view of the barns. I'm afraid we'll have to share a bath."

"All right." Images danced in his brain he'd probably have to scrub out with soap later.

Before he could move away, they heard the doorknob turning. A heartbeat later, she moved into his arms.

An old cowboy carrying their luggage caught them kissing. Just like Sunlan had planned.

"Sorry." Griffin managed to look like he wasn't sorry at all.

The old cowboy smiled. "No, sir, sorry I interrupted. It's good to see Miss Sunlan happy. If she were my girl, I reckon I'd kiss her any chance I got."

She smiled at the cowboy. "How are you doing, Sam?"

"I'm getting by. Arthritis finally took me off of a horse, but I stay busy."

Sunlan faced Griffin. "I'd like you to meet the man who taught me to ride. Griffin Holloway, Sam Fenton."

Griff turned loose of her long enough to shake hands. "Nice to meet you."

A woman, who had to be the cook, bumped her way in with a tray of food. She didn't bother to apologize. She simply waddled into what Sunlan had called the library and set the tray down. "You missed dinner, but this should work. If not, come to the kitchen. I'll be cooking for tomorrow till midnight."

"Thanks," Griffin said. "I'm starving."

The cook looked at him for the first time. "You're welcome, Griffin Holloway. Heard you were coming. My man says you've got a great spread up north."

"He did?" Griffin would have never thought anyone on this ranch would have any idea who he was.

"Yeah, he worked up near there a few summers. You still running wild horses on your ranch?"

"I don't have much choice. They were there before any Holloways were."

Sam joined the conversation with a story about trying to round up mustangs one time in Wyoming.

When the cook got in a word, she added, "Your friend dropped off the clothes, special delivery. Until then, I figured

Miss Sunlan would be bringing a girlfriend. Then I saw the name on the bags. Griffin don't sound much like a girl's name."

"No, ma'am," he answered as if he thought he had to say something.

"The delivery came about an hour ago. I had them pressed so they'd be ready for you, Mr. Holloway." She looked him up and down. "From the looks of it, you're in need of them."

"Thanks, call me Griffin."

"Allie." She smiled at him. "Allie Ray. I'm married to one of the trainers."

Griffin took Sunlan's bags from Sam. "Nice to meet you, Allie. When we drop by to see the horses later, as I know Sunlan will want to do, I'll look your husband up and say hello."

The round little cook smiled. "You do that, and, Griffin, if you need anything just ask. I got a kitchen stocked better than most restaurants."

"Thanks." He nodded at Sam and followed Sunlan to her room as the old cowboy and the cook left.

"Have a nice visit with the staff?" Sunlan asked.

Griffin grinned. "You jealous, Sunshine?" He set her bags by the bed.

Sunlan studied him. "Maybe I am. For all I know, you like older women with an extra hundred or so pounds."

He stretched his hands around her waist. "You guessed it. I might marry you all skinny, but I plan to fatten you up as soon as possible."

For a moment, away from all the responsibilities and pressure, they both seemed to just want to relax and have fun. She put her arms around him and whispered close against his ear, "Kiss me like you did in Mistletoe Canyon."

And he did. One long, delicious kiss that made them both forget the world for a while.

CHAPTER THIRTY-FIVE

Midnight Crossing

JAX WOKE A moment before Charlie pressed his nose into his face and whimpered.

"I heard it, too, Buddy. Someone's out there." He slipped from bed and pulled on his jeans and boots. The good part of living in an isolated place was it made you aware of every sound that didn't belong.

Moving with the dog by his side, Jax made it to the front door without even a creak on the wooden floor.

Mallory was curled up, hugging her pillow, sound asleep in her bed by the fire.

Jax slipped on his coat and picked up the rifle. His computer screen blinked the time: 2:00 a.m. Silently, he and the dog slipped outside. He knew his way without light. They crept to the side of the cabin where shadows laced over one another.

Beyond the shade of the hills, he could see a black car parked almost at the tree line bordering Holloway's land. Whoever was moving around wanted to make sure he didn't announce his arrival.

Charlie whimpered.

"Easy, boy." Jax touched the dog's head. "He's not close yet. Let him come. We'll be ready for him."

Slowly, almost as if the intruder was appearing out of a fog, a man came into view. Tall, thin, an athletic body. He wore black clothes, fitting tight like a professional skier might wear. His head was covered in a black mask. The disguise did the trick; the man moving over O'Grady's rocky land was almost invisible.

Jax saw no weapon, but the stranger carried what looked like a bat. The guy was cocky. He didn't see whomever Mallory was staying with as a threat.

Big mistake.

Forty feet away, the man must have stepped in mud. Jax could hear him cussing. He used the bat to scrape off the mud and moved closer. The light from the fireplace outlined the hospital bed inside the cabin. The predator could see his prey. Another mistake. He wasn't looking around. Casing the place.

Jax waited. The stranger took his time as he headed straight toward the window.

Judging from the moon, Jax guessed fifteen minutes had passed. There was moisture in the air, making the approaching stranger seem to quiver in and out of focus.

Jax felt the weight of the rifle in his hand, but he didn't raise it. One shot would probably frighten the guy off, but Jax wanted to know exactly why he was here.

Twenty feet out.

The stranger was bouncing the handle of the bat in his hand as if impatient to use it. He'd hurt Mallory badly once, but now, while she was weak, he might kill her. Curtis Dayson had come to finish the job he'd started a few weeks ago.

Jax silently widened his stance. He'd never killed anything in his life except a wild hog once. Violence wasn't in his nature. He'd spent his entire adult life trying to help people.

Ten feet.

He could see the intruder's breath now. Heavy in the air. His movements faster. More sure of himself. He still wasn't scanning the area. His focus was on the window. On Mallory sleeping.

Jax swore his fingers began to sweat on the rifle. He needed to act. Ten seconds from now, the intruder would be at the door. It wasn't locked. Curtis could break in and get in his first swing before Jax could reach him.

Five feet.

Jax stood frozen. If he acted too fast, he'd tip his hand. If he waited too long, it might be too late to help.

Three feet.

Out of the corner of Jax's eye, a flash flew from the darkness and bounded off the porch. For a blink, all Jax saw was the whites of canine teeth as a low growl penetrated the silence.

Charlie flew right into the intruder's face, ripping at the mask, tearing it away as he tumbled.

Curtis screamed and swung the bat, knocking the pup to the ground. He raised it one more time. "You're dead, mutt, even if you did lead me right to her."

Just as the bat began to lower, Jax doubled his fists around the barrel of the rifle and swung. A crack of wood sounded. A heartbeat later, Curtis Dayson hit the dirt.

Jax took a deep breath. He'd finally acted. Curtis lay spread-eagled on the ground as if he'd been staked out.

Moving closer, Jax heard the dog whimpering and knew his buddy was all right. Stepping over Curtis, he picked up Mallory's treasured pet and carried him to the light that suddenly spilled from the front door.

Mallory was up. She moved toward him as Jax set Charlie carefully on the porch. "What happened? I couldn't see anything, but I heard noises."

Jax saw her tears as she watched her pet limping toward her.

"I'll tell you all about it in a minute. Get Charlie inside," Jax ordered. "I'll take care of our intruder."

She glanced at the dark shadow of a man on the ground as she helped the dog through the doorway.

"This guy will be all right. He's just resting in the dirt." Jax didn't know if he was telling the truth, but she was upset enough, she didn't need to know that the intruder was her ex-boyfriend.

Jax dragged Curtis a few feet and tied him to one of the porch poles with several rounds of duct tape, then went inside to get a flashlight.

Mallory sat by the fireplace, holding Charlie, talking to him, telling him not to be afraid. The pup was looking up at her with his big brown eyes.

"He okay?"

She nodded. "I think he's just scared."

"Yeah." Jax grinned. The gentle puppy had fought like a wolf, but she'd probably never see him that way.

"I'll only be a few minutes." He grabbed the shoebox he used as his first-aid kit and went back to the porch.

There was a knot on Curtis's head the size of a duck egg and deep bite marks on his cheek. Charlie's teeth had punctured the skin completely through. The guy was spitting and dripping blood from the same hole.

Jax patched it up as best he could.

Curtis was cussing when Jax went inside and emailed Toni, hoping she'd be at her desk at the hospital. Send sheriff and EMT. Emergency.

Toni answered back in seconds. Is Mallory in trouble?

No, but our unwanted visitor needs stitches. Dog bite.

Sending sheriff and Tiny. Ambulance and both EMTs are out working a wreck.

No hurry. Looks like he's only in danger of cussing himself to death.

"It's Curtis out there, isn't it?"

Jax stood and closed the door so Curtis's screams were muffled. Without answering her, Jax moved close to the fire and brushed his hand over Charlie.

Mallory whispered, "I think he just had the wind knocked out of him. I don't feel any broken bones."

Jax checked, too, just to be sure. "He saved our lives tonight. Curtis came to finish killing you."

She hugged Jax.

He hugged her back. "I hate to think what might have happened if the dog had not attacked."

She kissed Jax's cheek. "You would have saved me. I have no doubt."

He nodded. "I would have, even if it meant my life. I couldn't let him hurt you again."

An hour later, the sheriff's cruiser pulled up in front of the cabin. Curtis had dripped blood all over his fancy ski clothes and had practically cussed himself out of a voice.

The sheriff left him tied to the pole while he asked questions. After Tiny unloaded two duffel bags, he went to work bandaging up the suspected intruder. "All are innocent until proven guilty, pal, but to tell the truth, I don't think you've got much of a defense. This ain't a place someone just happens to be walking past and you don't look like you're dressed as company."

Curtis would have a hard time explaining why he was on O'Grady property, in the middle of the night, with a bat in his hand. He tried to claim Jax attacked him, but the sheriff didn't seem to be listening to that theory.

Finally, Curtis mustered enough voice to complain, "You idiots care more about that worthless dog than you do me. I could have frozen to death out here waiting for you two to show up."

"No way," Tiny answered as he cut off the sleeve of Curtis's jacket. "This is high-dollar gear you got on. I've seen the commercials. It'll keep you warm in the Alps." The scissors accidentally slid open the material across Curtis's chest. "Sorry about that, pal. It's too dark out here to see what I'm doing. I just need to check your vitals."

"Cut the tape holding me to this pole, you fat moron."

"Oh, not till the sheriff tells me to. We may not be big-town professionals, but we got an order to this kind of thing." He felt the jacket's material. "This feels like seal skin. Hey, Sheriff, you think this guy killed a seal to get these clothes? That sounds like a crime if you asked me. Endangered species, maybe."

The sheriff was busy getting the facts from Jax, but he yelled back, "I don't know. Take a few samples."

Tiny whacked four inches off the knee and a hunk out of the side of the jacket. "No, on second thought, I think it's some kind of knit."

"We might need blood samples, Tiny," the sheriff added. "Have to make sure we cover every detail."

Tiny cut into the bloody lapel. "Got them."

"You don't need blood samples. I'm right here. I'm the one bleeding on my own clothes." Curtis fought to get free of the tape.

"Right," Tiny said. "You're real smart, mister, but then, I'm not the one tied up in the middle of nowhere with a bite mark on my cheek." He flashed a light in Curtis's eyes. "That's going to leave a scar. And if I was you, I wouldn't eat popcorn in the near future. It'll fall out while you're trying to chew."

Curtis closed his eyes as if he could make the entire night go away.

Sheriff Cline walked out on the porch, still talking to Jax. Mallory stood at the doorway, wrapped in a blanket, with the dog at her side. "Any idea how he found you?"

"Yeah. He tracked the dog. Mallory had Charlie chipped when she bought him. Curtis must have figured it out." Jax moved close to Mallory and put his arm around her. "I'm sorry he found us, but I'm glad no one in Crossroads turned Mallory in for the reward Curtis claimed her family was offering."

"How do you know they didn't ask me to help them find her?" Curtis spat.

"Because they're dead. If you'd talked to Mallory much, you might have learned that."

The sheriff pulled his knife and slashed the tape. Curtis didn't put up a fight as the handcuffs went on.

"I'll take him to the hospital and get him sewed up. Nurse Adams says she wants to have a talk with him, but I don't know, that might fall into cruel and unusual punishment. I'll book him into a cell before I head home for breakfast."

He turned back to Jax. "You did a good job, Jaxson. Some men would have fired and killed him. You got that right in Texas, you know. He was on your property, definite threat."

"I know. But no matter how mad I was, I couldn't do it. I couldn't let him kill Mallory's dog either. So I did what I had to do."

"You're a good man, Jaxson O'Grady. Someday you'll step back into the world and make a difference."

"Someday." He said the word, but there was no promise in it. "Right now, I have to get my guest back to bed and cook the pup some eggs."

Cline walked to his car. Tiny was sitting in the back seat with the prisoner belted in. The orderly took up three-fourths of the seat.

Jax stepped inside the cabin and helped Mallory into her covers. "Try to get some sleep."

She sat up and kissed his cheek. "Thanks. Sometimes I think you're my own private guardian angel."

"Maybe I am. I've been looking for a job." He tucked her in and turned out the light. The fireplace glowed in the room, settling the cabin down into peace again as if nothing had happened in the midnight shadows.

CHAPTER THIRTY-SIX

The Johnsons

WYATT REACHED FOR his cell the second time it rang. Jamie was in the shower, and he'd hoped to go back to sleep before dawn. He grinned. She'd probably wake him when she finished.

She'd woken him twice last night.

"This better be important," he said as he clicked on the phone.

"Captain Johnson, you've got you a flight out of DFW at midnight. That's the latest you can leave and get back in time. The mission you've been waiting for is a go. We need you half a world away ready to move out in forty-eight."

"I'll make the flight." He hung up the phone, his muscles already tightening up for the job he'd have to do. It wouldn't take long—a week, two at the most—but if everything didn't go just right, the exit plan might not work. His job was to follow orders and make sure all his men made it back. No small challenge. The others were younger than Wyatt by ten years or more, but they were like brothers to him. They'd go in as one team and they'd come out the same way.

He didn't want to talk about the flight or going back with

Jamie. She'd only worry, and he never wanted that. He'd told her enough, that she thought he installed listening equipment for a living. Which was true. He just hadn't told her where or that bombs and bullets were usually flying above him while he worked.

He had hours remaining with her. He'd talked his almost-wife into playing hooky for two days. They'd driven to Dallas and done just what he'd hoped to do. They'd spent the day together after checking into the most expensive hotel he could find.

Then they'd made love. Again and again. Man, he loved that part. But he also loved how they had a running conversation that drifted between them. He could never remember just talking to anyone nonstop in his life.

"Who was that?" she asked as she walked out of the bathroom wearing a towel.

"No one. Just a notice that I'll be leaving in—" he glanced at the clock "—eleven hours."

"Oh, what would you like to be third on our to-do list for that time?"

He grinned. "You got items one and two already planned?"

"Well, I have an idea for one." She dropped the towel and took a step toward him. "Two is order breakfast."

He liked the way she thought. "And three," he said as he lifted the covers, "is go shopping. I want to buy stuff you don't need. I want to get clothes other than my army stuff and wear them for one day. I want to buy you gifts." He almost added, *for every birthday and Christmas for the rest of your life*, but he didn't want to think about not being there to open them.

She moved against him. "Let's not count the hours. I couldn't stand to. For today, we'll just be Mr. and Mrs. Johnson on a holiday in Big D."

"I like that idea. We'll come back here and go to bed tonight. I'll leave you sleeping. I think I'd like remembering you that way."

She giggled as if it were only another day, another game they played.

They made love, then slept a few hours before ordering breakfast. Then they got dressed and went to the Galleria. He bought her fancy dresses she'd probably never wear and sweaters to keep her warm and sexy nightgowns.

She talked him into a suit and Western clothes and a leather jacket.

Wyatt wanted to spend money, lots of money, just because it made her smile. The laughter kept them from counting the hours. They walked the mall and watched the people, bought books they'd probably never read, went to a movie. As usual, he fell asleep in the middle of the movie, and she woke him up, laughing. They both knew they were living a lifetime in a day.

At nine, they went back to the hotel and tried on some of the clothes. Then they made a slow tender kind of love that was so beautiful, he felt her tears on his shoulder when they were finished.

"It's all right, baby," he said. "I won't promise you something I can't keep, but I do promise you that I will love you as long as I live. When I die, be it next month or eighty years from now, your face will be the last I see."

She pressed her body the length of his and kissed him.

"Don't wait for me. It wouldn't be fair. You can do a hell of a lot better than me. A soldier's life is hard on the spouses."

"When you come back…" she began, unable to finish.

"If I come back," he corrected. "We'll make plans then. But you got to promise not to wait. Just think about the time we had as a gift. It was the best. Go back to your perfect little house and put up your Christmas tree. Wrap your presents. When you open them, smile and remember that the two weeks I spent with you were the best I've ever lived. What a gift you gave me."

She nodded. "Me, too." She'd talked for two weeks, rattling on about everything, but now when time was so short, she grew silent.

He held her until her breathing slowed, then he slipped from the bed, dressed in his uniform and walked away. He left the clothes and boots and books he'd bought. There was no room for them where he was headed.

Four hours later, he was on a plane, flying across the ocean. He should have been thinking about the mission that he'd known was coming for weeks, but his mind was still full of her.

He couldn't even whisper *when this is over, I'll come back* to her. If something happened to him, he didn't want her remembering broken promises.

This mission was the one he'd always feared. The odds weren't in his favor. Staring out at the dark ocean, he'd decided this one would be his last. He'd walk away from the army when it was over or die in a hailstorm of bullets. Either way, he'd see Jamie's face when it ended.

CHAPTER THIRTY-SEVEN

Krown Ranch

GRIFFIN HAD EATEN half the snacks on the library table while waiting for Sunlan to come out of her bedroom. He thought the library area strange, nestled between two bedrooms, and then he realized all the books were about horses. The history, the breeding of horses, even art books of horses.

He might have found them interesting, but Griffin couldn't keep his mind off Sunlan.

After they'd kissed, neither seemed as tired as they'd been when they arrived. He worried that kissing his future wife could become an addiction. But then she pulled away, and he knew he'd probably become an addict without a supplier.

Sunlan seemed nervous in her not-so-homey home. She'd talked him into a moonlit ride over land that looked like a movie set. He might have enjoyed it more if he hadn't felt like they were being followed and watched as they circled the property. When they made it back to the barn, he was glad the ride was over.

As he had with Sam and Allie, Griffin took time to introduce himself to everyone he met. He was comfortable with working ranch people—he was one of them. But he had no idea how he'd relate to Sunlan's father and his crowd. Gentlemen ranchers weren't his type. When he'd been a kid, he'd once heard his dad say that a rancher without shit on his boots isn't worth his weight in hay.

But for tonight anyway, thanks to Sunlan, he did look proper in his new clothes. He'd been surprised how everything she ordered for him fit perfectly. The jeans weren't Wranglers, but they would do. The shirt had a hint of being Western and so did the jacket. She'd even ordered a belt and boots that were comfortable without him having to spend a few weeks breaking them in.

To his shock, she also ordered him underwear and socks. Again, not the kind he wore. They weren't white, but they'd do. Once she was out of their shared bathroom, he planned to shower and call it a night. The day had seemed endless.

He'd just finished pulling off his jacket when she finally walked out of her side of their apartment.

Sunlan was freshly showered, her hair still damp. She wore silk pajamas with slippers that matched. It crossed his mind that he was glad she had her own money; otherwise, he wasn't sure he could even afford to keep her in shoes.

"Did you open the wine?"

He did his best not to stare at the way the soft fabric clung to her body…all over. "I did. I wanted to let it breathe, but I think it's coughing."

"Very funny." She reached for a glass. "Aren't you drinking?"

"I've tried wine. Never developed the taste for it. By the time I was old enough to drink, I had a sick mother and two brothers to take care of. When Dad had his stroke, I felt like I needed to hang on to all the brain cells I had to keep up."

She sat down on one of the overstuffed chairs and folded her long legs in the seat, then unfolded them, as if nervous. "Griffin, don't tell me you've never been wild and drunk."

He took the matching chair and stretched his legs, touching

her fuzzy slippers with his boot. "I meant to. It was on my list. I order all kinds of drinks at hotel bars when I get away to the stock shows. I even drove to Lubbock once just to find myself a wild time."

"How'd that work out?"

"I went to a rodeo, ate half a dozen corn dogs, drank about as many beers, threw up in the parking lot, slept in my pickup, then drove home the next morning with my head feeling like a bull was sitting on it."

"You're a wild man, Griffin Holloway. Maybe I should marry you just to calm you down."

"I'd appreciate that." He studied her. "How about you, Sunshine? What's your wildest time? Tell me the craziest thing you've ever done."

She grinned. "When I was in boarding school, we used to sneak out and drink the beers the horse trainer hid in his old fridge in the barn."

"Who is *we*?"

"Girlfriends. All-girls school. Another fight my parents had. Father won. I didn't even kiss a boy until I got to college."

Griffin liked this casual private talk. He bumped her shoe again, and she smiled.

"Your turn," she said. "First kiss."

He shrugged. "That's easy. My second cousin. I was fourteen and she was fifteen. She took me up to the attic of our great-aunt's house to look for old pictures. I thought she knew all about sex because she wore lipstick, so I started asking a few questions. She wouldn't kiss me until I dropped my jeans and showed her what I had. I figured it was the price of admission."

Sunlan giggled. "And what did she do?"

"She showed me her chest. Wasn't much to see. Then she kissed me several times, explained the different kinds of kisses and where I was supposed to put my hands. It took me two years to even try to kiss another girl. I thought kissing might always come with a lecture."

Sunlan stood and poured out her wine, then replaced it with root beer. "I forgot. No wine. Not even at this house."

He clicked his glass with hers and smiled. "We'll save a bottle to have after the baby's born. Deal?"

"Deal."

She sipped her root beer. "You're a fascinating man. I'm surprised you learned to kiss so well."

"I didn't know I did."

"You do. Otherwise our first kiss would have been our last."

"So it's on the table as something we might do routinely when we're around each other? Not just when others are watching?"

She shrugged. "I guess. I wouldn't mind, as long as we keep it friendly."

He had no idea what she meant. He was friendly with the Franklin sisters, but he didn't want to kiss them the way he kissed Sunlan. Hell, he felt like he needed to go back to his second cousin and ask a few more questions. Only she was married, living in Tulsa, Oklahoma, with her fat husband and six chubby kids.

Sunlan sat on the arm of his chair. "What's the dumbest thing you've ever done, Griff?"

"I lied to the sheriff once. He caught me speeding in my dad's car. I wasn't even racing anyone, I was just seeing how fast I could go. I knew he'd tracked me. I was the only one on the road, so I couldn't claim he had me mixed up with another car. But I lied when he pulled me over. Swore I wasn't going fast. Got all mad that the sheriff even thought I would do such a thing. Called a good man a liar to his face. Said his radar gun must be broken."

"What did the sheriff do?" She leaned back and propped her arm on Griffin's shoulder.

"He took me home, banged on the door loud enough to wake

up my dad, then looked at me and told me to tell the truth. He said a stupid lie rots inside a man. After a few too many, a liar starts to smell. From then on, he's not a man anyone would trust. I saw his point. That night, I figured it was time for me to step up and be a man. An honest man. I told my dad the truth." Griffin put his hand on her knee. "What about you? The dumbest thing you ever did."

She was stone still, his frozen lady. He wasn't sure she'd answer, but he waited.

Finally, she started in a low voice, barely above breathing. "I went to an art gallery opening in Austin just as the leaves began to turn to fall colors. Several of my friends from college were showing their work at a little gallery downtown by the UT campus. The show wasn't big, but it was exciting, and I probably drank too much. My father had been furious with me over something that day and as always, stormed off yelling. I wouldn't even agree to meet another one of his picks for son-in-law. I wouldn't let him help with the running of Misty Bend. Who knows? I don't remember."

Griffin studied her, knowing what she was telling him now was important. He listened as she continued.

"When I left the gallery, I decided to walk along Sixth Street. I always love strolling past the clubs and bars with their windows and doors open and music playing from every establishment. It was a beautiful night, but I remember my mood was so dark. I saw all the couples and for once felt very alone.

"I finally reached the hotel and went straight to the bar. One more drink and I'd be able to get my father's voice out of my head. Two more drinks and I wouldn't feel so lonely. Three or four drinks later, I was talking to some guy from New York. You know the type—thousand-dollar suit, perfect hair, vocabulary he liked to flaunt."

Griffin really didn't know the type, but he didn't interrupt her.

"He walked me to my room, came in just to see that I was

all right. I wasn't that drunk. I knew nothing about the evening felt right, but I just didn't care. For a slick guy, he was a bumbling idiot in bed. I wasn't even turned on. He couldn't leave fast enough. Telling me he had a plane to catch. Saying we'd have to get together again, but he couldn't even remember my name. As he rushed out the door, he said, 'I'll call you, Sarah.'"

"And?" Griffin took her empty glass.

"And six weeks later, I realized I was pregnant and the last thing I wanted was that jerk to be my baby's father." She curled into his lap. "It hurts so bad to think how dumb I was, but I want my baby."

Griffin held her. "Our baby," he whispered against her hair.

"Our baby," she echoed.

"No one will ever hurt you again." He brushed the bruise on her forehead. "Except maybe runaway horses."

She managed a slight smile. "'Our baby' sounds so good, Griff. He, or she, will be a Holloway. An old Texas family."

"If you don't ever talk about that night in Austin again, I'll never mention it. I'm your baby's father. We're going to let one lie become our truth for a good reason."

She cupped his face with her hands. "I agree." She ruffled his windblown hair. "You are one good-looking man, Griffin."

"Sure. Everyone, including me, wonders how I found such a woman and how she could possibly agree to marry me. I may not be polished, but I'm thinking I'm very lucky."

She kissed his lips, featherlight. "And I'll tell them I knew from the first time I saw you that you were the perfect man for me."

They stood. They'd said all that needed to be said. Somehow in the fire and the flight and the silence of the evening they'd settled into a harmony together.

As Griffin turned toward his room, she took his hand. "Griff, would you hold me while I sleep? Just sleep like we did on the couch. I liked that. I always feel so alone in this house."

He didn't answer. He just changed directions.

They climbed into bed and he folded her in his arms. Without another word, they both fell asleep. Whatever came tomorrow, they'd face it together.

CHAPTER THIRTY-EIGHT

Krown Ranch

GRIFFIN WOKE AT dawn and slipped from Sunlan's bed. He'd checked half a dozen times during the night just to see if she was still there. The thought of truly sleeping with her had worn a rut in his brain. But he hadn't done more than hold her all night long. Somehow, after what they'd shared last night, holding her was enough.

As he looked down at her, he couldn't help but feel like he knew her better than anyone in her world. She wasn't easy to be around sometimes. Hell, she wasn't even friendly at times, and she was marrying him.

She was complicated, often frightened, bossy and a little broken. And, he added to himself, sexy as hell with her sunshine hair spread across the pillow.

He walked to the bathroom, pulling off the clothes he'd slept in as he moved. He needed a long hot shower and three or four cups of coffee before he faced what promised to be an interesting day.

Twenty minutes later, when he'd dried off and shaved, he

opened the bathroom door that led to his room. The half dozen outfits she'd bought him were still on his bed.

So was Sam. The old cowboy was sitting leaned back against the headboard, sound asleep. Hell, he'd probably been there all night.

Griffin pulled on underwear and a pair of slacks far too dressy to ever work in before he poked the old guy.

Sam came awake a muscle at a time, crackling like old newspaper as he unfolded. "Morning, Griffin."

"Did you sleep here?" Griffin asked. This was his bed, but Griffin hadn't used it last night. Not that it was any business of the old cowboy's.

"Nope. And neither did you."

Griffin ignored the comment.

The aging cowhand tried again. "I just thought I'd come in to tell you that if you hurt Sunlan, you'll answer to me. I may be shaky, but I can go a few rounds with the best of them. Me and the boys in the barn decided we'd better tell you how we felt about Sunlan. She grew up out in that barn. We all think of her as our kin."

Griffin relaxed. "I'm not going to hurt Sunlan. I'm going to marry her. We're here to tell her father tonight."

Sam grinned. "I'm glad to hear that. I was thinking I might have to hit you a few times to make my point."

"Well, don't tell anyone we're engaged. Krown probably thinks he should be one of the first to know."

Sam crossed his bony chest. "I swear, but maybe you should mess up these covers or the whole place will know you're sleeping together."

"I'll do that, but I don't care if they know I love her. That's how folks feel who get married. Now get out of here so I can finish getting dressed. I'll meet you in the kitchen for coffee. I've got a few questions."

"Will do. But you should know the guests and family take

breakfast in the dining room. They don't meet in the kitchen for breakfast like regular folks do."

"I said the kitchen. Coffee."

"I heard you."

Griffin turned to grab a shirt. When he glanced back, the cowboy was gone. Maybe Sam was the headquarters' ghost.

An hour later, Griffin looked up from a breakfast nook big enough to serve a dozen and saw Sunlan walk in. She was dressed in dusty green all the way down to her boots.

Griffin decided he'd better Google substitutes for *beautiful* or he'd wear out the word.

Before he could tell her all the interesting stories he'd heard about her growing up around horses, she was pulling him away from the small crowd surrounding him. Apparently, she had plans.

The cowhands made fun of him for tagging along. He just grinned.

For the next four hours, they visited with people arriving for the party, looked at pictures of all her ancestors and had tea with two of her great-aunts.

Just about the time Griffin was thinking of taking a nap, Sunlan informed him—calmly, without emotion—that they had to go to the airport, fifty miles away, to pick up her mother.

WHEN THEY ARRIVED, Griffin wasn't sure what he'd expected, but Sunlan's mother could have passed for her sister. She didn't look a day over thirty-five and had the same long slim body as Sunlan. Her hair was darker, but highlights made it shine. Her face looked like it had been polished to glass.

When her mother went to freshen up before the fifty-mile drive back to the ranch, Griffin whispered, "How old was your mother when she had you?"

"Twenty-six."

"But?"

"She's over fifty now, but never mention it."

Griffin spent the drive back trying not to stare. Marian Krown wore more makeup than most, he guessed, but she was still stunning. As the miles ticked by, he noticed something strange. Marian only talked about herself. Her health. The appointments she was missing to make this journey. The new diet she'd discovered. How much she loved yoga. How there was no good shopping in Dallas this season. Who she'd met lately. How someone had sworn there was no way she was old enough to have a grown daughter and that Sunlan must be adopted.

This mother, who hadn't seen her daughter in months and hadn't visited Texas in over a year, didn't ask a single question about Sunlan.

Sunlan drove ten miles over the speed limit and didn't say a word.

When they pulled up, it was almost dark, almost time for the party to begin. People were already filling the huge front rooms of the house decorated with crystal Christmas trees hanging from the ceiling.

Marian hurried off after her dozen bags, claiming she didn't have enough time to get dressed.

Griffin looped his arm over Sunlan's stiff shoulders. "She's nothing like you, Sunshine."

Sunlan managed a smile. "You're right. She's not. My father made sure of that."

An hour later, Griffin finally faced Sunlan's father. The Great Winston Krown. He wasn't what Griffin had expected, but he was the opposite of his wife. If they'd been about the same age when they married, the gap seemed to have widened. Winston looked sixty or more. Dark circles and wrinkles on a face that once might have been handsome.

"So, you are my daughter's friend?" Winston opened the real conversation after he'd welcomed Griffin and they'd talked about the weather.

Griffin figured he might as well lead with the truth. "I'm more than that, sir. I plan to marry her."

Winston's stone face blinked shock. "Does my daughter know about this?"

"She does. I wouldn't be standing here if she had any objections."

Sunlan's father puffed up a bit like a horned toad. "You get right to the point. You didn't wait for her to wander over and soften the blow."

"This is between you and me. I love your daughter. I'd like your blessing, but I'm not a child and neither is she. We don't need your permission. I've got a ranch—"

"I know about your ranch. One of the oldest in Texas. Struggling like most these days, but good land."

"We'll hang on." Griffin met Winston's stare. "We always have."

Winston nodded once. "Your great-great-grandfather built it when the fort line didn't even reach that far north. From what I've dug up since yesterday, there is not a single skeleton in any Holloway's closet. You're the kind of man who could run for office and win."

"I not interested in running for office. I just want to run my ranch and marry your daughter. The wedding will be right before Christmas. You're welcome to give her away."

Winston stared at him with the same light blue eyes as Sunlan's. "I could make this hard on you, son."

"You could. But that won't change a thing. I'm marrying Sunlan." Griffin knew he was coming on strong, but he didn't think a man like Krown would want it any other way.

Winston watched his daughter heading toward him. "She tell you I was hard on her when she was growing up?"

"She did."

"You plan to be?"

"No. I don't ever plan to try to make her do a single thing

she doesn't want to do. We'll be partners. I'm not a manipulator or a bully. She's a strong woman. She knows her own mind."

Winston smiled. "I know. That's why I was so hard on her."

Griffin looked over Winston's shoulder, and something dawned on him as he saw Marian come gliding across the room like the ball's only princess. Winston didn't want his child to grow up to be her mother. That's why he fostered her love for horses, sent her away to school, bought a library of books she'd love, let her fly at eighteen.

"Winnie," Marian shouted. "You must turn loose of Sunlan's handsome friend so he can dance with me. I simply have to dance in this dress. It almost floats."

Winston bowed slightly to his wife. "There is no music playing, dear. And don't call me Winnie."

Marian seemed confused for a moment. Apparently, she hadn't noticed music wasn't playing.

Sunlan stepped near and laced her fingers into Griffin's, and he pulled her close.

Winston turned away from his wife and faced his daughter. "I understand you had a fire at that worthless little place of yours in Colorado."

"What? No one told me," Marian said, but no one seemed to be listening to her. "Let the place burn, who cares."

Griffin felt Sunlan stiffen as she faced her father. "We did. I lost ten head."

"If she hadn't fought so hard, she might have lost more," Griffin added.

"You were there?" Winston raised an eyebrow.

"I was. My brothers and I flew up as soon as we heard. The barn was still burning when we arrived. Most of her herd was transported to one of our barns on Maverick Ranch, but others will take time to heal. She's got a great foreman there and my brother's staying over a few days to help out."

Winston looked impressed. "You have any idea what it'll cost to rebuild?" Marian looked bored.

"A great deal," Sunlan answered simply. "But I had insurance and with Griffin's barns, I won't have to worry about the horses."

Winston stared hard at Griffin, then glanced down to where his daughter's fingers were laced in Griffin's hand. When he looked up, he asked, "You two got it handled?"

"We do," Sunlan answered with a slight smile.

"Excuse me," Winston said as he stepped past them. "I have to make a few announcements."

"Oh, dear God, who is running for office now?" Marian pouted. "If it's not horses, it's politics. I come home every few years and the same conversations are going on."

Griffin held Sunlan close as they followed her father. He really wasn't all that interested in Winston's announcement, but he wanted to put as much distance between them and Marian as possible. The woman might be pretty, but every time she talked, she revealed inner ugliness. She was like the Wicked Witch's twin sister.

"Ladies and gentlemen." Winston stood three steps up on the grand stairs. "Before we begin the annual Krown Christmas party, I have a very important announcement to make."

The crowd grew silent.

"I've just been informed that my daughter has agreed to marry Griffin Holloway, who comes from an old Texas ranching family. I am very honored to welcome him into my family tonight, but I don't think I'll be able to give her away without a few tears."

Griffin glanced at Sunlan. She looked to be in shock. So did her mother, as people pushed past Marian to hug Sunlan.

"Sorry, I told him before you were there," he whispered in her ear. To his surprise, she rolled into his arms and hugged him so tightly around the neck he wasn't sure if she was happy or trying to choke him to death.

Finally, she pulled far enough away to kiss him, and people cheered.

"I told you he'd like you," she whispered.

"He likes me, Sunshine, but in his gruff way, he loves you."

There was no time to talk. They had a few dozen people who wanted to pat them on the back and ask questions.

Hours later, when all the guests had either left or gone to their rooms, Griffin lay on his bed, thinking about the night. It hadn't been all that hard to figure out that Winston's spies were everywhere. Old Sam had probably been taking his measure since he'd stepped on the ranch. Even the housekeeper was in on the game.

The only clueless one in the room was probably Marian. Griffin had a feeling at least some of what she'd told Sunlan about her father over the years were lies. A man couldn't run an operation this big and carry weight in politics and be a fool.

Sunlan's mother tried to get her to change the day to sometime in January, then finally gave up and said she'd try to make it, but that a place called Crossroads was not on her travel list.

Sunlan spent the rest of the evening close to Griffin's side. Marian passed her time circulating. Griffin had to wonder if Marian and Winston ever talked. No matter how rich you were, it'd be a hard life married to someone you didn't like.

A tap sounded at his door.

Before he had time to say anything, Sunlan slipped in. She was wearing red silk pajamas tonight, with red shoes to match. The way she moved in them now would definitely keep him awake tonight.

"Can I sleep with you tonight? Just sleep."

"Sure, but I should warn you, Sam comes in before dawn and perches on my headboard like an anemic vulture."

Sunlan climbed under the covers. "I can't believe it went so well tonight. My father even talked to me a few minutes ago about sending a few breeding horses to Misty Bend to replace the ones I lost."

"What'd you say?"

She was halfway under the covers, trying to pull off her slippers. "I said no, thank you. I couldn't believe he offered. First interest he's even shown in the place." One slipper flew across the room and thumped against the door.

He propped his head up with his arm and watched her. "Just out of curiosity, what do you and your mother do when you're together?"

"She usually calls and we meet somewhere a few times a year. You know, New York, LA, Paris. She's very busy, so we're usually only together a day or two. We go to parties or luncheons, sometimes a style show or a play. But when she visits the States, we shop."

"You like to shop?"

"Not really, but it beats sitting and talking to her."

He saw her point. The other slipper followed its mate and tapped against the door.

"You know, Sunshine, I don't want to just sleep with you, but that is exactly what we're going to do tonight."

"All right, but why are you announcing this?"

He smiled. "Because I want to do this right. I want to get to know you. Maybe fall in love like normal people do. We're going to make love because we can't even breathe if we don't, not simply because you want someone to cuddle up with."

"We'll talk about it in the morning on the way home."

He grinned again. "On the way home." He liked the sound of that.

The next afternoon, her father drove them to the plane and hugged his daughter goodbye. Neither said much. Griffin decided the little they had said was enough. Winston would be at their wedding in Crossroads.

Sunlan talked about her plans to rebuild at Misty Bend and Griffin tried to sleep.

When they landed at Maverick Ranch near dusk and drove around the white barn, Griffin caught sight of his headquarters. For a moment, he thought he was at the wrong house. No, the place was right but the year was wrong. His headquarters glittered in the night almost like he remembered it had at Christmas when he was a kid.

Huge evergreen wreaths hung from every window. Mistletoe twirled in big balls from the center of each circle of green. Red ribbons danced in the breeze below the windows and a string of white lights ran the roofline.

"You decorated," he said as he saw a twelve-foot tree in the great room shining through the windows.

"It's time, Griff. I found several boxes of ornaments going back generations. They'd been carefully stored in a closet that looked like it hadn't been opened in twenty years," she said. "It's time the Holloways celebrated the holidays again. I had Cooper and the boys help hang them. They had to find a tree big enough to hold all the generations. I hope your dad won't mind if they took one of his trees from Mistletoe Canyon."

"I'll plant another dozen come spring. If he glances down from heaven, he'll like watching them grow."

They stepped out of the ATV and walked up the steps. She hugged his arm and he thought about how much he liked the simple gesture.

"Do you mind, Griff?"

"No. I said you could decorate the house any way you wanted. I just didn't know that what you did would look so right. We got to do this every year. Our kids are going to love this."

"Our kids?"

"Sure."

As they stepped inside and stopped beneath a mistletoe ball, he paused and kissed her. When he pulled away, he smiled. "I could get used to doing that."

"Good." She laughed. "There's mistletoe hanging in every room."

CHAPTER THIRTY-NINE

Midnight Crossing

MALLORY STAYED WITH Jax for almost a week after Curtis had tried to get to her. Though the sheriff fought to keep him in jail, Curtis brought in lawyers from Dallas. It took a week, but he bonded out.

He'd told several people in Crossroads that his lawyers assured him he'd never serve any more time than the week. After all, it was just a lovers' quarrel. His word against hers. The bruises might have been from the wreck. Curtis even claimed he'd gone to the O'Grady cabin to win her back and he'd taken the bat along because her dog was vicious.

When Tim drove out to Midnight Crossing to tell her Curtis was out, Mallory didn't bother to ask questions. Now he wasn't just mad at her; Curtis would also come after Jax for helping her. She knew what she had to do.

"The guy is even threatening to sue the county for wrongful arrest, but that'll go nowhere." Tim, as always, loved being part of the team at the sheriff's office. "You might want to get that old .30-30's stock fixed, Jax. You might need to use it as a club again."

"I have another idea." Mallory looked directly at Jax. "I've decided I am going to call my old roommate in Galveston. I haven't talked to her in a few years, but when we were close, she was always inviting me to come down and stay with her. If I could borrow Tim's phone, I could call her. Maybe the offer is still open."

Jax was silent, but he nodded once. They both knew she'd be safer somewhere else.

Tim agreed. He even offered to take Charlie into the vet to get the chip removed. "The sooner we get you away, the better."

While Jax and Tim moved onto the porch to plan how they'd get her out of town unseen, she called her college roommate and took her up on the longstanding offer to visit Galveston.

Jax came back inside alone. "We've got a cousin in Plainview who said he'd rent you a car and then lose the paperwork. You can drive it to the coast. My cousin's sons go to Sam Houston State in Huntsville. It's not far from Galveston, so they'll drive down and pick the car up next week when the semester is over and they're heading home for Christmas. Their dad said they could probably use the extra trunk space for hauling dirty laundry anyway."

"You have cousins everywhere?"

"Pretty much."

He joined her in the small kitchen, where she was starting supper. As soon as she'd been able, she'd taken over cooking the evening meal. Told him it was the only way she'd survive.

Jax leaned against the counter and watched her work. "I still don't know about you driving so far. It's all the way across Texas."

"I'll be fine. If I get tired, I'll pull over at a motel where I can pay cash." She put her hands on his shoulders. "I'm okay, Jax. You took good care of me. Saved my life when I needed a friend. But at twenty-seven, it's time I grew up. Opened my eyes. I've got a degree in business. I can start over."

There were still shadows of bruises on her face, but the hard cast on her arm had been replaced by a brace that she could remove when she showered. She was healing, mentally as well as physically.

Saying goodbye to Jax was hard. He'd touched her body and heart. He'd held her when she was hurting. He'd seen all her scars, inside and out, and never judged her. He'd saved Charlie's life. "Jaxson, you do know that you're my hero?"

He shook his head. "I should have shot the guy. Now you'll be looking over your shoulder."

"Not for long. Curtis will forget about me. And I'm glad you didn't shoot him. He wasn't worth it. There's a kindness in you. I'd hate to see you lose that."

He touched her hair. "Midnight curls," he said, more to himself than her, she thought. "You taught me a great deal, Mallory. I don't know if I'll ever step back into the world, but I've been asked to present a paper on fire investigations next mouth. I thought I might leave the day you do and check out Seattle for a while before the conference."

She nodded. "The town will think we left together. That's how you're planning it, isn't it?" He was still thinking about protecting her. Curtis wouldn't know where she'd gone, and he'd think she had Jax with her. Two reasons keeping Curtis from trying to find her. She felt like she was building a wall around herself and Jax was helping.

"We'll keep in touch." She hugged him. "I don't want to lose you."

"We'll keep in touch," he echoed but didn't hold on as hard as she did.

Two days later, as she stood ready to drive away, she whispered, "You know I love you, Jax. We both do." She patted

Charlie's head. "I think I have since that morning you carried me back into the hospital and said I'd be safe with you."

"I know. I love you, too. It was good having you both here. I felt I was helping out for a change. Doing something good."

"Any chance you'd come to see me after you get back from Seattle?"

He shook his head. "I'm the county hermit, remember? But I won't forget you, not ever. A few times in life, someone comes along that changes the shape of your heart. You did that for me. I'll always remember you."

She kissed his cheek. "I'm not giving up on you, Jaxson O'Grady. One day I'll walk out of my office building in a big city and there you'll be waiting to take me on a date."

"I'm too old for you."

"Nine years isn't so much."

"It's a lifetime, kid."

"I'll still watch for you. Think about it. You take me on a date. I might cook you breakfast for a change."

He laughed. "That'd be a switch."

She climbed into the car Tim's cousin had rented her. While Jax strapped Charlie in his riding seat, she added, "I'll send you a note now and then. I've got enough savings to buy what I need and get an apartment when I settle somewhere. I'll let you know when I take a job. My friend says she's already got some possibilities lined up."

Jax didn't know how to say goodbye. He simply nodded and waved as she drove away.

As she disappeared, Tim stepped off the porch and joined him. "Why didn't you tell her you loved her like you meant it? You said it like friends say they love each other."

"She can do better than me."

"Yeah, like the guy who hit her?"

"She's broken. She needs time to heal. I'd just be in the way."

"Right, Jax. What are you planning to do while she's heal-ing?"

Jax looked at his redheaded cousin. "I think I should go to town and get a haircut. Then you can drive me to the airport."

Tim raised his eyebrow. "You've already packed your bags?"

"I won't need a suitcase until I buy clothes. I've got a month in Seattle to do that."

"You got your speech ready?"

"I got time."

"What about talking to a crowd? That doesn't seem much like your style."

"I'm thinking I'll show slides. That way it will be dark and I won't see the audience. It'll be like talking to myself. I've been doing that for two years. When I finish at the conference, I thought I might buy a car and drive back. Take some time to see the country."

Tim shrugged. "Sounds like something to do while you're putting off going after Mallory."

Jax reached inside the cabin and grabbed his computer. "I'm not putting it off. I told her I'd think about it. Someday."

Tim looked confused. "Let me get this straight, Jax. You're going the opposite direction while you're thinking about it. You're not taking any clothes, but you are taking a laptop."

"I've got to stay in touch with you and Mallory."

"A phone might be easier."

Jax shook his head. "This works. It's got all my research in it for the talk, as well."

They walked out to Tim's truck. "You know, Jax, you are far more complicated than I thought you were. No wonder Mallory was crazy about you. She likes puzzles."

As usual, Jax didn't comment on Tim's rambling.

"Promise me one thing. In one year, if Mallory hasn't written to tell us she's found someone, you'll go wherever she is and at least have that one date."

Jax stepped into the truck without answering, but he knew Tim didn't miss the slight smile he couldn't hide.

CHAPTER FORTY

Maverick Ranch

WHEN THEY ARRIVED HOME, Griffin and Sunlan had stepped right into chaos. With the wedding to plan, paperwork to be done, Sunlan flying back and forth to check on her wounded horses, there was little time to talk.

They talked on the phone for a few minutes every night. She'd ask his advice on what to do at Misty Bend and then, as likely as not, she'd argue with him.

When she was home at his ranch, she'd slip into his room after the house was quiet and curl up beside him. She'd be gone before dawn, but Griffin had got used to holding her and, when he knew she was asleep, he'd whisper how he loved her.

About the time things calmed the week before the wedding, her mother appeared. Griffin was tempted to dart outside to see where she left her broom. The first day, both his brothers just stared at the beautiful woman. The second day, they avoided her.

Having Marian in residence was like having a circus move in. She invited people she barely knew over and talked to them as if they were old friends. She flirted with Elliot and Cooper as if

she were their age. Both his brothers were polite and always remembered to call her ma'am, which irritated her into wrinkles.

After two nights with her on the ranch, Sunlan moved to the
bed-and-breakfast and took her mother with her. Griffin missed
Sunlan, but he had a feeling she'd made the move to save all
three Holloway men.

The Franklin sisters loved Marian and treated her like a queen.
Marian loved the attention and the sisters were her adoring audience.

No one on the ranch mentioned Marian. It was almost like
each one feared if they said her name, she might reappear. The
three brothers had a ranch to run, with double the normal crew
of cowhands and a thousand wedding details to check off the
Franklin sisters' list.

A few inches of snow fell on the morning of the wedding,
making the world white and perfect. At dawn, Griffin stood
beside the preacher and watched Winston walk his daughter
down the stairs for their rehearsal. She was all in white and had
never looked so beautiful.

He thought about how they'd started, both wanting to solve
their own problems by getting married. Neither giving much
thought to the other's feelings. Somehow, in just over a month's
time, everything had changed. First, he'd respected her. Next,
he'd understood her. Then slowly, he'd grown to love her.

As he watched her coming closer, he realized something more.
He cared about Sunlan so deeply he would give up his ranch
for her. The most important thing in his world didn't matter if
she wasn't by his side.

She met his gaze and smiled. There was no one else in the
room as far as he was concerned. She hadn't said a word, but he
knew she felt the same way. They'd each found their mate on a
road neither had expected.

Marian stood beside Cooper and watched them practice. "It's

bad luck for the bride to see the groom before the service. Winston should have come in last night and done this."

Cooper whispered back, "You're right, it could be bad luck. Something terrible might happen. Something like the mother-of-the-bride might disappear in this snowstorm and no matter how hard we searched, we'd never find her."

Marian looked out the window. "What snowstorm? We've only got two inches."

"We can always hope for more."

Griffin grinned and tried his best to ignore Cooper. All he wanted to think about today was Sunlan. That first day in the café, he'd thought this day might never come. It seemed they'd already lived a lifetime together in a month. All he wanted for Christmas was her.

CHAPTER FORTY-ONE

Franklin Inn

JAMIE HAD NO idea why she'd been invited to Griffin and Sunlan's wedding. She barely knew the couple. Wyatt and the Holloway boys had become friends while Wyatt was in town, but that had been a few weeks ago. The last week Wyatt had stayed with her, while she was in school, he'd driven over and done everything from digging fence posts to fixing computer problems at the Holloways' place.

They asked about her husband when they saw her in town. Jamie always said he was fine, even though she had only heard from him once. The day after she'd returned from taking Wyatt to catch his flight, she'd gone back to teaching and found three dozen red roses on her desk. The card simply read, *I'll remember.*

He hadn't promised he'd return, but he'd mentioned it once. They hadn't had enough time to talk about the future. They'd just lived and loved. And made memories.

He wouldn't talk about his mission, but she sometimes saw the worry in his eyes. Dark thoughts shadowed even his smile.

That last day, she'd known Wyatt must have thought he was

somehow saving her future pain by not talking about the some-days they might share. He didn't want her imagining all the could-bes. If something did happen to him, he must have not wanted her to have to mourn the might-have-beens.

Only he hadn't known that her imagination was already working. In her heart, she really was married to him and not talking about it didn't make it less real.

Tonight, she'd worn one of the fancy dresses he'd bought her in Dallas. He'd told her she looked like an angel in it. She'd seen her own beauty in his eyes that last day when she'd mod-eled the dress just for him.

Part of her didn't want to go to a wedding. She just wanted to be alone in her little house. But Griffin had called saying that they'd really like her to come and Jamie knew if she was to make her life in this town, it was time she made friends. If Wyatt had liked Griffin, she probably would also. Maybe if they talked about him, a part of Wyatt would stay with her a little longer.

Jamie moved into the parlor, which was all decorated for a wedding in white lace, red ribbons and evergreen, with a few dozen chairs set up. Understated but lovely.

She was early. Great. Alone and early. She could have sworn the invitation had said six, but she was the only one here. The sisters were somewhere in the back, setting up for the recep-tion. She could hear people moving around upstairs, but no one was in sight.

Her thoughts were filled with memories of Wyatt tonight, so she welcomed the solitude. Maybe Wyatt was somewhere that didn't allow personal communications. That made sense.

She thought of all the things she knew about him that he hadn't told her. The scars on his body for one. A man work-ing with just installing computers wouldn't have so many scars. He'd said he wanted peace, but deep down she knew he wanted someone to care about. That's why he'd bought her presents that last day.

She'd wrapped them all, like he'd asked her to, but it wouldn't be the same without him there. She'd even hung all the clothes he'd left behind in her closet and put his new cowboy hat on the hook by her front door. Then she could see the hat and almost believe he was still there.

As she had every day since he'd left, she went over everything he'd said to her that last day. He'd said he loved her. That she was his world. That no matter how long he lived, hers would be the last face he saw when he finally closed his eyes.

But he had never mentioned that they'd have a life together. He'd never said he was coming back to her. He'd never talked of the future. He'd never said much about it, but she knew he feared that for him there would be no future.

Jamie closed her eyes and let her imagination take over. If he'd come back to her, they'd have three kids and keep the lake house for weekends. Every Thanksgiving, they would make all the dishes just like they had this year. He'd carve the turkey, and their kids would laugh when they'd tell the story of their first Thanksgiving together.

If she kept making up a future, it might happen, she told herself. She didn't have to face any facts. Not now. Not when she remembered everything he'd said that last day. She had her memories. That was enough for—

"Is this seat taken?" a low voice asked.

Jamie bolted out of her daydream. She stared at a tall man in a tux. His shoulders were wide. Almost as wide as... "Wyatt!"

He grinned. "It's good to see my wife recognizes me."

She was in his arms before he could say more. Hugging him. Kissing him.

He laughed. "I'm home, Jamie. I wasn't sure I'd make it out of this last mission. It was bad, but every time I closed my eyes, I saw your face. I think you were the reason I made it through. I'm home, honey, for good if you'll have me."

Jamie decided she must still be dreaming. When she pulled him closer, she noticed his limp. "What's wrong?"

"Nothing. It'll heal. I may not be able to dance at our wedding, but I'll do my best to stand. That is if you'll marry me for real. No more pretend. Not for you and me."

"I will marry you." She almost said that she already was his wife in her heart.

Wyatt pulled away a few inches. "That's good, Jamie, cause I brought a few witnesses."

She looked at the back of the parlor where four young soldiers stood in full dress uniform as Wyatt continued, "I told them about you when we were pinned down, taking fire. They all swore they'd come watch me marry for real this time even if they had to carry the groom out." Wyatt grinned. "Which they did."

Jamie hugged each one with tears rolling down her cheeks.

In the stillness of the parlor, while all others got ready for Sunlan and Griffin's wedding, Wyatt and Jamie stood in front of the Christmas tree with the preacher. Wyatt had asked the minister if he'd take a few minutes so they could renew their vows.

The preacher grinned. "Of course, Captain. I'd be happy to."

Slowly, he said the words and they each repeated their wedding pledge.

For the first time, for forever.

CHAPTER FORTY-TWO

Franklin Inn

GRIFFIN FELT LIKE they'd practiced their vows so many times that when he said the words for real, he could hear an echo. He fumbled with the ring and swore he heard Marian huff. But the exchange of two plain gold bands went fine. He even kissed his bride, almost politely, but he couldn't stop looking at her. Somehow, being near her was as vital as breathing now.

She looked up and laughed. Mistletoe hung above them. "Kiss me one more time like you did in Mistletoe Canyon, Griffin. Kiss me like it's just you and me here."

He smiled. He knew what she wanted. A real kiss.

Griffin was just getting started when Winston cleared his throat, reminding the groom that there were other people in the room. When Griffin pulled away, he glanced over Sunlan's shoulder and Winston smiled, then winked.

The evening seemed to glide by. Griffin was glad there was a photographer present, because he barely remembered the friends cheering or what the cake looked or tasted like. None of it mattered. All he saw was his Sunshine.

Finally, when they drove away in his pickup, with Just Married painted on the back, both were silent.

Griffin had to say what was weighing on his mind. "I have to tell you this, Sunlan. I met you that day at the café because I needed money for the ranch, but from that first day, it was never about the money. It was always about you."

She looked straight at him in the low glow of the fading town lights. "So, if I have no money to put in your account?"

"We'll survive somehow. I'm not letting you out of your promise to stay married to me. No matter what happens, we're partners in this life. We'll make it through the good and the bad times."

She smiled. "I believe you, Griffin, but the money is already there. I paid off the loan the day I met you. Because I never planned to let you out of the bargain. I figured you wouldn't check until January first when the payment was due. Elliot got the payoff papers but I asked him to keep quiet. You had other things on your mind. Like my fire and meeting my dad and a wedding."

"I'm nothing special, Sunshine."

"You're wrong, Griffin. You're an honest man. I fell for you when the sisters were telling me about you."

"Does that mean we're not sleeping together tonight? That was part of your bargain, too. I'll hold to it if that's what you want."

"Right. I've planned on you keeping your word. We're not sleeping. It's our wedding night. I think we'll be far too busy to sleep."

He thought about it as he drove toward the ranch. "I don't think one night will ever be enough, Sunshine. I think either you move downstairs or I move upstairs. We're sharing quarters."

"What do I get if I agree to this bargain?"

Griffin grinned. "You get me."

She moved closer to him. "Sounds like a fair agreement.

We'll take turns sleeping in each other's beds. I'm not mixing my clothes in with yours."

"As long as we're together, I don't care if we sleep on the porch."

She hugged his arm. "I'll need a little more privacy than that. I plan to wear the same thing you usually wear to bed."

"Nothing?"

"Yep."

Griffin pushed on the gas. It was about time they got home.

CHAPTER FORTY-THREE

Houston

MALLORY MAYWEATHER WALKED out of her office building and turned into the winter wind. She'd been climbing the ladder at a great company for the last several months. Loving her work, moving on with her life. But now it was December, almost Christmas, and the memory of her few weeks in Jax's cabin filled her thoughts.

Every now and then, she scanned the street, looking for a shaggy-haired hermit. He'd never mentioned finding her to claim that date she'd told him she wanted, but she hoped he remembered that she'd invited him to come see her.

She knew he wouldn't come, but that didn't stop her from looking. He'd been the kindest man she'd ever known. When she'd go out with friends, she'd occasionally meet someone, but they could never measure up to Jax O'Grady.

Sometimes, late at night, halfway between sleep and thought, she would swear she could feel him spreading cream over her injured leg or tucking her covers around her. He'd simply been helping her wounds to heal, but his touch washed over her, making her feel cherished.

She'd sent him a dozen emails but Jax never answered back. If she and Tim hadn't been Facebook friends, she'd have no idea how Jax was doing. Now and then Tim would drop a few lines about how his cousin was doing and Mallory knew he was talking about Jax.

Tim told her Jax still lived at the cabin from time to time, but he now traveled, doing seminars on surviving fires. He still didn't have a phone. But he had finished his master's and was thinking about teaching. Jaxson O'Grady was now a specialist in his field.

She bought a few of Tim's books and wrote to tell him how much she loved them. He wrote back asking her to marry him. When she turned him down, he asked if she'd leave a review.

The seasons changed and she grew used to driving in Houston traffic, but she never forgot the man who'd carried her out of the hospital one midnight. The man who'd gotten up every morning and made sure she was okay before he even got dressed. A man worth loving.

Mallory bought her afternoon coffee, then bundled up to face the wind as she crossed the street heading back to her office. Out of the corner of her eye, she caught the form of a man sitting on one of the granite benches. For a moment, she thought he looked like Jax. But his hair was short. He wore a suit with a tailor-made wool coat.

As she passed, he looked up and she froze.

"Jax?"

The man stood. "Hello, Mallory. I came for that date, if you're not busy."

She tossed the coffee and flew into his familiar arms. "I thought you would never come." Tears ran down her face, freezing in the wind, but she didn't care.

He held her so close, as if he couldn't let go, and she did the same.

"You okay?" he finally whispered against her ear.

"I am now," she answered as she rubbed her cheek against his clean-shaven jaw.

"Me, too," he answered. "I was worried you wouldn't recognize me."

"You're always there, Jax. In my memories. In my thoughts."

He rubbed his thumb across her cheek, shoving away tears. "How about we get out of this cold?"

Laughing, she linked her arm with his and they ran to her car. As soon as they were inside with the heater running, she asked, "How did you find me? All I told Tim was my email address."

"It wasn't easy. You changed your name. Just M. Weather is it now? Changed occupations. Never sent me your new address."

"But I emailed you?"

"I dropped my email account after your first email that simply said you were safe. I thought staying away from me, the guy Curtis probably hates most in this world, would keep you safe."

She smiled. "We don't have to worry about Curtis. He went to federal prison for fraud a few months ago. I think when the police started looking into his past behavior with women, they also checked his finances. He'd been embezzling for years. If he ever gets out of federal prison, there are several women who will probably file harassment charges."

"Couldn't have happened to a nicer guy."

"So, how did you find me?" Mallory studied him, thinking he'd changed a great deal in a year. But she could still see kindness in his eyes, and something else now. Love, she thought. When he looked at her, she saw pure love. She'd always known how much he cared about her, but he must have hidden his love before.

Jax shrugged. "I asked Tim. He had your office address from when he mailed you some of his books. If you hadn't come out soon, I fear I'd have been frozen to the bench."

They laughed as she drove home to her apartment. She told

him all about her new job and the friends she'd made in the city. She couldn't wait for him to see her place. It might not look anything like his cabin, but she had a fireplace and a view of Houston.

After just one step inside the door, Jax dropped to his knees and hugged Charlie. "I missed you, Buddy."

The dog seemed just as happy to see Jax. He barked and ran around him.

"Every time I say your name, his ears perk up, like we're going to go looking for you." She shrugged. "I sometimes call him Buddy just to make him happy."

Jax looked around while she made him a strong cup of coffee. She didn't miss how he smiled at her Christmas decorations. A small tree decorated with tiny log cabins and pinecones. The only stocking hung had Charlie's name on it. And on one wall were three frames holding copies of the puzzles she'd left behind at his cabin. Horses running over a snowy field. Kittens playing under the Christmas tree. A starry night shining over a lone cabin.

"I could have mailed the puzzles to you," Jax said.

"I know, but I kind of liked the idea that the same pictures were on both the cabin walls and here."

He grinned. "Me, too."

They sat on bar stools, looking out at the city lights and talking like old friends. He told her of his travels and how he was getting used to having people around when he wasn't at the cabin. She talked about her dear friend who'd put her up for two months at a beach house in Galveston.

Neither wanted to go out, so she made him an omelet while he burned toast. He talked about his work, but mostly he just seemed to be studying her as if he couldn't get enough.

At midnight, she realized he was never going to make the first move, so she stood, took him by the hand and tugged him toward the bedroom.

"Mallory, I don't know about this. I can't see where this is going."

"Me either, but I do love you, Jax."

"But there are questions that don't have answers. A million things we've never talked about. I don't want to be a complication in your life. I just had to see you. Make sure you were all right. I—"

"I know, Jax." She faced him. "Before we go any further, I have one question that has to be answered."

He seemed to relax. "All right. I'll be as honest as I can in answering. I'm not involved with anyone, but I'd be happy for you if you've found someone. You mean a lot to me, but I'd understand if you want to go slow—"

"One question, Jax." She stood on her toes and kissed him on the check.

He squared his shoulders. "All right."

She stretched and kissed him on the mouth this time. "What do you want for breakfast?"

★ ★ ★ ★ ★